The JOYS of LOVE

The JOYS *of* LOVE

Madeleine L'Engle

FARRAR STRAUS GIROUX

NEW YORK

Copyright © 2008 by Crosswicks, Ltd.

All rights reserved

Distributed in Canada by Douglas & McIntyre Ltd.

Printed in the United States of America

Designed by Robbin Gourley

First edition, 2008

1 3 5 7 9 10 8 6 4 2

www.fsgkidsbooks.com

Library of Congress Cataloging-in-Publication Data

L'Engle, Madeleine.

The joys of love / Madeleine L'Engle.— 1st ed.

p. cm.

Summary: After graduating from college in 1946, Elizabeth Jerrold pursues her dream of becoming a stage actress, landing a position as an apprentice in a summer theater company where she hones her acting skills and falls in love with an aspiring director.

ISBN-13: 978-0-374-33870-1

ISBN-10: 0-374-33870-1

[1. Theater—Fiction. 2. Acting—Fiction. 3. Love—Fiction. 4. Apprentices—Fiction. 5. Orphans—Fiction.] I. Title.

PZ7 .L5398Jo 2008

[Fic]—dc22

2007014331

INTRODUCTION

I REMEMBER THE FIRST TIME I read *The Joys of Love*. It was 1978 and I was ten, curled up on the couch, listening to the tap-tapping of my grandmother's typewriter keys, and reading—no, devouring—her unpublished manuscript about summer theatre in the 1940s. My nine-year-old sister, Charlotte, was on the opposite end of the couch, eagerly waiting for me to pass the next page to her. We were honored that Gran thought we were mature enough to read this novel, and we had promised to be quiet so that she could write. We had a history of spending time with her while she was working, whether it was at her home, Crosswicks, in northwestern Connecticut, or in the Cathedral Library at St. John the Divine in New York City, where she was the librarian and writer-in-residence. My grandmother lovingly referred to her office above the garage at Crosswicks as an "ivory tower," one in which she could harness her wild, abundant imagination through the craft of writing. In

1978 she used a gigantic typewriter, atop a big desk with piles of paper everywhere. Large windows overlooked green fields and the peak of Mohawk Mountain. Crosswicks was a magical place for us, having served as much of the setting for her best-known work, *A Wrinkle in Time*.

Sitting and reading *The Joys of Love*, I was thrown back into the world of the 1940s, and through the character of Elizabeth I felt able to catch a glimpse of my grandmother as a very young woman. She became more than the woman who made the best hot fudge sundaes and liked cats and dogs, more than the writer of my favorite books. She inhabited this character, Elizabeth, and reading the manuscript made me feel closer to her than ever before.

After we finished, Charlotte and I grew restless, daring to break the sanctity of quiet.

"Gran, we're so mad that this was never published!" rose the cry.

"Well, my darlings, then this can be just for you two to share, a special book just for you." We loved that idea then, to have a literal piece of my grandmother that nobody else could have. We had begun to realize how famous she was and how generous she was with that fame, and we could get a little jealous!

Gran had struggled as a writer until the early 1960s, when *Meet the Austins* and *A Wrinkle in Time* were published and she won the Newbery Medal for the latter. She had had a modicum of success with her first novel, *The Small Rain*, published in 1945, but after a lukewarm reception to her second novel, *Ilsa*, she had a terrible time getting her novels published, suffering rejection after rejection. She was able to publish *And Both Were Young*, but then *Camilla*, *Meet the Austins*, and *Wrinkle* made the rounds of countless publishing houses before being accepted. Publishers did not know how to classify her. Her spirit suffered badly with those rejections, but she never stopped writing, never stopped trying. Hers remains a legacy of discipline and dogged persistence. She has always said that being published doesn't make you a writer—writing does.

After Farrar, Straus and Giroux took a chance on *Wrinkle*, she who couldn't be classified was in a class by herself, and en joyed an immensely successful writing career, which opened the way to speaking and teaching around the world. By the time Charlotte and I were born, her professional, public persona as Madeleine L'Engle had been firmly established. We loved her both as our grandmother and as Madeleine L'Engle. We didn't have to share our grandmother, but we certainly had to share Madeleine L'Engle, and having *The Joys of Love* to ourselves became a delicious secret!

When Charlotte and I uncovered that old copy of *The Joys of Love* two years ago, we looked at each other and smiled, remembering how much we had loved reading it over and over again, and how much it had shaped us. I know it inspired me to read Chekhov and become an acting junkie, practicing the same monologue from *The Seagull* that Elizabeth does, and using it when I auditioned for a theatre camp when I was a teenager. Now, thirty years later, our "secret" is out, and we couldn't be happier to share with everybody this sweet novel about coming of age at a summer theatre.

The first incarnation of *The Joys of Love* was written in 1942 as a short story called "Summer at the Sea." In that first version, Elizabeth was as close to an autobiographical portrait as you could get. Madeleine had spent two summers doing theatre in Nantucket, and the setting for *The Joys of Love* is also at the ocean. Elizabeth was primarily a writer, as was Madeleine. (In this penultimate version, Elizabeth is an actress.) Madeleine describes herself as "tall, gawky, [and] myopic" in *Two-Part Invention*, as is Elizabeth. Madeleine's own father died when she was a teenager, and she describes Elizabeth repressing her grief, just as she had done. Madeleine's mother had been nervous about Madeleine pursuing a theatrical life, although to a lesser degree than Elizabeth's Aunt Harriet. Elizabeth, like Madeleine, went to Smith College and is impossibly well-read, able to quote Shakespeare, Chekhov, and others at the drop of a hat. Madeleine was also starstruck by an older, established actress, as Elizabeth is. In fact, Madeleine's idol, Eva Le Gallienne, was the prototype for Valborg Andersen.

In 1941 Gran graduated from Smith College and left that world of cozy intellectualism for Greenwich Village, in New York City. Imagine a hunger and passion for the writing life that drives you beyond all other things. My grandmother was tenacious, loyal, and fierce. Believing the theatre could be her best training ground as a writer, she worked selling war bond certificates in the theatres so she could see all the plays of the day for free. She took acting classes, and wrote several plays that she would workshop with friends. Perhaps this is why she has a keen knack for dialogue, enforcing the dictum for good writing: show, don't tell.

She wrote an early play with Eva Le Gallienne in mind for

the title role, then spent a tremendous amount of energy trying to get the script to her—she even befriended the stage manager of the theatre Miss Le Gallienne was working in! Her persistence got her noticed, even though the script was never used. (The script ended up becoming *Ilsa*.) She was given a chance to audition as an apprentice for Miss Le Gallienne's company. She wrote her own monologue, culled from the letters of Katherine Mansfield, and, standing out from the other young hopefuls, was given the job. How she thrilled to be earning her own living in the theatre, being paid the Equity minimum of sixty-five dollars a week, all the while understudying various roles and playing some small parts herself.

And she constantly wrote. I don't know of anybody else who supported their writing career by working in the theatre.

Eventually, she met my grandfather, the actor Hugh Franklin, in that company's production of *The Cherry Orchard*, in which she was an understudy. My grandmother turned to writing full-time after she married him in 1946. Life in the theatre can be unpredictable, and my grandparents felt they needed more stability to raise a family. They had bought a summer house in Connecticut the year after they married; in 1950, they decided to live there year-round. They settled into Crosswicks, and my grandfather ran a country store.

It was during those years that Gran had the hardest time getting her work published. She picked up "Summer at the Sea" again that first summer, and it became *The Joys of Love*. She had also been hard at work on *Camilla*, which her agent loved and sent out again and again, only to have it rejected. It was hard for Gran to feel this near constant sting of rejection. While

Camilla was classifiable at the time as a young adult novel, her agent felt that *The Joys of Love* was not. The agent suggested that my grandmother rewrite it with some more adult themes, to be sold as a serial to a magazine. But Gran wasn't happy with the idea; she felt that *The Joys of Love* was much fresher as a young adult novel. Thus Gran put *The Joys of Love* away and moved on to writing new novels, plays, and poems. *Camilla* was eventually published and compared to J. D. Salinger's *Catcher in the Rye*. I know my grandmother would be thrilled that after all these years *The Joys of Love* will finally find its audience.

It is also no coincidence that Gran picked up writing *The Joys of Love* the same year she and my grandfather moved away from New York. I see it now as her love letter to the theatrical world, expressing her ambivalence about giving that world up. In *The Joys of Love*, Elizabeth talks to Ben about her own ambivalence:

> "I've always thought about the theatre like a Christmas tree, all shining and bright with beautiful ornaments. But now it seems like a Christmas tree with the tinsel all tarnished and the colored balls all fallen off and broken. That's a corny way of saying it, but you know what I mean."
>
> "Sure, I know what you mean, Liz. And it's both ways . . . Some of the ornaments fall and break and some stay clear and bright. Some of the tinsel gets tarnished and some stays shining and beautiful like the

night before Christmas. Nothing's ever all one way. You know that. It's all mixed up and you've just got to find the part that's right for you."

Ultimately, my grandparents were able to find the part that was right for them, selling the store after ten years in Connecticut and returning to New York, where my grandfather resumed his working life as an actor, and my grandmother's writing blossomed into an extraordinary career. Her body of work is astounding.

Her legacy is not limited to her books, but encompasses her fierceness of spirit: her love, her discipline, her belief in herself, and her creative generosity in lifting up the world.

As *The Joys of Love* is an early work, I hope that readers will catch that same glimpse of my grandmother in Elizabeth that I did—vibrant, vulnerable, and yearning for love and all that life has to offer—and feel inspired.

—Léna Roy

Act I
FRIDAY

THE SUMMER THEATRE was on a pier that jutted off from the boardwalk over the sand. Sometimes when there was a storm and the tide was unusually high the actors could hear the soft swish of water underneath the stage; and the assistant stage manager, one of whose duties was to sweep the stage, was always in a rage at the sand which blew up between the floorboards and through the canvas floorcloth so that ten minutes after he had swept there would be a soft white dust over everything.

On the warm summer nights after the curtain had come down on the evening's performance, the actors would hurry out of costume and makeup and stroll down the boardwalk, stopping for ice cream or Cokes, or drifting into town where there were restaurants and nightclubs. The apprentices, who served as ushers, would walk along in their bright summer evening clothes, and in the ice cream parlors would talk loudly of the evening's performance and of the problems of acting, so that everybody would know that they belonged to the theatre.

Sometimes, if Elizabeth had received a tip, she would go with the other apprentices; sometimes she would walk into town to a midnight movie with Ben Walton, the assistant stage manager, who was also an apprentice actor; but usually she stayed backstage, doing odd jobs for any of the professional actors who needed anything, waiting for a word or a gesture from Kurt Canitz.

Kurt Canitz was the director at the theatre, but occasionally he would take a role that appealed to him and then he would have Elizabeth cue him. When he grew tired of that, he would say, "I'm sick of working. Come and talk with me, Elizabeth." And then he would take her to the restaurant in his hotel, the Ambassador, and talk to her for hours about the theatre, about the productions he had directed on Broadway, about Elizabeth's own talent as an actress.

I have never lived before, Elizabeth thought. Until this summer I did not know what it was to be alive.

One Friday night in the beginning of August, Kurt, his face smeared with greasepaint and cold cream, said, "Elizabeth, I want to talk to you. Go wait for me on the old boardwalk."

The old boardwalk was about a hundred feet closer to the ocean than the regular boardwalk. It had long ago been washed away and consisted now of perhaps a dozen barnacled piles sticking haphazardly up out of the sand.

Elizabeth climbed onto one of the piles and sat facing the

ocean. She had on the full long yellow dirndl skirt and peasant blouse she had worn for ushering, and the sand had come in through her sandals and settled between her toes. The tide was coming in and small, precocious waves crept closer and closer to her. From farther down the beach came the sound of two recorders playing a duet, and the delicate notes of an old English madrigal floated up to her, so faint and so blown by the wind that the music seemed to be part of the night, one with the lapping of the small waves against the piles, the roar of the breakers muted in the quiet night, rather than a sound produced by two human beings blowing into wooden pipes. Behind her and up the boardwalk Elizabeth could still hear voices from the theatre, stragglers from the audience standing around on the boardwalk talking, members of the company coming out of the stage door and discussing plans for the evening.

Elizabeth raised her head as a voice called, "Elizabeth Jerrold, is that you?"

She tried to keep the disappointment that it wasn't Kurt out of her voice as she called back, "Hi, Ben, where are you off to?"

Ben dropped off the boardwalk and clambered up onto the pile next to Elizabeth. "Hey, the tide's coming in."

"I know it is."

He turned and tried to look at her face, which was only a pale shadow in the starlight. "Come on down the boardwalk to Lukie's and have a hamburger with me."

"I'm broke."

"I'll treat you," Ben said, still trying to read her expression.

"I can't." She put her head down on her knees.

"Waiting for Canitz?" There was a trace of anger in Ben's voice.

She nodded.

"Listen, Elizabeth," he said, "maybe I'm the last person to speak to you about this, but I've been around and I just want to tell you you're riding for a fall."

"Anything else you wanted to say?" Elizabeth asked him.

"Nope. Where do you suppose Jane and John Peter dug up those recorders? That melancholy stuff they're playing's bad for my mood. My gosh, the divine Sarah Courtmont stank tonight, didn't she? She blew her lines twice." Ben reached down the length of his immensely long, immensely thin legs, took off one of his shoes, and shook out the sand, almost losing his balance and toppling off the pile. "I don't know why that dame thinks she can act," he muttered as he managed to put the shoe back on without falling.

"I'm not a big fan of hers either, but most of the kids think she's magnificent," Elizabeth said, looking surreptitiously at the luminous hands of her watch. It was almost midnight.

"What a dump this is," Ben said. "What made you come here anyhow, Liz?"

"It was the only place I could get a scholarship."

"Scholarship, my eye," Ben snorted. "You're paying J. P. Price twenty bucks a week for room and board, aren't you?"

"Yes." Elizabeth looked at her watch again. Barely a minute had passed. And Kurt had not come.

"I swore I'd never be an apprentice," Ben said. "So J. P. Price offers me room and board in exchange for being assistant stage manager and all I am is an apprentice who works harder, that's all. And we're so much better than the professional company and the stars—I mean you and me and Jane and John Peter—that's the worst of it. I've never seen such a bunch of second-string hams in my life." He pulled off his other shoe. "There's more sand in my shoes than on the beach."

"What about Valborg Andersen?" Elizabeth asked, reaching out to steady Ben as he struggled to tie his shoelaces. "Don't you think she's good?"

"Now there's an actress," Ben admitted. "I am enjoying watching her rehearse, so I guess it's worth the rest of the summer just to see that, but I don't think she should be doing *Macbeth*. Her Lady Macbeth stinks."

Elizabeth scratched a mosquito bite on one of her long suntanned legs—her legs, though less skinny, were almost as long as Ben's—and looked at her watch again. Then she turned around and looked back across the boardwalk at the theatre. Now the last of the audience had dispersed and the building was dark, except for a light in J. P. Price's office. She couldn't see the back where the dressing rooms were. Perhaps Kurt was still talking to someone in one of them. "I guess Miss Andersen knows what she's doing," she told Ben.

"You're so wrong," Ben said. "It's just the great ones like Andersen who *don't* know what they're doing."

"Okay. You've been around and I haven't, so I can't argue with you," Elizabeth agreed, infuriated, "but you are lucky that you get to watch Miss Andersen rehearse. All the apprentices wish they could watch the professionals and the stars rehearse, but Mr. Price won't allow it." Elizabeth then laughed and said,

"When I saw Price about coming here I told him I'd played Lady Macbeth at school and he told me he wasn't planning to produce *Macbeth*. I can hardly wait to see it on Monday."

"I bet you pray to that big picture of Valborg Andersen you have on your bureau," Ben said.

"If I'd lived a few thousand years ago when graven images were still permitted, I probably would," Elizabeth admitted.

From the direction of the theatre they heard a voice, too blown by the wind to identify, calling, "Hoo-oo, Liz Jerrold!"

Elizabeth twisted around on her pile, cupped her hands to her mouth, and called back, "Hoo-oo!"

"Telephone!" the voice said.

"Okay," Elizabeth yelled, disappointed once again that it wasn't Kurt. She jumped off her pile, landing lightly in the wet sand. A wave licked at her sandals. "Now, who on earth would be telephoning *me?*" she asked Ben, and a vague feeling of unease spread over her. "If Kurt comes, tell him I'll be right back, will you please?" she added.

"Sorry, toots," Ben said, scrambling down from his pile. "The gaseous activity of my stomach will not be denied. I'm going down the boardwalk for some food."

Elizabeth crossed the sand to the boardwalk, pulled herself up, and stood, a tall slender shadow in the darkness, looking down at Ben.

"Give me a hand," Ben said plaintively. "You know I am not athletic."

Elizabeth extended a hand, which Ben clutched as he managed to clamber up beside her, panting. "It's the awful life I lead, turning night into day, as my dear grandmother would say. Come down later to Lukie's and tell me who the call is from."

"Maybe," Elizabeth said, and turned and ran toward the theatre.

In the office Mr. Price was putting away some papers. "Call operator twenty-three," he told her, "and put out the lights and lock up when you're through."

"Okay, Mr. Price."

"And be in the box office at nine tomorrow morning, will you, Elizabeth?"

"I'll miss my classes—" Elizabeth started, then stopped. "Okay, Mr. Price."

"Good night, darling," Mr. Price said with automatic affection, and left.

Elizabeth picked up the telephone and asked for operator twenty-three.

"You have a call from Jordan, Virginia, Miss Jerrold," the operator told her, and Elizabeth's heart began to beat with apprehension. If the call was from Jordan, it meant that it must be from her aunt with whom she had lived since her father's death, and Aunt Harriet Jerrold would not call except for bad news. Elizabeth heard the telephone ringing and she could imagine it ringing in the dark, narrow hall of the house in Jordan. It's after midnight, she thought. Why on earth would Aunt Harriet be calling me at this time of night?

The phone kept ringing, and after a while the operator said, "There doesn't seem to be any answer, Miss Jerrold. I've been trying to get you since eight o'clock this evening and either the line was busy or you couldn't be reached. Do you think I should try again in twenty minutes?"

"No," Elizabeth said, "it's too late now. I'd better call in the morning. Shall I ask for you?"

"I won't be on in the morning, but ask for operator nineteen and she'll take care of you."

"All right. Thanks." Elizabeth hung up and a sick feeling of apprehension settled in the pit of her stomach. She looked around the small office, starkly painted white. On the wall was a calendar, opened to the month of August, 1946, showing the schedule for the rest of the summer. Most summer-stock theatres did a play a week, and this theatre was no exception. There are four more plays to learn from, Elizabeth thought wistfully. Next to the calendar was the box office window.

Elizabeth reached up to the neat cubbyholes to touch one of the stacks of pink and blue and green tickets which she would be selling the next morning. Under the green money box was a large mimeographed seating plan of the theatre, and on this she would mark off all the tickets she sold. She rather enjoyed sitting on the high stool by the ticket window and chatting with the people who would be seeing the play that night or later on in the week; she had come to know several who returned each week, and tried to always give them the choicest seats. I love everything about this place, she thought. Ben can say anything he likes about it, but I've loved every minute of this summer so far.

"Liz!" a voice called. "Are you there?"

"I'm here," Elizabeth called back.

After a moment Jane Gardiner's slight figure appeared in the doorway. Ben had been in the theatre since he was a child, only taking a break for college at his father's insistence, but it was Jane, fresh out of drama school, who seemed to have the wisdom the rest of them lacked. Elizabeth always felt tall and clumsy beside her, though Jane said that Elizabeth was a Viking, and she herself the product of a decadent civilization.

"Ben told me you had a long distance call," Jane said, "so I thought I'd come over and make sure it wasn't bad news."

Elizabeth shook her head. "The operator said she had a call from Jordan for me and that she'd been trying to get me all evening. But when she rang just now, there wasn't any answer. It must have been Aunt Harriet. And Aunt Harriet never answers the phone after ten o'clock. If anybody called to tell her the house was on fire, it could just burn down if it depended on her answering the phone. I do hope she isn't ill or something."

"Probably just wants to talk to you," Jane said.

"Not Aunt Harriet. It's bound to be something bad or she wouldn't call." Elizabeth frowned and tried to imagine what particular bad thing might be responsible for the call.

"Now, don't go brooding, Liz," Jane told her severely. "John Peter says you worry too much about things, and he's right."

Elizabeth sat down in Mr. Price's swivel chair. "Aunt Harriet hated having me come here this summer. She'd do anything in the world to get me back. She thinks, as I believe I have told you before, that the theatre is an invention of Satan."

"What gets me," Jane said, sitting on a corner of the desk and resting her delicate feet on the edge of the big tin wastepaper basket, "is if she hates the theatre so, why did she let you come here in the first place? She gives you the twenty a week room and board, doesn't she?"

"I wouldn't be here otherwise." Elizabeth picked up a glass paperweight that had a snowman in it, and shook it to set up a cloud of snowflakes falling inside. She watched it intently. "Father didn't have a penny when he died. Teachers don't make much money, as you know, and Father didn't even teach in a university—he taught at a boys' school—and he didn't have any sense about money anyhow. Aunt Harriet took me because it was her Christian duty, and not because she wanted me. Please, Jane, if you ever see me doing anything because it's my Christian duty, stop me."

"You aren't apt to," Jane said. "You're too good a Christian."

Elizabeth smiled at her, then looked at the snow that was still falling, very gently now, inside the glass globe. "It was kind of a bet. Aunt Harriet doesn't make bets, of course, but that's what it was."

"What was the bet?" Jane asked, upsetting the wastepaper basket and spilling papers all over the floor. "Darn," she said, and got down on her hands and knees to clean up the mess. It always amazed Elizabeth that in positions that would make anybody else look awkward, Jane still managed to be graceful.

"She said that if I'd major in chemistry at Smith instead of dramatic arts, and if I graduated with honors, she'd let me go to a summer theatre." Elizabeth, too, was now down on her hands and knees, helping Jane cram papers back into the basket. "I guess she thought if I majored in chemistry I might forget about the theatre. Well, I didn't forget about the theatre and it was kind of a challenge, so I just managed to squeak through with honors, no magna or summa cum laude, just plain cum laude, but anyhow it was honors and she hadn't specified. She made a fuss and tried to get out of it but I'd already got my scholarship here so I threw a scene about her word being no good and how hard I'd worked and how little twenty dollars is to her and all that. I was really stinking, Jane. I feel terribly ashamed whenever I think about it. But I had to do it, and no matter how guilty I feel I know I'd do it again."

"Yes, I know," Jane said, sitting down on the floor and leaning back against the wall. "I've never seen anyone look more determined than you did last spring in Price's office."

That day in Mr. Price's office in New York, Elizabeth thought now, had been the turning point of her whole life. If it had not been for that day last spring, none of the summer—working in the theatre, getting to know Kurt, beginning a completely new life—would have been possible.

Even then she had been aware of it. Sitting in the anteroom of Mr. Price's office, she had thought, How strange to know that the whole course of my life can be changed today in this dingy office.

But it was true. It was so frighteningly true that her hands had felt cold with fear and her heart had beat so fast that for a moment she was afraid that she might faint in the hot stuffiness of the little room. Although it was an unseasonably hot April day, steam hissed in the radiator, and there was no window in the anteroom. Even the office door to the main hallway was closed.

Because she had not been able to sit still another moment, she went over to the receptionist. "My appointment with Mr. Price was at one o'clock and it's after two now," she said.

"Yeah?" The receptionist looked at her with a hot, annoyed face.

"I mean—he's still going to see me, isn't he?"

"You've got an appointment card, haven't you?"

"Yes."

"Okay, then, relax. Sit down. Though why you want to see him I don't know. I'm sure he doesn't want to see you."

Elizabeth sat down again. She felt miserable and young and more than snubbed. She looked at her feet because she was afraid that if she looked at the others waiting in the room she would find scorn in their faces.

"Don't let it get to you," the girl next to her said. "I've just been in an office where the receptionist was nice enough to say 'Thank you for coming in' after she told me the cast was all set. They're not all like the sourpuss here. Though with the second-rate theatre Price is running, I don't know why we're all hanging around here like a lot of trained seals waiting for him to throw us a fish."

The door to the hall opened and a young man entered. The moment he came in, a slight, pleasant smile on his face, Elizabeth saw that there was something different about him, that he was not like anybody else in the room. And then she realized what the difference was: he was the only one who was not nervous.

He walked over to the receptionist's desk and said, "Hi, Sadie, how's my duck today?" He had a slight accent.

The sour face was surprisingly pretty when it smiled. "Oh, dying of the heat, Mr. Canitz. Otherwise I guess I'll survive. You want to see Mr. Price?"

"If he's not too busy."

"Oh, he always has time to see you, Mr. Canitz. Go right in."

The young man smiled his pleasant smile at the room full of hot, nervous people, and opened the door to Mr. Price's office. Elizabeth looked in quickly and saw that it was very like the anteroom, except that it had a large open window and a brief, welcome gust of cool air blew in at her. Mr. Price was sitting at his desk talking to a young woman with blond hair, and he waved his hand genially at Mr. Canitz. "Oh, come in, Kurt. I want you to meet this young lady."

Then the door shut and heat settled back over the room.

"If I had any sense," the girl next to Elizabeth said, "I'd leave this hellhole and go home. And so would you."

"Home," Elizabeth found herself answering, "is the last place I'd go."

"Well, then, I guess you have a point in hanging around. Why don't they at least open the door into the hall?" She appealed to Sadie. "Couldn't you turn off the heat or something?"

"No, I can't," the receptionist snapped. "The radiator's broken. And I'm just as hot as you are. Hotter. If you don't like it here, why don't you leave? I tell you, he isn't going to hire anybody else. He's got the whole season set. You're wasting your time."

The girl turned back to Elizabeth. "That's the way people get ulcers. People with vile natures always get ulcers. If I stay here much longer, I'll get ulcers, too."

"But is it true?" Elizabeth asked.

"What?"

"That he has the whole season set."

"Of course it isn't true. She only said it because she's in a vile mood. What's your name? I'm Jane Gardiner."

"I'm Elizabeth Jerrold."

"Listen, I don't mean to butt in," Jane said, "but don't be nervous. You're practically making the bench shake. After all, the world isn't going to end if Price doesn't give you a job. Nothing's that important."

"But it is," Elizabeth said. "For me it is."

The door to the office opened again and Kurt Canitz and the blond woman came out. Mr. Canitz had his arm protectively about her, and he ushered her gallantly to the door and said goodbye. Then he sat down and smiled at Sadie and looked slowly around the anteroom. His eyes rested on Jane, on Elizabeth, on a little man in a bowler hat. Sadie picked up a stack of cards and called out, "Gardiner."

Jane rose. "That's me. Well, this is only the fifteenth office I've been in today. What've I got to lose?"

Elizabeth watched her as she walked swiftly into the office, shutting the door firmly behind her. Yes, Jane was obviously a person who knew her way around theatrical offices. She had a certain nervous excitement, like every actor waiting to hear about a job, but it was controlled, made into an asset; it gave a shine to her brown eyes, a spring to her step. Elizabeth felt that Jane was dressed correctly, too. She wore a pleated navy blue skirt and a little red jacket. Her hair was very fair, a soft ash blond, and on her head she wore a small red beret. Elizabeth felt forlorn in the other girl's absence, and suddenly foolish. She herself wore a simple blue denim skirt and white blouse, and she felt that she belonged much more on a college campus than she did in a theatrical office on Forty-second Street in New York. If someone as desirable as Jane had been in fifteen offices that day and still did not have a job, then what was Elizabeth thinking of when she was letting everything in the world depend on whether or not Mr. J. P. Price took her into his summer theatre company?

But Mr. Price was Elizabeth's only hope after her twenty letters of inquiry to summer-stock companies. Many of the managers had sent back form letters that offered her opportunities to apprentice—but at a two- or three-hundred-dollar tuition fee. Mr. Price had simply sent her a card telling her to be at his office at one o'clock, April 14, and he would see her then.

Elizabeth looked around at the dingy anteroom; the buff-colored walls were cracked and some of the cracks were partially covered with signed photographs of actors and actresses of whom she had never heard. There were no familiar names like Judith Anderson, Katharine Cornell, Eva Le Gallienne, Ethel Barrymore. The air smelled like stale cigar smoke from the little man in the bowler hat who sat stolidly on a folding chair and surrounded himself with a cloud of heavy fumes.

Elizabeth noticed Kurt Canitz was writing busily in a small notebook. He looked up and stared directly at her for several seconds, then scribbled something else in the notebook, tore off the page and gave it to Sadie with a radiant smile, and left.

Elizabeth wondered what his connection with the theatre was. Was he an actor, a director, perhaps a producer? Certainly he was connected with Mr. Price's summer company.

Again the door of the office opened and Jane came out. She grinned at Elizabeth.

"Did you get a job?" Elizabeth asked eagerly.

"Well, not exactly the job I went in for, but at this point it'll do. I'm going as an apprentice, which I swore after last summer I'd never do again, but this time at least it's a scholarship."

"Oh, I'm so glad!" Elizabeth exclaimed. "That's wonderful!"

"Thanks," Jane said. "Good luck to you, too."

Sadie was looking at her cards. "Jerrold," she called.

Elizabeth stood up.

Jane took her hand. "Good luck," she said again. "Good luck, *really*. I hope I'll see you there."

"Thanks," Elizabeth answered, and went into the office.

"Well, what can I do for you?" Mr. Price asked, looking Elizabeth up and down until she flinched.

"You can give me a job," Elizabeth said, and was surprised at how calm her voice sounded.

"And what kind of a job are you looking for, my dear?"

"A job in your summer theatre. As an actress." Elizabeth felt that her voice sounded flat and colorless; anxiety had wiped out its usual resonance.

"And what experience have you had? What parts have you played?"

Elizabeth ignored the first part of his question. "I've played

Lady Macbeth and Ophelia and I've played Hilda Wangel in *The Master Builder* and Sudermann's *Magda*, and the Sphinx in Cocteau's *The Infernal Machine*."

"A bit on the heavy side, wouldn't you say?" Mr. Price asked her. "And aren't you rather young for Lady Macbeth or Magda? How about something more—recent—and perhaps a little gayer?"

"Well—I've played Blanche in *Streetcar*—oh, I know that's not very gay, but it's recent—and—and—I've done some Chekhov one-acts. They're not very recent but they're gay—"

"And where did you get all this magnificent experience?" Mr. Price asked her. "Why, after all this, have I never heard of you?"

"At college," Elizabeth said, looking down at her feet.

"My dear young lady." Mr. Price sounded half bored, half amused. "Perhaps you do not realize, but I am running a professional theatre. I am sure you were very charming and very highly acclaimed at college, but I am really not contemplating producing *Macbeth* or *Magda* or even *The Infernal Machine*. So what do I have to offer you?"

"All I want," Elizabeth said desperately, "is—*anything*."

"Anything what?"

"Maids, walk-ons, working in the box office. Anything."

"I take a certain number of apprentices," Mr. Price said. "They take classes from the company actors. We use the star system. We do a new play every week and the company professionals rehearse all week in bit parts. Then the star arrives on Sunday. The stars have one rehearsal with the company before the show. Although one or two of them will direct the plays they are starring in, and those actors will be there longer. If I can, I use the apprentices in at least one walk-on part during the summer. The fee is three hundred dollars."

Elizabeth shook her head. When she spoke her voice trembled. "I—borrowed the money to come to New York to see you today. I—I—"

"And I suppose if I didn't give you a job you'll jump off the Empire State Building? Or into the Hudson River? Or perhaps the East River would suit you better."

"That's not funny," Elizabeth said with a sudden flare of anger. "Would you really laugh if you were responsible for someone's death?"

"If you did anything so foolish as to kill yourself, I wouldn't be responsible. You would." Mr. Price's voice was calm and reasonable.

"As it happens," Elizabeth said, anger still directing her words, "I agree with you. And I do not approve of suicide under any conditions. However, a weaker character in my circumstances might."

Mr. Price smiled. "Are your circumstances so very particular?"

"To me they are. You never know what people's circumstances are."

"Perhaps I can guess some of yours. You go to a good college and major in drama. Your family has a thoroughly adequate income."

"Wrong," Elizabeth said. "I go to a good college but I major in chemistry and I am on scholarship and I have no parents. I was president of the Dramatic Association and took some theatre courses in Theatre Workshop at school. I graduate later this spring."

"I stand corrected."

Elizabeth looked at him, tried to smile, and said, "And now, since you haven't a job to offer me, I'll say goodbye and go throw myself under a Fifth Avenue bus."

The door to the office opened and Sadie thrust her head in. "Say, Mr. Price, I almost forgot. Mr. Canitz left me a note to give you."

Mr. Price read the note and handed it to Elizabeth. Kurt Canitz had written, "Give the tall girl with glasses a scholarship. I have a hunch about her."

Mr. Price looked at Elizabeth. "You are tall—rather tall for an actress, incidentally—and you wear glasses, so I assume Kurt means you. By the way, how does it happen that you don't take off your glasses for an interview?"

"I forgot," Elizabeth said. "I don't always wear them, but I really can't see well without them. I never wear them onstage, of course."

"I suppose I'll have to answer to Kurt if I don't at least have you read for me. All right. Read for me."

"If you like me, will you give me a scholarship?" Elizabeth asked.

"I'm known for—shall we kindly call it being shrewd?—about money, but as far as the theatre is concerned I also have a conscience," Mr. Price said. "I collect as many three-hundred-dollar tuitions from the apprentices as I can. If a girl can afford it, why shouldn't I take it? However, if I think a kid has possibilities, and they can't afford the tuition, I give them a scholarship for the summer and I work her—or him, as the case may be—like a dog. There are usually two scholarships for young men and two for women. I have both my men set and one of my women. You might possibly fit the other scholarship. The apprentices and most of the resident company live at a cottage a few blocks from the theatre. Of course the scholarship apprentices pay twenty dollars a week for room and board. Could you manage that?"

"I'll have to," Elizabeth said.

"I have a feeling that you are a hard worker," Mr. Price told her. "Also, believe it or not, I have a healthy regard for Kurt Canitz's hunches—and also for his dollars, which help finance the theatre. More of a respect for his hunches and his dollars than I have for his acting, I might add, though I could pick a worse director. Okay, now read something for me." He picked up a dog-eared copy of *The Voice of the Turtle*. "This is pretty much a classic in its own way," he said. "Maybe you won't feel too much above it."

Elizabeth stood up. "Mr. Price, I know you're laughing at me, and I know you have a perfect right to. Maybe the parts I've played are silly. I didn't do them because I expected to repeat my college triumphs on Broadway, but because they're parts anyone who really cares about being an actress ought to study, and because it was my one real opportunity to work on them—until I'm an established actress and can really do them if I want to. I have learned a lot from them that I can apply to anything I do."

"Pretty sure of yourself, aren't you?" Mr. Price asked.

"No. But I have to talk as though I were."

Mr. Price sighed. "Darling Miss Jerrold—it is Jerrold, isn't it?—there are so many like you. So many who believe in themselves as potential great ones—and many who don't have the handicap of being tall and wearing glasses—so many who have real talent. Do you know that with ten young women of equal talent only one of them can possibly succeed?"

"I'm willing to risk it," Elizabeth said.

Mr. Price sighed again. "All right. Read for me."

"What shall I read?" Elizabeth took the book from him.

"Just hunt for a longish passage. One of Sally's. Are you familiar with the play?"

"We did it in college. I directed it, though; I didn't act in it."

"Good. That means you ought to know it pretty well but you won't be giving me a rehash of an old performance. Found something?"

"Yes. Here's a speech of Sally's." Elizabeth read the speech slowly, not trying to force a quick characterization. She made her voice low and pleasant, her words clear and well-defined, but she felt that she was failing thoroughly, that Mr. Price expected a performance. When she had finished the speech she said, "I'm sorry it was so bad. I can't plunge into a character right away."

"No, and you had sense enough not to try," Mr. Price told her, and for the first time his smile was for her and not at her. "One of the greatest banes of my existence is the radio actor who gives a magnificent first reading and then deteriorates until his performance is thoroughly mediocre. Each time I cast a show I say that I won't be fooled, and each time I am fooled.

Okay, Miss Jerrold. If you want to come under the terms I've outlined—as a scholarship apprentice—you may."

Elizabeth sat down abruptly. "Yes. I want to," she said, and her voice sounded as though Mr. Price had punched her in the stomach.

"Good. Give Sadie your address and she will drop you a line about trains and when to arrive and so forth. Also I will have her send you a note confirming all this so that once you get back to that good college of yours you won't worry about my forgetting you. Goodbye, Miss Jerrold. I'll look forward to seeing you at the end of June, and you, in the meanwhile, may look forward to a summer of hard work."

"Yes. Thank you," Elizabeth said, still sounding winded.

Mr. Price smiled at her again. "And one more thing. I hope you realize that I am offering you this opportunity not because of your reading, which, as you were aware, was barely adequate, but because of Mr. Canitz's hunch and my own whim. The theatre is not a reasonable place. You may as well learn that now." He held out his hand to her.

Elizabeth shook it and then, after giving Sadie her address, left the office. She almost missed Jane Gardiner, who was standing in the dim hallway leaning against a fire extinguisher.

"Hello, how'd you make out?" Jane asked her. "Thought I'd wait and see."

"I've got a scholarship," Elizabeth told her, beaming, and very pleased at Jane's friendly interest.

"Oh, good, I'm awfully glad. Look, let's go have a cup of coffee at the Automat to celebrate."

Elizabeth hesitated, then said, "I don't think I want any coffee, but I'd love to come while you have yours."

"Fine."

They went down in the elevator, both smiling with a vague and dreamy happiness at the prospect of the summer ahead of them. And to Elizabeth New York was no longer frightening but suddenly full of excitement and glamour, and the starkness of the Automat was vested in glory because Elizabeth Jerrold and Jane Gardiner were going there and perhaps one day other struggling young actresses would say, "Do you know, the great and famous Elizabeth Jerrold and Jane Gardiner used to come here!"

Elizabeth sat down at one of the tables and waited until Jane came back with two cups of coffee. "Just thought you might have changed your mind," she said casually. "If you don't want it, I'll drink it. Or, if you're broke or something at the moment—and heaven knows almost everybody in the theatre is—you can pay me back sometime."

"But that's just the trouble. I probably can't," Elizabeth said. Her voice sounded rather desperate.

Jane looked at her with friendly curiosity, then said lightly, "What's a cup of coffee between friends? Anyhow, I was referring to the golden future when we're both rich and famous and have our names in lights. Look, let's get to know each other. I'll give you my autobiography and you can give me yours. Though as for me, I'm a lot more exciting than my autobiography."

Elizabeth laughed. "Me, too."

"I'm just a damn good actress," Jane said. "How about you?"

"I'm a damn good actress, too."

"Good. Now we know the most important thing about each other. As for the unimportant details, I was born in New York and I've lived here most of my life. My father teaches higher mathematics at Columbia and I can't count up to ten. Neither can my mother, who is terribly beautiful but has never made me feel like an ugly duckling. I graduated from Columbia against my will and on my parents' insistence, though they're both very nice about my wanting to be an actress, and last winter I went to the American Academy of Dramatic Arts and fell madly in love with a great young actor named John Peter Toller who also—and for this I got down on my knees and begged and it's why I took this scholarship rather than a job anywhere else though I *did* honestly and truly *try* to get a job; I told you I'd been to dozens of other offices today—anyhow where was I? Oh, yes, John Peter has a scholarship with Price this summer, too. He's been away for two weeks visiting his parents and during these fourteen days my life has been blighted. I feel as though I'm not breathing when I'm out of his presence. He's the oxygen in my air, the sun in my universe, the staff of my life. From this you may gather that he means a great deal to me, but please don't tell him because he knows it far too well already. Now tell me about you."

A sober, rather sad look came over Elizabeth's face. Then she said lightly, "There isn't much to tell. My parents are dead and when I'm not in college in Northampton, I live with my aunt in Virginia. She doesn't approve of the theatre. I graduate this year. As for men, I'm footloose and fancy-free, and I've no idea of letting an emotional entanglement hamper my career."

Jane laughed. "Now if that doesn't sound like a college student. *My* emotional entanglement, if you want to call it that, hasn't hampered my career a bit. It's helped it. I know more about life and humanity and understanding and compassion and knowledge—and therefore about acting too—since I've known my darling John Peter than I ever dreamed of knowing before. Just you wait, my girl. You'll see." Jane pushed back her chair. "I've got to dash now, I promised my mother that I'd meet her. Maybe we'll room together this summer. I do hope so. Anyhow, I'll be seeing you at the end of June."

"Right," Elizabeth said. "Good luck till then."

"And good luck to you, too."

They shook hands. Elizabeth watched Jane walk swiftly out of the Automat, erect, graceful, assured, and somehow more alive than anyone else in the restaurant. Elizabeth realized that Jane was probably well in advance of her as an actress, and then thought happily, But I'll learn! Now I'm being given my chance to really learn with a professional company!

Everything began then, she thought, stuffing the last few papers into Mr. Price's overturned wastepaper basket. That was even the first time I saw Kurt. She watched Jane get up, push the wastepaper basket under Mr. Price's desk, and perch again on a corner of the desk.

"Jane," Elizabeth asked abruptly, "did you notice if everybody's gone, backstage? Is anybody left in the dressing rooms?"

"They've all gone ages ago," Jane told her. "You ought to know that. Ben locked up before he left. He always does."

"Did Kurt"—Elizabeth turned her face carefully away and

made her voice overcasual—"leave any message for me with you, maybe?"

"Nope," Jane said.

Elizabeth stood up. "I think I'll go on back to the Cottage and go to bed." She seemed suddenly to droop like a wilted sunflower. "I'm kind of tired and Mr. Price wants me in the box office at nine. Got a handkerchief, Jane? My glasses are filthy."

"Apprentices aren't supposed to work in the mornings," Jane said, handing her one of the small white squares of linen she always carried. "We're supposed to have classes in the morning."

"Sure, I know, but if Mr. Price tells me to be in the box office at nine, there isn't much I can do about it. Maybe he won't keep me long. I love being in the box office any other time." She blew on her glasses and wiped them with Jane's handkerchief.

"If Price is going to work you at all hours of the day, he shouldn't make you pay room and board."

Elizabeth sighed, handing Jane back her handkerchief. "I'd give my eyeteeth for room and board. I'd feel okay about Aunt Harriet, then. It's a lousy business, accepting money from people, especially when they don't want to give it. Let's go." She took the key out of the cash box and turned off the light, and they left the office. Elizabeth locked the door behind them and put the key in the pocket of her skirt.

"Want something to eat before we go back to the Cottage?" Jane asked.

"No, I don't think so."

"Dinner was a long time ago. I'll treat you."

"Thanks a lot, Jane. But I really don't want anything. You go ahead, though."

Jane shook her head. "I've already had a hamburger with John Peter and I told him to wait for me in the Cottage."

The Cottage, where all the apprentices and most of the professional company lived during the summer, was several blocks from the theatre and the beach. The theatre had once been a casino and the Cottage had first been a private home and then an orphanage. The casino went bankrupt and the orphans were moved to a larger and newer building. Even though the Cottage was set back from the beach, the floors were always sandy under the rugs and the sheets damp in cold weather, and it constantly smelled musty.

Elizabeth and Jane walked side by side on the sidewalk. "I'll bet your Aunt Harriet doesn't approve of your staying up late like this," Jane said.

Elizabeth grinned. "I *think* Aunt Harriet's fond of me—in her own way—but I *know* she doesn't approve of me. Your parents sound so wonderful, Jane, the way they really like you, and don't mind about your wanting to be an actress."

Even the darkness could not hide the forlorn look that suddenly fell on Jane's face. "They don't approve of John Peter," she said.

"Why not?"

"I don't know, but it makes me unhappy anyhow."

"But they let you come here with him this summer," Elizabeth said.

Jane shook her head sadly. "It's just their way of doing things. They know if they tried to keep me away from him it'd just make it worse. But it's like your aunt hoping you'd like chemistry better than the theatre. I'll never like anyone better than John Peter."

They had reached the Cottage now and they climbed the stone steps in silence. There was only one dim light on in the large living room, which the apprentices, and occasionally the company, used for rehearsals. Dorothy Dawne, also known as Dottie, the same blond woman Elizabeth had seen in Mr. Price's office, and Huntley Haskell, another one of the professional actors, were sitting together on one corner of a sagging sofa, embracing passionately. This was nothing unusual, and Elizabeth and Jane, barely glancing in their direction, went slowly up the stairs. Elizabeth felt suddenly very tired. It wasn't a physical tiredness but a tiredness in her heart, because Kurt had asked her to meet him and then hadn't come.

Maybe he left a message for me with one of the others, she thought, and started to hurry.

The professional company lived in rooms on the second floor and the ten girl apprentices lived on the third floor. The male apprentices lived in a big dormitory room over the garage. Most of the paying girl apprentices had single or double rooms, but Elizabeth and Jane lived with two of the paying apprentices in a lopsided room under the eaves. The two paying apprentices had the large half and the big closet. Elizabeth and Jane had the small half and a curtained-off alcove for a closet.

The door to their room was open and the lights were blazing. John Peter and Sophie Sherman, one of Elizabeth and Jane's roommates, sat on Jane's bed. Ditta Coates, a paying apprentice who lived down the hall, sat sprawled across the bed of their other roommate, Bibi Towne. Ditta was a plain girl of about twenty-nine who taught dramatics at a boarding school. In the large half of the room, Ben, draped in a sheet, Jane's blond hairpiece pinned to his dark hair, was doing the vial scene from *Romeo and Juliet*.

" 'Stay, Tybalt, stay!' " Ben cried, waving his long arms wildly as Elizabeth entered. " 'Romeo, I come! This do I drink to thee.' " Draining a paper container of coffee, he fell, all arms and legs, across one of the beds. Elizabeth and Jane joined in the applause.

Ben laughed happily. "It's certainly the *vile* scene, isn't it?"

" 'O wonderful, wonderful, and most wonderful wonderful, and yet again wonderful, and after that, out of all hooping!' " Elizabeth said.

Ben raised one of his dark, peaked eyebrows. "And what, may I ask, is that from?"

Elizabeth grinned. "Celia, in *As You Like It*."

"Be careful of my hair," Jane warned, as Ben reached up and began tousling the hairpiece that looked so incongruous against his dark locks, his eyes as alive and eager as a puppy's.

"Now I'm going to be Melisande."

"Not with my hair you aren't," Jane said. "Give it here."

"What a brute you are." Ben reluctantly unpinned the hair. "What was your telephone call, Liz?"

"It was my Aunt Harriet and she'd gone to bed. I'll have to call her tomorrow morning."

"Bed at this time of night!" Ben cried, tossing Jane the hair.

"It's the shank of the evening." He took a brown paper bag off one of the bureaus. "I brought you a hot dog, Liz. It's all covered with mustard and pickle the way you like it."

"Ben, you're an angel," Elizabeth said, and pulled the hot dog, wrapped in innumerable paper napkins, out of the bag. "I'm going to have to eat this out the window or I'll drip all over the room." Bless Ben, she thought. He knows how I hate to sponge off people, but he always sees that I get fed.

Sophie, who had hay fever and was always accompanied by Kleenex, threw her a box. "Here, Liz."

"Thanks, Soph." Elizabeth took a large bite of the hot dog, then asked with pretended casualness, "Any messages for me?"

Ditta shook her head. "Not a thing."

Sophie said indifferently, "What did you expect?"

But Ben turned to Elizabeth and said bluntly, "I saw Kurt Canitz going into the Ambassador with Sarah Courtmont."

For a minute Elizabeth looked at him furiously, then she turned away.

"That was mean, Ben," Ditta said.

"Well, it's the truth."

Ditta rose, saying, "If I'm going to keep awake at any of the classes tomorrow morning, I've got to get my beauty rest. Good night, all." She yawned widely and ran her fingers through the rather stiff permanent in her brown hair, hair that was already beginning to show a few threads of grey.

As she left, Elizabeth yawned, too. "If I don't get to bed, I'll never get to the box office by nine. Come on, kids."

"You mean you want us to go?" Ben asked with incredulity.

"In words of one syllable, yes. It's our turn to set tables to-morrow morning, Ben. Mind you don't oversleep."

"And mind you don't wake me when you get up, Ben," John Peter said. He bent over Jane and gave her a quick kiss.

"Good night, darling," Jane said.

"Good night, sweetheart."

Ben patted Elizabeth clumsily on the shoulder. "It's a pity your attention is otherwise occupied, Liz. We might have made such a lovely couple." Then he raised one of his peaked brows and looked around. "Where's the charming fourth roommate, by the way?"

Sophie shrugged; she had a petulant way of lifting her shoulders whenever she was envious or discontented that particularly annoyed Elizabeth. "Bibi is probably at the Ambassador or Irving's," Sophie said, "fraternizing with the professional company."

It's amazing, Elizabeth thought, how Sophie can make anything she says sound unpleasant.

Ben lounged in the doorway and said, "Why, I'll never know. The professional company stinks. Good night, kids. See you over the canned orange juice, Liz."

A voice from down the stairs shouted up, "Elizabeth Jerrold!"

Ben stuck his head out the door. "What?" he shouted back. Jane winced, as she always did at loud noises.

"Is Liz there?"

"Yes."

"Mr. Canitz wants her."

"Damn it, what does he want at this time of night?" Ben said. "Tell him you're asleep, Liz."

"But I'm not," Elizabeth said, and ran to the door. "Tell him I'll be right down," she called. Elizabeth's voice, though she raised it only slightly, easily reached down the two flights of stairs; instinctively she understood projection and during the summer had learned to add more to her native knowledge. Then she said, not looking at the others, "He probably wants me to type some letters for him or something."

"At this time of night?" Jane asked.

"Why not? Mr. Price had me taking dictation till two o'clock one morning." She looked hastily in the mirror, and ran her brush over the soft brown waves that never, to Jane's envy, had to be put up in bobby pins at night. "Well, goodbye," she said, and hurried out the door. Ben's clarion-clear voice floated down the stairs after her—and what Ben lacked in projection, he more than compensated for in volume—singing:

> "Love is a little thing
>   Shaped like a lizard.
>   It runs up and down
>   And tickles your gizzard."

Elizabeth quickened her footsteps and felt the color mounting to her cheeks.

Kurt Canitz was waiting for her at the foot of the stairs. He stood leaning against the balustrade, his dark head as sleek and beautiful as a black leopard's, and held out his hands to her.

"Elizabeth," he said, "Liebchen, sweetheart. I'm sorry I didn't meet you after the show tonight."

Elizabeth said nothing.

"La Courtmont asked me to go up to the Ambassador with her for a drink and everybody else was going down to Irving's. It was my one chance to see her alone. I wanted to talk to her about the lead in a show I'm thinking of producing this fall." His voice was childlike and pleading.

"Sure," Elizabeth said. "It's okay, Kurt."

"She's certainly a beautiful creature," Kurt said as he put his arm about Elizabeth and led her out of the Cottage. They walked through the deserted streets to the boardwalk, and then in the direction of the Ambassador, at the other end of the boardwalk from the concessions and soda fountains.

"I hope you've been watching Courtmont this week, Elizabeth," Kurt said. "You can learn a lot about makeup from her. And lighting. That woman knows more about lighting than most electricians. A lot of good actresses don't know when they're in a spot and when they're in shadow. Courtmont manages to get all the light on her face and everybody else slightly shadowed. And she knows how to make up those big blue eyes of hers so that they look like two small individual spotlights of her own. Your eyes are——" He stopped for a moment, then asked in a tone of wondering surprise, "What color are your eyes, my Liebchen, my Elizabeth?"

"Grey," Elizabeth said.

Kurt laughed, rather apologetically. "It's odd how one remembers what eyes are like but doesn't remember what color they are. You have good eyes, Elizabeth. Wide apart. And nice lashes. And nice wavy brown hair. But you should put in a rinse to make it redder."

Usually Elizabeth seized on any of Kurt's suggestions like a seagull diving after a fish, but now she shook her head. "If I put in a rinse, it would look dyed. This way, what red there is is my own."

"It wouldn't look dyed if you had it done properly."

"I can't afford that sort of thing, Kurt." People with money never understand that other people don't have it, she thought. Even Kurt, who usually seemed to understand everything. Aloud she said, "I don't like dyed hair anyhow."

It was the first time she had ever disagreed with Kurt, and she felt quickly upset and unhappy.

But Kurt's arm tightened about her waist in an affectionate gesture, and he said softly, "It was just an idea, Liebchen. You're perfect as you are. I'm very fond of you, funny one, did you know that?"

Elizabeth's heart winged with happiness as it always did when Kurt spoke to her in that gentle, loving way.

But as to his question, she could give it no answer, because to think that Kurt Canitz was really fond of her was too exciting and too wonderful a thing to be believable. All she wanted to do was to cry out, I love you! but she just leaned against him and continued to walk beside him on the lonely boardwalk with the salty night wind pushing her hair back from her face.

I wonder when I first began to love him? she thought, and it seemed to her that it had been from that very first moment she saw him, that April morning when he had come walking into Mr. Price's office and she had realized at once that he was different from everybody else in the room. And then there was the first night they went walking on the boardwalk together. They had barely been there a week and it was opening night of the season.

That whole evening had been a wonderful one for Elizabeth, starting with the moment when the apprentices put on their long summer evening dresses in preparation for ushering in the first audience of the summer. Elizabeth was grateful that she had been on the Ivy Chain at college and that being on Ivy meant a pastel evening dress. She had made her own, a long corn-colored dirndl skirt and a deeper yellow blouse that bared both her shoulders.

"The reason I stick to dirndls is that they're inexpensive and easy to make," she had confessed to Jane, "and I'm really no seamstress."

"They look wonderful on you," Jane said, rather wistfully, "and they make me look dumpy. Look, honey, I have a big sort of dark amber cummerbund thing that would look gorgeous with that outfit. You take it. I never wear it."

"Oh, but I couldn't—"

"Listen," Jane said, rather sharply, "don't get your back up again. It is also blessed to receive. We're all perfectly aware that at the moment you are—shall we say—short of cash. Okay, that's a fact and what difference does it make? We know you aren't trying to milk us dry or take advantage of us or anything. Now take the dratted cummerbund or I'll think you think I don't have any taste. Oh, lawks, maybe that's the root of it. Do you think it would look awful?"

"No. I think it would look wonderful," Elizabeth said. "I thought of a sash of a darker color when I sewed the outfit, only for Ivy we had to be all one color."

"Well, will you take it then?" Jane asked. "Please. Or you'll really hurt my feelings."

"Thanks ever so much." Elizabeth knew that her gratitude was clumsy and ill-expressed. "I—just thanks, Jane."

"Oh, forget it," Jane said. "Here, let me put it on for you. Oh, Liz, it does look elegant! Come on, hon, we have to dash. If you're head usher you ought to be there before anybody else."

The opening went beautifully. The audience loved Mariella Hedeman, the company's character woman, as the crotchety old lady in the wheelchair, and Kurt Canitz as her murderer got three solo curtain calls and several shouts of "Bravo." The apprentices, standing in the back, jumped up and down and shouted and cheered. Afterwards they all went backstage. They were imbued with a glowing sense of vicarious importance. After all, Ben was really one of them and he was assistant stage manager; and Mariella Hedeman gave them voice lessons; and Huntley Haskell, who played the rather sweetly pompous young Englishman, was their acting coach. Even Marian Hatfield, their movement teacher, who had not been in this play, had joined everyone backstage. The apprentices felt they belonged in this company; they were part of a professional theatre; these were their friends and colleagues who had just given the audience a pleasant and exciting evening.

Ben had met them anxiously. "Did you notice I was a little late on the second act curtain?" he asked with a worried frown. His blue shirt was moist with nervous perspiration and his shadow loomed grotesquely on one of the flats like a beanpole of a giant.

"No," Jane said, "it looked perfect to me. I don't think it should have come down a second earlier."

"You mean you don't think anybody in the audience noticed it, then?"

"For crying out loud, no." John Peter sounded exasperated.

"Well, Kurt swore at me like mad. I didn't think it was late. Maybe he just had the jitters like the rest of us," Ben said, sounding relieved. "We're in, anyhow. They loved it, didn't they?"

"Wasn't Kurt wonderful?" Elizabeth cried.

"Oh, he was okay," John Peter said. "I've seen the part done a lot more subtly. Kurt doesn't know the meaning of shading. And of course his accent was out of place."

Elizabeth knew better than to argue with John Peter in the backstage crowd, especially as Jane was nodding in agreement. John Peter was opinionated at all times, and here, with people milling around, she would have no chance even if she shouted. "We'll discuss his performance later," she said. "I want to go see Miss Hedeman now. See you later, kids." She moved across the stage toward the long passage off which the dressing rooms were located.

Kurt Canitz's dressing room door was open. He was sitting at his table in his dressing gown, his makeup still on, talking to a group of people. He looked up as Elizabeth passed and called out to her.

"Yes, Mr. Canitz?" She stopped and waited to hear whether he wanted a cup of coffee or a fresh tin of Albolene.

"I want to talk to you. Wait for me, will you? I won't be long," he said, and smiled at her.

"Yes, Mr. Canitz."

Elizabeth went down the corridor and spoke briefly to Miss Hedeman and Huntley Haskell. A group of apprentices was in Dottie's dressing room. Elizabeth had not liked her performance. "You can't play that girl with glamour," she had whispered indignantly to Jane. "The thing that gets her audience's sympathy is that she's pitiful and frustrated and doesn't know the score. Wouldn't you think that Kurt—or somebody— would have stopped her? Dottie, I mean?"

"It's a tough job trying to direct *and* act in a play," Jane whispered back. "Anyhow, I don't imagine La Dawne's easy to direct."

Elizabeth was rather disgusted at the overgracious way Dottie (and whatever *was* her real name? No one was christened Dorothy Dawne) was holding forth, and she was angry with the apprentices for fawning over her simply because she had made two or three grade-B movies. I don't suppose she's any older than Jane or I, she thought, and she certainly doesn't have as much talent. Either of us would have been better in that part.

She did not admit to herself that Dottie's lack of talent was not the only thing that annoyed her.

In spite of his promise not to be long, it was after one on opening night when Kurt was ready to leave. Most of the apprentices and the company had already departed. They had gone down the boardwalk to Irving's, the nightclub that was very popular among the company and the more affluent apprentices. Jane and John Peter had been there once that first week, and had said that once was enough, but this evening they tagged along with everybody else.

"After all, there's only one opening night to a season," John Peter said. "Coming, Liz?"

Elizabeth was glad she had a legitimate excuse. "Nope. Can't. Mr. Canitz asked me to wait."

"What for?" Jane asked curiously.

Elizabeth shrugged. "I don't know. Letters to type or something, I suppose."

"As long as he doesn't ask you over to his hotel to show you his etchings," Jane said.

Elizabeth laughed. "Don't be a nut."

She waited in the corridor outside Kurt's dressing room. When his last visitor left he stuck his head out and saw her.

"There's my good little Liz," he said, "though not so little, are you, Liebchen? Come in and sit down."

She went into the dressing room and watched while he finished removing his makeup, wiped it off with cotton saturated with witch hazel, and repeated the process three times.

"Elizabeth," he said, "how old are you?"

"Twenty."

"And this is your first experience in the professional theatre?"

"Yes, Mr. Canitz."

"Are you enjoying it?"

She nodded. "Terribly."

"Yes. You look happy." He leaned back in his chair and sighed. "This tiny little dressing room! Really, it's more like solitary confinement than a place for an actor to prepare for a role. Do you suffer from claustrophobia?"

She shook her head.

"Well, I do. I thought if that mob of well-meaning but stupid people didn't leave me alone I'd scream or at least be stupidly rude. And the thought of going to Irving's, that mediocre little *boîte de nuit*—I should get claustrophobia all over again if I went there. I think that I shall telephone and say that I have a headache and have had to go home to bed, and will everybody please have a drink—two drinks—on me. No. Better yet. I shall donate the entire party. That would more than make up for my absence, don't you think? That would make up for anybody's absence."

"No, they'll be disappointed," Elizabeth started, and meant it.

"Rubbish," Kurt said. "Anyhow, it is myself I am thinking of. I saw you passing by, looking so fresh and cool and clean as I was surrounded by that ravening mob, and I thought to myself, Kurt, if you could do as you chose this evening, what would you do? And my answer was, I would go for a walk and a talk by the ocean with Elizabeth Jerrold. Will you go for a walk and a talk by the ocean with me, Elizabeth Jerrold?"

"Yes, thank you. I'd like to very much." Her heart beat with excitement. Me, she thought unbelievingly. He wants to go for a walk with me! And on opening night!

As though reading her thoughts, he said, "So much is made of opening nights, and by now opening nights and stupid parties are an old story for me. I'm going to call Irving's and then we can go."

Afterwards they walked on the boardwalk. Kurt talked and Elizabeth listened. He told her of his childhood in Sweden, of the beautiful castle where he had been born and brought up, of the cold, tragic woman who was his mother and the lecherous degenerate who was his father. His voice was taut with remembered unhappiness.

"Did you have a happy childhood, little Elizabeth?" he asked her. "The pastoral childhood that seems to be the birthright of all American children?"

She shook her head. "I don't think all American children have such happy childhoods, Mr. Canitz," she said. "That's just a myth."

"Please, please," he cried. "To you I am Kurt! Everybody else calls me Kurt, so why should you, you the most charming and unusual of all, be formal with me? Say 'Kurt.' I want to hear it from you."

"Kurt," she said softly.

He put his arm tenderly around her and felt the sudden uncontrollable rigidity in her spine. "Liebchen," he murmured, "you are twenty and you are bursting with a great talent and yet you stop suddenly still when I touch you, like a young doe startled by the sight of a hunter crouched in the hill. Why?"

She shook her head mutely.

"No answer?" he asked, and he took her face in his hands and turned it toward him and kissed her gently. Still holding her face, he pulled away, holding her gaze. He put his arm back around her and they continued walking in silence until he asked, "Elizabeth, forgive me, but was that the first time you have been kissed?"

She answered in a low voice. "No. But it might just as well have been."

"What do you mean?"

"It was the first time it meant anything to me."

"It did mean something to you?"

She nodded. "Yes."

"It meant something to me, too," he said.

That had started it, that evening, that first evening on the boardwalk. With that kiss it had been as though Kurt had reached bodily into her and taken her heart, as though he had procured it for his personal possession. She felt helpless when she was with him, whenever she thought of him, and now she understood the blind look that came over Jane's face whenever she talked of John Peter.

"What are you thinking?" Kurt asked her.

"I was remembering opening night," Elizabeth told him, "when we went for our first walk on the boardwalk."

"So was I," Kurt said. "Oh, Liz, what a nice kid you are!"

Elizabeth laughed. "What brought that on?"

"Every once in a while I realize all over again how nice you are, and I just thought I'd tell you."

"Thanks." She tried to keep the upsurge of pleasure out of her voice. In spite of everything, Jane took John Peter for granted, but Elizabeth could never take Kurt for granted, could never be sure from one moment to the next that the wonderful times she had spent with him had existed in actuality and not in her imagination. For one thing, professionally John Peter and Jane were on a par, but whenever Elizabeth thought of her own relationship with Kurt she was reminded of the stories of her childhood, the prince and the daughter of the woodcutter, the peasant's child and the lord of high degree.

"Want to turn back?" Kurt asked.

"Not unless you do." She did not want to turn back ever. She wanted to walk on and on with the houses thinning out so that on one side of them were sand dunes covered with harsh wild beach grasses and on the other the ocean reaching out in an ever-changing pattern to the horizon. "Look at the stars, Kurt. There are always more stars when there isn't a moon. Don't you love stars? Sometimes I love them so much I want to reach up and pick them and hug them the way I used to do with flowers when I was little; and then I cried because I crushed the flowers when I hugged them. Flowers don't like to be loved too hard. And my Aunt Harriet always tells me that people don't, either." Although her voice carefully ended the sentence as a statement, there was a question in her heart.

Kurt did not answer it. "Your Aunt Harriet's an old maid, isn't she?"

"Yes. She was engaged once, but her fiancé died of typhoid fever before they were married."

"I like being loved," Kurt said, though his voice was light. "How about you?"

Elizabeth tried to match the lightness of her voice with his. "I think it's wonderful."

Kurt stopped walking and turned her around so that she faced him. Then he bent toward her and touched her lips very lightly with his own. "You sweet child," he whispered.

Elizabeth leaned against him, her heart beating wildly long after the kiss was over.

"It's getting chilly," Kurt said. "There's a wind off the ocean tonight."

"Yes. We'd better go back," Elizabeth whispered regretfully.

"What are you whispering for, Liebchen?"

"I don't know."

"Let's not go just yet. Let's walk and talk for a little longer."

"Yes." She slipped her hand into his.

Kurt's voice became easy and conversational; Elizabeth often wondered at his ability to make transitions from one mood to another. "You and Jane Gardiner are the only apprentices in this place with a scrap of talent. Acting is an important thing to you, isn't it, my darling?"

"Yes," Elizabeth said seriously. "The most important thing in the world."

"The very most important?" Kurt asked.

Elizabeth nodded.

Kurt leaned forward and pressed his lips to hers again. Then he said, "We should head back."

"All right."

They walked hand in hand until they came to the Cottage. The light was now off in the living room and the night light glowed dimly in the hall, casting long shadows across the walls.

"Shall I come in with you and talk for a while longer?" Kurt asked.

She shook her head. "No. It's terribly late. I've got to go to bed now. Good night, Kurt."

"Good night, Liebchen." He did not kiss her again, but

squeezed her hand. Then he went out, and she could imagine him, a solitary figure, walking back up the boardwalk to the Ambassador Hotel.

Jane and her other two roommates were already asleep when Elizabeth went up, and she undressed quietly in the dark. Her alarm clock was set for the morning and she put it by her bed. The light in the boys' room over the garage was still on and she could see in her mind's eye Ben and John Peter and the others lying on their beds in the hot garage room, talking about the theatre, and life, and the theatre, and the world, and again the theatre . . .

She lay in her bed and stared at a patch of faded, peeling wallpaper, and happiness blew over her like the breeze from the sea. I am in love, a voice in her sang over and over again. I am in love.

She never once remembered that she had to call her Aunt Harriet in the morning.

Act II
SATURDAY

ON SATURDAY most of the professional company slept through breakfast, since their rehearsal call was not until eleven. But the apprentices' classes began at nine thirty and the majority of them came down to eat, along with the professionals who taught their classes. Ben and Elizabeth, both in a haze of sleep, set the tables and filled the small glasses with canned orange juice.

When they went back in the kitchen, Mrs. Browden, the cook, said, "I've squeezed some fresh orange juice for you, my pets. Drink it quick before anyone else comes down and finds out."

"Mrs. Browden, you're an angel," Elizabeth cried.

Ben flung his arms about Mrs. Browden's solid body. "Light of my life! You know I can't abide that canned stuff!"

"And how will you have your eggs this morning?" she asked.

"Eggs, joy of my heart!" Ben exclaimed. "This is Saturday. We have puffed rice on Saturdays."

"And so we do," Mrs. Browden said, taking down a frying pan and setting it on the stove. "But you and Liz could both do with more flesh on your bones. How will you have them, Liz?"

"Scrambled would be wonderful, Mrs. Browden."

"Ben?"

Ben pulled thoughtfully at one of his ears. Perhaps by nature and perhaps because of the fact that he pulled it whenever engaged in thought, that particular ear did not curl over in the usual fashion at the top, but was pointed, giving him a lopsidedly elfin look. "Now let me see, Mrs. Browden. Ah, I have it. Poached in sour cream with anchovies. And just a soupçon of Pernod."

Mrs. Browden looked at him dotingly and set about scrambling four eggs. "Pour yourselves some coffee, my pets, and there's a wee bit of heavy cream left in the icebox from Mr. and Mrs. Price's breakfast. They'll never miss it. How they expect you to work all day on empty stomachs I do not know."

"My joy," Ben said, pouring cream into his cup, measuring it out carefully so that he left exactly half for Elizabeth, "you'd never let that happen. Thanks to you I shall put off going into a decline for at least another summer."

"Here's your eggs. Get along in the dining room with you now. Mrs. Price doesn't approve of your being out in the kitchen with me so much."

"Lulu and J. P. Price. What a pair," Ben muttered, pushing through the swinging door into the still-empty dining room. "She was made from a tack and he was made from a nail."

Elizabeth and Ben sat down at a table. Ben took a large mouthful of eggs and shouted into the kitchen, "These eggs are but divine, Mrs. Browden."

Jane came in, yawning behind her small, delicate hand. "John Peter not here yet?"

"He was sleeping the sleep of the just and the unjust when I left," Ben started, and then turned to the entrance of the dining room with the sudden quiver of anticipation that always betrayed him when he prepared to tease anyone. "Well, well, Soapie," he said. "Good morning! And good morning, Bibi, my little Pekingese!"

Sophie and Bibi came into the dining room and sat down at the table, each wearing an expensive cotton dress. Jane had on knee-length blue denim shorts and a soft shirt, the color of pale corn, matching her hair. Elizabeth, since she had to work in the box office, had forsworn her usual uniform of blue jeans and a white shirt and wore a flowered dirndl skirt, tiny multicolored flowers on a black background, which she had made at college from a piece of material left over from the Dramatic Association's production of *Autumn Crocus*.

"Look at Liz all dressed up!" Bibi cried, ignoring Ben.

"And very nice she looks, too," Jane said quickly.

"Well, anybody knows they look better in a dress or a skirt than they do in blue jeans. Why don't you get some more dresses, Liz? You look real cute in them." The edge of maliciousness to Bibi's voice was so slight as to be almost undetectable, but Ditta, who had just entered the room, looked at her sharply.

"Oh, I like my jeans," Elizabeth said casually. "Comfort first."

Jane poured skim milk into her coffee, looked at it distastefully, and said, "Liz has the figure for blue jeans. Most females don't. Have some puffed rice, Bibi. How's tricks, Soapie?"

"Don't call me Soapie," Sophie said automatically. "Ben Walton, is that egg on your plate?"

"Egg, certainly not," Ben said, "nothing but a mirage." He stood, picked up his plate, whisked Elizabeth's from in front of her, and disappeared into the kitchen.

"If Mrs. Browden's given you eggs and the rest of us have to eat puffed rice, I don't think it's fair; I think it's just mean," Bibi complained.

"Eggs, eggs." Ben came back from the kitchen with a pot of fresh coffee. "Who said anything about eggs?"

"Well, it's not fair and I've a good mind to speak to Mrs. Price." Tempers were always shortest over the breakfast table, especially when there had not been enough sleep the night before.

"I wouldn't if I were you, honey bunch." Ben stood behind Bibi, tilting the coffeepot dangerously.

"Watch out for that coffeepot!" Bibi screamed.

Ben stood very still; only the coffeepot leaned menacingly toward Bibi. "Then I'd just forget about Mrs. Price if I were you, angel foot," he said.

Bibi shrugged petulantly. "Gee, couldn't you see I was just kidding?" she said.

Elizabeth stood up, took the coffeepot from Ben, filled Bibi's cup, and went around the table filling the rest. Other apprentices and a few members of the professional company were beginning to straggle in. Elizabeth took the coffeepot out to Mrs. Browden, calling over her shoulder, "I've got to get to the box office, kids. See you later."

The theatre was deserted. Aunt Harriet, she thought. I've got to call her first thing. She quickly unlocked Mr. Price's office and let herself in, pulling up the shades and opening the windows. Picking up the telephone, she asked for operator nineteen. Again she heard the phone ringing and ringing. Then there was a faint click. "Elizabeth." She barely heard her aunt's voice, muffled as it always was when her aunt talked on the phone because Aunt Harriet never deigned to talk directly into the mouthpiece.

"Aunt Harriet," Elizabeth shouted, "is there anything wrong?"

"There certainly is," the thin-sounding voice said, "and you don't need to bellow, thank you. I am not deaf."

"What's the matter?" Elizabeth asked, controlling her voice; it was difficult not to shout back to that faint tone on the other end of the wire.

"You are the matter," Aunt Harriet said, and Elizabeth had to strain to hear. "You are to come home at once."

"But what—why—" Elizabeth's voice rose.

"I never should have let you go to that place. If I'd known you were going to go out alone with strange men at all hours of the night—"

"But, Aunt Harriet, I used to go on dates when I was in college!"

"Don't bellow. You never had men in your bedroom."

"Aunt Harriet," Elizabeth tried to explain, "it's different here. Our bedroom's big and we use it as a living room. That way we don't get under the professional company's feet in the Cottage living room."

"Don't try to make excuses, Elizabeth. There is no way to condone men in your bedroom. In your last letter you actually said something about some Ben . . ." The voice trailed off.

"I'm sorry," Elizabeth said. "I couldn't hear you."

"Of course you could hear me. There's no reason why you shouldn't be able to hear me. I said that some Ben admired your pajamas."

"But, Aunt Harriet, I'm far more covered up in pajamas than I am in a cotton dress, even."

"Elizabeth, don't argue with me. How do I know you don't undress in front of these men?"

Elizabeth's voice was icy. "You ought to have more faith in me than that."

Aunt Harriet's voice, through its dimness, was also icy. "Perhaps you have forgotten your background. I expect you home on the train tomorrow evening."

Elizabeth's jaw set. "I'm sorry, Aunt Harriet, but I am not coming."

"I haven't yet sent you next week's money, which makes it impossible for you to stay. I knew I had made a mistake in allowing you to go to a theatre in the first place. After what happened with your mother, I should have learned my lesson."

"You promised me I could have this summer."

"I'm sorry, Elizabeth, but I have to act according to my own lights. And please realize that I am making this decision for your own good."

"Please, Aunt Harriet," Elizabeth begged. "Please let me

stay—even just one more week. I'll come home without a word if you'll just let me stay one more week. Valborg Andersen is playing here and I want so terribly to see her. She's a great actress and she's doing a great play and if I could just watch it all week I'd learn so terribly much."

"I'm sorry, Elizabeth. Believe me, I'm sorry. But I've made up my mind."

"But—"

"Elizabeth, I will not argue with you over long distance. I would not have spent this much time discussing a closed matter except that I realize your disappointment. Goodbye."

At the other end of the line the phone was hung up abruptly. Elizabeth held the receiver numbly before replacing it in its cradle. Just then, Mr. Price came in. "Time to get to work, Elizabeth," he said.

Without a word, Elizabeth opened the ticket window and sat down on the high stool in front of it. She startled as the phone rang. Aunt Harriet? She picked the receiver up. "Hello? . . . Yes, I can give you six tickets for tonight . . . I could give you better locations if I have you three and three . . . They'd be right behind each other . . . Good, I'll reserve them for you. In whose name, please? . . . They'll be at the box office. They should be picked up by seven forty-five . . . Thank you very much."

Ditta came up to the window and leaned in toward Elizabeth. "Listen, Liz, do me a favor, will you? Seven of my kids from school are here on vacation and they want to see the show tonight. Can you give me some tickets?"

Elizabeth jerked her head slightly to indicate J. P. Price sitting at his desk behind her in the office. "What do you mean, give?"

"Oh, they'll pay for them. I mean, I know this is Saturday night and everything. Can you squeeze them in?"

"If they don't mind being divided up."

"Oh, sure, anything'll be fine. Leave the tickets in my name, okay?"

"Okay," Elizabeth said. "Will do." She bent over the seating chart.

Ditta was looking at her probingly, in a way in which she might look at one of her students. "What's the matter?"

Elizabeth's voice was strained. "Nothing."

"You aren't your usual radiant self. I can tell something's wrong."

Again Elizabeth indicated Mr. Price. "I can't talk about it now," she whispered. "Are classes over?" she asked in her regular voice.

"All but voice. I reneged on that. No use trying to do anything with my voice. I'm tone-deaf. Rehearsal this afternoon?"

"Three till six. Will you be there?"

"Well, my students are here, so I'll have to miss it today. But actually I think I'm learning more from those rehearsals you kids thought up than I am from Huntley Haskell's classes. He's good when he bothers to be, but most of the time it seems to me he doesn't bother. Are you liking it here this summer?"

"I adore it," Elizabeth said, and tears welled up in her eyes.

Ditta looked at her sharply again, saying, "I don't think I picked such a hot place to sink my money in this summer. Most of what I am learning I wouldn't dare to teach my kids at school. I was at a marvelous theatre last summer but I thought it would do me good to try a different place this year. Next year I'd like to try a place that doesn't use the star system. It isn't enough to have the stars rehearse only one day with the professional company. I swear my high school kids have given more creditable performances than some of the stars I've seen here this summer."

"Valborg Andersen's been here all week rehearsing," Elizabeth reminded Ditta, her tears now under control.

Ditta nodded. "Well, she's the exception so far. Maybe we'll be given a great show Monday night," she said. "You've got some more customers. I'd better get going. See you at lunch."

"Right."

Elizabeth was leaning her head rather wearily against her hand when Ben came up to the window.

"Hi, Liz," he said. "What's wrong?"

She looked up at him in surprise. "How do you know anything's wrong? Not getting psychic, are you?"

"Bumped into Ditta."

"Ditta should keep her mouth closed."

"I had to twist her wrist," Ben said. "What's the matter, Liz? No nonsense, now. You aren't the crying type, so I know it's more than J. P. Priceless bawling you out about something. You're too used to that to let it upset you anyhow, so don't try that as an excuse."

Elizabeth looked behind her at J. P. Price's desk, but it was empty.

"He's in watching rehearsal," Ben said. "Now tell me what's up."

"Oh—" Elizabeth tried to keep the strain out of her voice. "Remember my long distance telephone call?"

"Yes. What about it?"

"It's all my own fault," Elizabeth said. "I've just been elected Miss Dope of the Year. Please don't tell the others how stupid I've been. I wanted—well, I wanted to make Aunt Harriet see what fun we all have here and how grateful I was to her for letting me have this summer and everything, and I wrote her about you and—and Kurt, and John Peter and Jane, and how we all sit up in our room talking half the night and everything, and she's got the idea that the Cottage is a House or something."

"Maybe she's not too far wrong at that," Ben said. "Some of the company down on the second floor ought to change their profession. But that doesn't have anything to do with you. She's not blaming you for *that*, is she?"

"She thinks *I'm* immoral, Ben. She says I have to come home."

"Do you have to do what she says?"

"This time I can't help myself. I haven't any money for room and board."

Ben's face darkened with anger. "Is the old witch poor?"

Elizabeth looked puzzled for a second. "The house in Jordan's big and all her furniture's beautiful and everything. I don't think money has anything to do with it, Ben. She's always been—oh, what you'd call eccentric; and she's always been against the theatre or any kind of a so-called bohemian life. When I first went to live with her, I was thirteen, and whenever I talked about wanting to be an actress she'd make me sit in my room for an hour to contemplate my evil spirit. But it's really understandable in her case, Ben. I don't mean to make her sound like an ogre—she isn't. She's truly tried to do the best she knows how for me. But she can't bear anything to do with the theatre because of my mother."

"What about your mother?" Ben asked.

"This the box office?" a voice behind Ben said. "Is this where I buy tickets for the Valborg Andersen play next week?"

"Yes, right here, sir," Elizabeth said, and Ben stepped aside.

When Elizabeth was relieved at the box office, there was about an hour until lunch. Mr. Price was back in the office so she told him the awful news from Aunt Harriet. When he grumbled about it being a "damn inconvenience," she hoped that he would offer to keep her on without paying the twenty dollars room and board. She held her breath, but he kept grumbling and stormed back into the theatre. Crushed, she went to see if Ben was through with rehearsal; as assistant stage manager he was the only one of Elizabeth's particular friends who actually had the opportunity to work daily with the professional company. He was standing by one of the open side doors talking to Valborg Andersen. Elizabeth watched them for a moment—Ben, tall and lanky with a lock of heavy dark hair falling across his forehead, and the smallish woman, dressed in a simple blue cotton dress, drinking coffee out of a paper cup and laughing heartily at something he was saying. Standing there in the shadows, rather wistfully looking at them, Elizabeth remembered very well the first time she had seen Valborg Andersen.

Almost every year during the Christmas holidays, Elizabeth's father would leave the small house across the street from the school where he taught English literature and go to New York to see as much theatre as he could, sending an unwilling Elizabeth off to Jordan to spend Christmas with Aunt Harriet. But when Elizabeth was ten her father started taking her with him, and the first Saturday evening they went to see Valborg Andersen in *Romeo and Juliet*. Never would Elizabeth forget the excitement and glamour of that evening. Perhaps Aunt Harriet's disapproval lent it an added charm.

Elizabeth had sat beside her father in the balcony, first row center ("My favorite place to see a play," he told her), holding his hand, half listening as he talked about the play, half looking about her at the audience, at the privileged glamorous people who were accustomed to going to plays, who sat there so calmly, talking to each other or glancing casually at their programs.

When the lights began to dim, Elizabeth clutched her father's arm in anticipation as the footlights came up and the red velvet curtain began to rise. At intermission her father said, "Are you enjoying it, dear? Andersen is giving a magnificent performance. It's a wonderful introduction to the theatre for you."

As usual when she was tremendously moved, Elizabeth could not speak. She knew only that the question of the future had been finally and definitely decided for her; she was going to be an actress. She nodded solemnly and waited for the curtain to rise again.

After that she went with her father to New York each Christmas until he died. Then there was no more theatre, except in her imagination, until she went to college. At college, in spite of chemistry, there was the Dramatic Association, and the Theatre Workshop, where she managed to take a few elective courses for credit. And occasionally a professional company came to the old Academy Theatre in Northampton where Sarah Bernhardt and Eleonora Duse had once played, or to one of the auditoriums in nearby Springfield.

Valborg Andersen came to Springfield to the high school auditorium as Portia in *The Merchant of Venice* the same year that she published her *Shakespeare Prefaces*. She came on a Saturday and played both a matinee and an evening performance. Elizabeth left college with her roommate at eleven o'clock in the morning, so afraid was she that they might not be on time for the rise of the afternoon curtain. The roommate sighed but did not attempt to reason with her. They were so early that they saw Valborg Andersen standing on the cold stage wearing an old raccoon coat and watching while the stage manager set the lights. Somehow that made the day even more wonderful than it had promised to be, this unofficial glimpse of the professional theatre in action.

Elizabeth sat through the matinee in a state of ecstasy and insisted that they stay for the evening performance, too. Quite a group of other students came over to Springfield for it and afterwards went backstage.

"Coming, Liz?" they asked her.

She shook her head.

"But why on earth not? You're so crazy about her! And she said we could go back."

She shook her head again. "I just can't." She could not explain her reasons even to herself.

"Liz, you should have come back," her roommate told her afterwards. "She was wonderful to us. And even when I made a couple of criticisms about the production, she took it perfectly seriously as though my opinion meant something, and discussed it with me. She's—oh, Liz, you should have come back. Why didn't you?"

"I don't know," Elizabeth repeated. "I—I admire her too much. I couldn't have said anything if I'd gone back there."

"But there were lots of things about the production you said you'd give anything to ask her about."

"Yes—but I couldn't have done it, just going back with a bunch of kids, when she's so busy and tired."

Elizabeth still couldn't explain why she hadn't gone backstage that night any more than she could explain why, during the past week that Miss Andersen had been rehearsing, she had not, like most of the apprentices, made some sort of excuse to speak to her. Bibi had brought her coffee; Ditta had found an opportunity to talk to her about using *Shakespeare Prefaces* for her students; Ben reported wonderful talks with her; and Jane had gone down the boardwalk to buy her cigarettes.

Now she watched Ben and the actress for a moment longer; then, afraid that she might be noticed, she turned away from the theatre and walked back to the Cottage. Four of the apprentices were out on the stone porch, wearing wet bathing suits and rehearsing a scene from *Mourning Becomes Electra*, which they had been practicing in their class with Huntley Haskell. Elizabeth watched them critically for a moment before heading inside. The living room was dark in the daytime and smelled cool and damp and musty. The furniture was covered with very old and very faded chintz and was always being pushed around for one rehearsal or another. The ceiling light, which reminded Elizabeth of some horrible overfed spider with its seven weak bulbs at the end of rusty iron legs, was on, and Jane and John Peter, setting the dining room tables for lunch, waved at her as she started upstairs.

I can't go back to Jordan, Elizabeth thought. Oh, please, I can't.

The bedroom was deserted. Elizabeth stood looking at the pictures on the chest of drawers which she and Jane shared. Jane had a picture of her parents in a silver frame. She looked, oddly, amazingly, like both of them. There was also, on Jane's portion of the bureau, a picture of John Peter, dark and moody, his nose an aristocratic beak, his eyes brooding and troubled. Elizabeth liked and respected John Peter, but she was never completely comfortable with him.

On Elizabeth's side of the bureau was a small double frame with a snapshot of her father seated at his desk in his office at the boys' school, and a newspaper picture of her mother. Her father, as he appeared in the snapshot, was a serious-looking man, with a humorous quirk to his mouth, and eyes stained

with sadness. Her mother, in the newspaper picture, had a boyish bob and a gamine's face with huge grey eyes like Elizabeth's. In spite of the fact that her mother's hair was straight
and obviously blond, as blond as Jane's, and Elizabeth's was
reddish and wavy, Kurt had assumed, the first time he had seen
the picture, that it was Elizabeth.

"No, it's my mother," Elizabeth had said. "She—she's dead."

"She looks like an actress," Kurt had said, and turned to the
pictures of Jane's parents.

Behind the pictures of her mother and father Elizabeth had
a picture of Kurt from a publicity release, looking handsome
and blasé and also rather sinister with a slight droop to one
eyelid. Next to Kurt's was a picture of Valborg Andersen as
Shaw's Lavinia, simple and serene and shining. Elizabeth looked
at the two of them, Kurt posing as the worldly director and
Valborg Andersen as the early Christian martyr. If only I could
stay, she thought passionately. If only I could stay!

She would have liked to fling herself on her bed and weep
with rage at her Aunt Harriet and disappointment in general,
but she felt that crying was a sign of weakness and she had had
more than her quota for the day, so instead she reached for her
volume of Chekhov, from which they were rehearsing *The
Seagull* in their informal afternoon sessions, and began studying
her role. She concentrated with a kind of desperation until
John Peter knocked on the door.

"Liz!"

"I'm here."

"Are you decent?"

"Yes. Come in."

John Peter and Jane, arms entwined, entered and sat on Jane's bed.

"We missed you this morning," John Peter said.

Elizabeth shut her book. "Learn anything new?"

"Not a thing." Jane leaned back against John Peter. "Did you ever get your telephone call?"

"Yes." Elizabeth stood in front of the bureau and began to brush her hair.

"What did Auntie want?" Jane asked.

"I have to go back to Virginia."

Jane was appalled. "What do you mean?"

"Just what I say, unfortunately."

"But why?" John Peter asked.

Elizabeth hesitated. "Well—Aunt Harriet isn't sending me any more money for room and board."

Jane pushed away from John Peter and stood up. "But, Liz, you *can't* leave! When do you have to go?"

"Tomorrow, I guess. I'd been kind of wondering why my check for next week hadn't come."

"But, Liz, you'll miss *Macbeth*! You'll miss seeing Andersen!"

"You're just making it harder for Liz," John Peter said.

Jane sat down again and asked, more quietly, "What are you going to do?"

"I'm going to Jordan. I'm going to get a job. I think I can get work at the lab at the hospital. Maybe there was a real reason to all that chemistry in college. And when I have enough money saved, I'm going to come to New York and get another job until I can find work in the theatre."

John Peter reached over and took Elizabeth's hand. "Liz, it's a shame. Isn't there anything we could do to coerce the old girl into letting you stay?"

Elizabeth shook her head. "It's not Aunt Harriet's fault. It's my fault for ever having asked for this summer in the first place. I can't give her anything in return—if I make a success in the theatre it will pain her and not please her—so why should I expect her to help me in something she dislikes so intensely? I shouldn't have let my wanting it so much make me want or hope for help from her. Well, the world won't come to an end just because I have to go back to Jordan, Virginia, where Aunt Harriet thinks I belong. I'll see you in New York anyhow."

"Did you tell Mr. Price?" John Peter asked.

Elizabeth nodded. "I did."

"How did he take it?"

"He was really—filthy—about it. I don't know why he had to be so horrible when sometimes he can seem so understanding. He made me feel as though I were committing some unspeakable crime by leaving in the middle of the season."

"He doesn't want to lose you," Jane told her. "You're the most useful apprentice he has. You do twice as much work as the rest of us put together."

"I can't be too useful," Elizabeth said. "He didn't suggest that I stay on without paying my twenty bucks a week."

"That man's tighter than a wad," John Peter said with disgust. "I don't see why he doesn't take you on for props or something. When the paying apprentices do props—with a few exceptions, such as Ditta—they never get anything right."

Downstairs they could hear Mrs. Browden ringing the bell

for lunch. "Come on," John Peter said, "we're having hamburgers and it's going to be nice and quiet. Ben just took a big box of grub over to the theatre for the professional company."

Elizabeth put her hairbrush down on the bureau, carefully in line with Jane's. "It's a pity one must eat to live. I'd much rather go for a swim than eat. I haven't had a chance to get in the ocean for days."

"Don't tell me you've lost your appetite," John Peter said. "There are no classes tomorrow morning, so we can all swim before you go."

Jane put her arm affectionately about Elizabeth's waist. "We're going to miss you. Life will be very drab around this dump. And it seems awfully peculiar to me. Why'd she send for you all of a sudden like this?"

Elizabeth sighed wearily. "I told you, Jane. I never should have asked it of her anyhow, the way she feels about the theatre."

Jane persisted. "But *why* does she hate the theatre so?"

"Honestly, Jane!" Elizabeth's voice was exasperated. "Lots of people hate the theatre!"

"Now don't be mad at me, Liz," Jane said, grinning at her ingratiatingly.

"I'm not mad at you, idiot. Come on. Let's eat."

After lunch Ben came back from the theatre and found Elizabeth. "Joe is letting me off for a few hours. I'll help you clear and then we can set the table for tonight and get it over with. I'll be able to rehearse *The Seagull* with you guys after all."

"Great," Elizabeth said.

They worked quickly and in silence, Ben pausing every once in a while to stare with anxious affection at Elizabeth. Apprentices and members of the company who were not at rehearsal moved in and out of the living room, but there was little noise. The quiet of a hot summer afternoon pressed over them; only the ocean talked incessantly with restless insistence. When they were finished, Ben watched Elizabeth pour herself a glass of water from a huge pitcher, and then nudged her, causing her to spill water on the floor. He jerked his head at Dottie, who was in the living room. Elizabeth followed his gaze and grinned.

Dottie was sitting on the couch she had occupied with Huntley Haskell the night before, writing a letter, with an intent and rather idiotic look on her pretty face. Her long blond hair, which she dyed to get the same color that Jane's was naturally, swirled over her bare shoulders, covering her with much more modesty than the man's silk handkerchief she had tied around her bosom.

"Why is it that when people bleach their hair it always makes their faces look hard?" Elizabeth asked Ben. "But when it's natural, like Jane's, it doesn't at all. Jane looks—well, as easily bruised as lily of the valley, but Dottie looks like a sharp little paring knife."

Ben strolled over to Dottie, lifted the veil of hair, and dropped it so that it hung over her eyes. "The sun's gone in, Dottie," he said.

Dottie swept her hair back impatiently, but didn't look up. "Quiet, child. I'm writing home."

"Home for delinquent females?"

Dottie said, still without looking up, "I know you don't think much of me, but Courtmont's going to have dinner in the Cottage tonight. You'd better curb your saucy tongue around her. She's a star and she's used to being treated like one."

A wild look came into Ben's eyes. "And how would *you* treat a star, my angel?"

"With more respect than you would," Dottie said, pulling her hair over her shoulders as a slight breeze came in the window behind her.

"Don't you want my sweater, my fair maid of Perth?" Ben asked her. "You'll have gooseflesh in another minute, and think how unattractive those cozy arms of yours would look with little goose pimples all over them."

"You're disgusting," Dottie said.

"If Courtmont is rude to me when I'm serving her supper tonight, I shall throw the potatoes in her face," Ben said.

"You should be grateful," Dottie told him sententiously. "She's only coming because of you apprentices."

"It's a lovely idea of the Pricelesses, having the stars eat with us the Saturday night of their last performance. Too bad they aren't allowed to sit with us and we can't talk to them. I wish Courtmont'd bleary well stay at her ritzy thirty-dollar-a-day hotel and leave us to our squalid peace."

Elizabeth grinned and thought, I can't leave tomorrow. I can't. Ben and all his idiotic yammering. I'll miss him. I'll miss him almost as much as I'll miss Kurt.

At the thought of leaving Kurt, a cold stone of misery settled in her.

"Why this venom?" Dottie asked with curiosity.

Ben's voice quivered with indignation. "Courtmont called me a 'sweet little boy'!"

"Well, you are." Dottie combed her long red nails through her hair.

Ben glared at her. Then he turned to Elizabeth. "Thank God Courtmont's going home tomorrow." He flung himself down and lay flat on the floor. "Hey, it's nice and cool here."

"She's going home tonight," Dottie said, never averse to any tidbits of gossip, no matter how slight. "Looks like she doesn't like being here any better than you like having her."

"The thing that gets me"—Ben began doing the exercises the apprentices were taught in body movement classes—"is that the woman can be such a damn good actress when she wants to. I've always had kind of a thing about her and then she comes up here and disillusions me. She's been rude and up-stagey offstage and all she's done *onstage* is admire herself and her position in the Theatah. If Valborg Andersen disillusions me too, I'll want to puke, but she's been here almost a week and my allegiance has certainly switched."

"Ever hear of the famous Andersen temper?" Dottie asked. "We may see it in action yet."

"I like a temper when there's a reason for it," Ben said. "And there's always a reason around here." It didn't seem to occur to him that this was logic nohow contrariwise. Satisfied that he had put Dottie in her place, he turned around just in time to see Sophie slinking down the stairs in a dark suit and an elaborate fur piece, and, what was even more striking, carrying two large suitcases.

"My sainted hat, Soapie," he said. "Where are you going?"

Sophie got very red. "I wish you wouldn't call me Soapie, Ben. And I'm going home."

"Home!"

"Yes."

"Whatever for?"

"I'm sick and tired of paying a large tuition and then some more for room and board every week and not getting one thing out of it. Old Mariella Hedeman gives us those silly voice lessons and Marian Hatfield gives us body movement and she's always mean to me and you scholarship kids always get the best parts in the scenes with Huntley Haskell and it isn't fair and we're told we might get a walk-on with the company but I can't see that one maybe walk-on's worth wasting the rest of the summer to wait for. So I'm going to find another theatre where the paying apprentices get better treatment."

Ben whistled. "You really are upset, aren't you, Soapie? That's the most impassioned speech I've ever heard you make. When did you pack?"

"After lunch."

"We asked you to work with us in the afternoons," Elizabeth reminded Sophie, "but you said you'd rather stay out on the beach and get a tan."

"I don't want to work on your silly old plays," Sophie said, "but none of the professional company ever pays any attention to me in their classes and we've never even *had* makeup classes yet."

"I can't blame you for leaving." Ben clambered up onto the

newel post and perched there, trying to posture like a statue as he looked down at Sophie. "Is J. P. Price refunding your tuition?"

"No," Sophie said, "and I'd already paid room and board through next week."

Ben whistled again. "Throw it around, girl!"

But Elizabeth turned on Sophie eagerly. "You've paid room and board for next week?"

"Yes."

"Oh, Sophie, please, you could do me the most wonderful favor if only you would!"

"What?" Sophie asked suspiciously.

"Sophie," Elizabeth clasped her hands in her intensity. "Tell J. P. Price you want me to have it, will you?"

"Why?"

"Listen, Sophie, I don't expect you to understand such sordid things, but I'm broke. I haven't got twenty dollars to pay my room and board next week, and if I can't get it I have to leave. If I could stay on the twenty dollars you've already paid, it would mean another whole week here."

"I don't want to speak to Mr. Price," Sophie said. "I've already said goodbye to him and he was real mean to me."

"Then let me tell him you said I could stay on your twenty dollars." It was the first time Ben had ever heard Elizabeth ask for anything, and the effort it cost her was painfully apparent.

Sophie looked at Elizabeth with unfriendly eyes. "I don't see why I should do you any favors, Elizabeth Jerrold. You and Jane and your gang are always all over the room and sit on my bed and you tease me and call me Soapie."

"We haven't teased you to be mean," Elizabeth said. "I'm awfully sorry if we've hurt your feelings. Truly. And we only called you Soapie for fun, the way we tease Ditta about being a schoolmarm or John Peter about having a nose like a hawk."

"I don't see why I should do you any favors," Sophie repeated.

Elizabeth looked at Sophie and then said flatly, "As a matter of fact, neither do I. I never should have mentioned it. Forget it."

But Ben climbed down from his newel post and advanced menacingly toward Sophie. "Shut up, Liz," he said. "Now listen to me, Sophie Sherman. Are you going to let Liz tell Price you want her to stay on your room and board next week or not?"

Sophie looked at Ben's angrily flashing eyes and then down at her feet in high-heeled suede pumps. "I don't care what she tells him," she said sulkily.

"Okay."

"Soapie, it's terribly nice of you," Elizabeth said.

"Don't call me Soapie!"

Elizabeth laughed apologetically. "Sorry."

The screen door with its torn rusty screening was pushed open, and Joe McGill, the stage manager, stuck part of his huge bulk through and said, "There's a taxi over at the theatre for a Miss Sherman. That you, by any chance, Sophie?"

"Oh, yes, Joe," Sophie said. "Tell it to come over here."

"If you want to go anywhere, I advise you to go over there, see. Where you going?"

"Home."

"Couldn't take it, huh? Can't say I blame you. Okay, I'll

take your bags over to the taxi for you." He turned to Dottie, who was again engrossed in her correspondence. "Just a word of warning to the wise, Dorothy Toujours L'Amour. I'd amble over to the theatre if I were you, see. Andersen's about to call your scene, and she won't like it if you're not around."

"She's not going to call my scene this afternoon, Grandpa." Dottie folded her letter and put it carefully in a lilac envelope, then licked the flap, transferring thereon a considerable quantity of the red from her lips. Her lips were naturally full, and she painted well over the original line so that Ben was not far wrong when he referred to Dottie's mouth as an overblown rose with the petals about to fall.

"Okay. Don't say I didn't warn you, see," Joe told Dottie. "Come on, Sophie. Say goodbye to your friends and let's go."

"Goodbye, Liz and Ben." Sophie's voice was suddenly a little wistful. "I—I'll miss you. Say goodbye to Bibi and Jane and John Peter and the others for me."

"Goodbye, Sophie," Elizabeth said. "Good luck. And thanks for helping me out."

"That's okay."

"Maybe we'll see you in the casting offices in New York," Ben said.

Sophie turned to Dottie. "Goodbye, Dottie. I'm awfully glad to have met you."

Without looking up, Dottie addressed her envelope. "Goodbye, Soapie. See you at supper."

Ben and Joe raised their eyebrows and grinned at Elizabeth.

"If Dottie concentrated when she's acting the way she does when she's writing love letters," Ben said, "the theatre would benefit greatly."

Joe picked up Sophie's bags. "Come on, kiddo. Ben, I'll see you after dinner." He went out, pulling Sophie after him.

"And the sad part of it is," Ben said, "that no one's even going to know she's gone."

"She couldn't have picked a better time or a better way." Elizabeth's face shone with relieved pleasure. "Thank goodness some people have money. Now I can see Miss Andersen every night next week!" And I can have another week with Kurt, she added in her mind.

"Do you think Half Price will let you stay on Soapie's dough?" Ben sounded worried.

"I don't see why he shouldn't. And if I can stay next week, maybe I can figure out a way to stay on a bit longer—" she broke off, flushing, as Kurt bounded in with a graceful leap.

"Kurt!" Elizabeth ran over to him but stopped herself short from flinging her arms around him. "Are you going to help us rehearse this afternoon?"

"Of course, Liebchen. That's what I came over for."

"Oh, Kurt, I can stay another week—I thought I was going to have to leave tomorrow."

"Her sainted aunt has stopped paying room and board," Ben said.

"But Soapie's just left and has already paid for the week! And she said that I could use it!"

"The theatre has claimed you, Liebchen. It would be terrible to have you ripped from its arms so violently." He touched her cheek and smiled. "Where is everybody?"

"Ditta's got students visiting here this afternoon, so she can't come. I think Jane and John Peter are upstairs. I'll go get them," Elizabeth said. As she turned toward the stairs, Kurt pirouetted across the room toward Dottie. Elizabeth paused on the landing and watched him lean over Dottie, running his fingers through the fountain of blond hair, and was amazed at the rage that welled up in her. Dottie frequently cuddled up to Kurt; Dottie frequently cuddled up to every man in the company. Elizabeth pushed her fingers viciously through her hair, in anger at her anger.

"Looks like you'll have to tear Kurt away from Dottie if he's going to help us," Ben said.

"I'll tear him." A gleam came into Elizabeth's eyes. She started to go upstairs but paused again as the screen door creaked open and Huntley Haskell peered in. He was almost as nearsighted as Elizabeth but refused to wear glasses; he was handsome in a rather dissipated, puffy way, and Elizabeth liked him because he liked her as well, and because, on the first day of the season, he had decided that Dottie was his own particular piece of property; and that was something for which Elizabeth was frequently grateful.

"Have you seen Dottie?" he asked now. "Oh, hi, honey. There you are."

"Hello, lamb. Rehearsal over?" Dottie drawled lazily, stretching herself to best advantage on the faded chintz of the couch. "What do you want?"

"Andersen wants you onstage. She's not in too good a mood," Huntley said.

Dottie stretched again. "The old slave driver. I don't see why I should run at *her* beck and call. I bet they wouldn't even have her out in Hollywood."

Elizabeth came down a few steps. "She's a magnificent actress."

"Valborg Andersen? Oh, I don't know about that," Dottie said, winking at Kurt.

"Well, I do." Elizabeth was fierce as an angry puppy.

Kurt ran his fingers through Dottie's hair again and said to Elizabeth, "Okay, Liebchen. Calm down."

"Don't take hysterics," Ben added, winking at her and putting on a strong Brooklyn accent.

Dottie leaned lovingly against Kurt and looked up through her eyelashes at Huntley. "She's going to be a letdown next week after Sarah Courtmont."

Elizabeth's voice cracked with rage. "That superficial, insincere—"

"Liz, don't let them egg you on," Ben said.

Kurt put his hands under Dottie's arms and raised her off the sofa. "You'd better run along, angel face."

"I'm going up to powder my nose first," Dottie said. "Huntley pet, go and tell her I'll be right over, will you? And I'm not egging you on, Liz. I don't like neurotic actresses like Andersen. Courtmont's the gal I like to work with."

Elizabeth came downstairs and turned to Ben. "Which scene are we doing this afternoon?" she asked in a frigid voice.

"We got to where Nina comes back in the last act. Hey, Dottie, shout upstairs at John Peter and Jane to come down when you go up to powder your nose, will you?"

"And you'd better hurry," Huntley called as he slammed the screen door.

Dottie walked slowly over to the staircase, swinging her hips provocatively. "I'll shout at 'em for you. Though why you want to waste time like this I don't know. And you, too, Kurt. What's in it for you?"

"The future," Kurt said. "It isn't any waste of time for me. These kids are good, aren't you, kids? Price isn't giving them too good a deal on their summer, so if I can give them anything extra it's my pleasure. And my investment."

Dottie started upstairs. "Chekhov. *The Seagull.* You can have 'em."

"Thanks," Elizabeth said. "We will. And thanks, Kurt." Her voice softened as she turned to him. "You know how much it means to us to have you work with us."

Ignoring Ben's ill-concealed snort, Kurt said, "What do you want to start with?"

"Jane does Nina's part, so would you read Masha's first scene with me till Jane and John Peter get here?"

"Sure," Kurt said. "Give me the script."

Ben glared up the stairs after Dottie's disappearing figure. "That dame. The way she thinks a few stinking pictures give her the right to put on airs gives me a pain in the posterior."

"Dottie's got a big career ahead of her," Kurt said.

"Yeah." Ben nodded sagaciously. "But not as an actress."

"Listen," Kurt said, the easygoing humor momentarily

gone from his voice. "You kids have got to stop thinking you know so much. You're not as good as all that. It's okay for you to talk now when everything's still ahead of you, but wait until you've been around a few years longer and really come up against it. Then maybe you'll think more of people like Dottie."

"Come on. Let's forget Dottie and start to work," Elizabeth said. "Come on, Kurt."

Ben curled up on Dottie's vacated sofa to watch. Elizabeth sat down on a folding chair, leaned her elbow on a small rickety table, and placed her head on her hand. To Ben, watching, it was amazing how with a brief gesture she stopped being Elizabeth Jerrold and became the bitter young woman in Chekhov's play, always a little drunk so that she never actually seemed drunk, but so that one knew there was something strange about her; always darkly intense, passionate.

" 'Why do you always wear mourning?' " Kurt read from the play.

" 'I dress in black to match my life. I am unhappy.' " The extravagant words seemed inevitable and right as Elizabeth spoke them.

" 'Why should you be unhappy? I don't understand it.' " Kurt put the same overemphasis into his reading that often marred his acting.

Dottie called as she ran down the stairs, "John Peter and Jane aren't around." She ran across the room, tying a bright wraparound cotton skirt over her white sharkskin shorts, and slammed out the door.

"They must be at the beach with their recorders," Ben said.

"It's not fair of them to be late like this!" Elizabeth cried.

"We can do plenty without them," Kurt said easily. " 'Why do you always wear mourning?' "

"Oh, Kurt, I can't just bounce in and out of it like that."

"Okay," Kurt said. "Ready now?" He cleared his throat, then asked again, " 'Why do you always wear mourning?' "

" 'I dress in black to match my life. I am unhappy.' "

This time it was the screen door slamming on Bibi that jarred Elizabeth out of Masha. Bibi came rushing into the room, swirling the skirts of her pink-and-white dotted swiss dress, and screeched, "Did you know Sophie's gone?"

"Yes," Ben snapped. "And we're working."

"When did you find out?" Bibi persisted. "My goodness, I can't believe I'm one of her roommates and she never said a word about it. She didn't even mention it at breakfast. Did she tell you or Jane, Liz?"

"No. We just happened to see her leave," Elizabeth said patiently. "She said to say goodbye."

"Oh, listen, don't set a place for me, Liz. I'm going out." Bibi flitted from thought to thought as quickly as a mosquito.

"I already have."

"Oh, I'm sorry. I meant to tell you sooner, but I forgot."

"Don't mention it."

"Anyhow, you've got the tables set awful early today."

"Who're you going out with?" Kurt asked.

"Oh, Jack. Do you know what I've been doing?"

Ben yawned. "Don't know, don't care."

"I've been watching the rehearsal of *Macbeth*."

"What!" Elizabeth and Ben pounced on her.

"You wouldn't've if I'd been around," Ben said. "How did you sneak in?"

"I didn't sneak in at all," Bibi exclaimed in righteous indignation. "I went to Mr. Price and he gave me special permission."

"Some people—" Ben started, and shut his mouth tight.

"He wouldn't give *me* special permission," Elizabeth said grimly.

"You just don't know how to handle him right, Liz. I can wind Mr. Price around my little finger. Anyhow, he couldn't let *all* the apprentices watch rehearsal, could he? And Miss Andersen's in a rage at Dottie," Bibi added with importance.

"Why?" Kurt raised one of his dark, flexible eyebrows.

"Because she wasn't there when they came to Lady Macduff's scene. Gee, I think Miss Andersen's wonderful. She let me go get coffee for her again and she made me buy some for myself, too. I don't blame you for having that big picture of her on your bureau, Liz. I'm going to get her to give me one next week and ask her to autograph it. She was so mad at Dottie. Do you think Dottie's a good actress?"

"My opinion of Dottie's acting is not fit to print," Elizabeth said.

"Listen"—Bibi lowered her voice—"why do you suppose Sophie left?"

"She couldn't keep up with your conversation," Ben said. "Look, Bibi, didn't I tell you we were trying to work? If you're going out for dinner, you'd better go get ready."

"Okay, okay, I guess I'll go up and change now. This dress is kind of wrinkled. Gee, I've got a lot of stuff to send to the laundry this week. One good thing about Soapie leaving is that I'll have the closet all to myself. Will you call me if Jack comes before I'm ready, Liz?"

"Yes, I'll call you." Elizabeth sighed heavily as Bibi went upstairs.

"Not much above the eyebrows," Kurt said, and put his arm about Elizabeth's waist. " 'Why do you always wear mourning?' "

Ben came over to them. "I don't like to interrupt you again, Kurt, but I guess one more interruption more or less won't make a difference. Listen, Liz, you know Nina's lines in that last scene as well as Jane does, don't you?"

"Mm-hm. I've been kind of working on her a bit by myself. And I love *The Seagull* so much I think I know the whole thing by heart."

"Well, do that bit with me, will you? I don't think John Peter and Jane are going to turn up this afternoon, drat their hides, and I want to go over the scene at least once. I've thought out a couple of new things I want to try."

Elizabeth looked quickly at Kurt, then back at Ben. "I'd adore doing it with you. You know how I love Nina even if I'm all wrong for her." She turned eagerly to Kurt. "Would it be all right if I do it, just for now, Kurt?"

"Of course, Liebchen. I'd like to see you."

He sat down on the old couch to watch as Elizabeth and Ben started the scene. And so persuasive were they in their intensity that he hardly noticed as Jane and John Peter slipped in the door, their recorders under their arms, their hair blown and their skin red from too much sun, and sat down next to him. None of them noticed when Valborg Andersen opened the door and stood quietly just inside, listening.

" 'Why do you say that you have kissed the ground I walked on?' " Elizabeth was crying, and she was no longer Elizabeth, but a wild beautiful creature with a light burning inside her which adversity had not been able to extinguish. Elizabeth felt closer to Nina than to any other character in fiction or even to many living people, not through experience but through instinct—Nina who loved so desperately, so foolishly, and who was rejected.

Then Nina turned to the stage, and in her work finally found comfort and strength. She came home again, exhausted and half ill, to see the boy who loved her and whom she had been unable to love once she met the famous writer who casually took and destroyed her. " 'He does not believe in the theatre; he used to laugh at my dreams, so that little by little I became downhearted and ceased to believe in it too. Then came all the cares of love, the continual anxiety about my little one, so that I soon grew trivial and spiritless, and played my parts without meaning. I never knew what to do with my hands, and I could not walk properly or control my voice. You cannot imagine the state of mind of one who knows as he goes through a play how terribly badly he is acting.' "

Then exhaustion overcomes Nina. " 'I am a seagull—no—no, that is not what I meant to say. Do you remember how you shot a seagull once? A man chanced to pass that way and destroyed it out of idleness. That is an idea for a short story, but it is not what I meant to say . . . What was I saying? . . . Oh, yes, the stage. I have changed now. Now I am a real actress. I act with joy, with exaltation, I am intoxicated by it, and feel that I am superb. I have been walking and walking, and thinking and thinking, ever since I have been here, and I feel the strength of my spirit growing in me every day.' "

Elizabeth paused for a moment before she said the last words of the speech, the words which were her creed. Kurt leaned forward, his mouth slightly open, a habit of his whenever he was excited. John Peter reached over and took Jane's hand. Valborg Andersen remained quietly in the doorway.

" 'I know now, I understand at last, Constantine, that for us, whether we write or act, it is not the honor and glory of which I have dreamt that is important, it is the strength to endure. One must know how to bear one's cross, and one must have faith. I believe, and so do not suffer so much, and when I think of my calling I do not fear life.' "

As Elizabeth finished, Valborg Andersen made a slight sound and all heads turned toward her. Elizabeth looked quickly around the room and when she saw Miss Andersen, she turned scarlet.

Valborg Andersen came into the room. "You. The tall girl," she said. "Nina."

"Y-yes, Miss Andersen," Elizabeth stammered.

"I want you for *Macbeth*. To play the Gentlewoman in the sleepwalking scene. I am putting Marian Hatfield in Miss Dorothy Dawne's place as Lady Macduff, and we'll need someone else to replace her as the Gentlewoman. You'll do very well if you'd like to do it. You have the right quality."

Elizabeth stood still, not saying a word, and Valborg Andersen went on.

"Small though the role is, the Gentlewoman is exceedingly important to the scene and I was quite in despair over it. It can throw off the whole balance of the play, and there was no one in the company to replace Miss Hatfield. Joe McGill suggested I might find someone among the apprentices and told me you were rehearsing here. I liked the way you did Nina. What's your name?"

"Elizabeth Jerrold."

"That's a beautiful speech."

"Yes."

"And a beautiful play. Are there enough of you to cast it?"

As Elizabeth remained speechless, Ben answered for her. "Oh, no. We just do bits of it among ourselves, Miss Andersen."

"Is it part of your work? What you're supposed to do?"

"Oh, no. We just do it for ourselves. It was Liz—Elizabeth's idea."

With a great effort Elizabeth spoke. "Miss Andersen—"

"Yes, Miss Jerrold?"

"Nina isn't really my part. It's Jane Gardiner's." She indicated Jane sitting next to John Peter. "I just do Masha. Jane's a better actress than I am. I was just doing Nina with Ben because Jane and John Peter hadn't come. So—so Jane really ought to play the Gentlewoman."

Jane was making unhappy gestures of dissent and Valborg Andersen looked intently at Elizabeth.

"Don't you want to do it?"

"Yes, of course!" Elizabeth cried. "It's not that! It's just that Jane's a better actress than I am."

"Please don't listen to her," Jane said. "Please."

Valborg Andersen raised her eyebrows as she looked at them. "I think I'd rather have you as the Gentlewoman, any-how, Miss Jerrold. Your height will give an interesting quality to the role. But I'd like to see the whole of that scene, and if Miss Gardiner and Mr. . . ." She smiled at Ben. "I'm sorry, I've only heard you called Ben around the theatre."

"Walton," Ben said.

"—Mr. Walton would care to do it for me, I'd be glad to see it tomorrow morning. Dress rehearsal doesn't start till the afternoon."

"Golly, that would be wonderful," Ben said. "We—we can't thank you enough, Miss Andersen."

"There is nothing to thank me for. Can you be there by ten o'clock? At the theatre?"

"Any time." Ben was nodding furiously. "The set from Courtmont's play should be down by then and *Macbeth* should be up. I'll make sure of it, so we'll have the time."

"All right. The theatre, at ten o'clock. You, Nina, Miss Jer-rold, I'm assuming you are familiar with the lines, but you'd better come back to the theatre with me now. We'll do a quick run-through before dinner and then we'll have to work very hard tomorrow afternoon at dress rehearsal. Mr. Walton, in view of the change of cast, Mr. McGill would like you back at the theatre, too."

Elizabeth and Ben followed Miss Andersen out. The others

looked after them, excitement and affectionate amusement mingling on their faces.

"She's completely crazy, that girl," Kurt said. "Perhaps that is why I am rather nuts about her."

When Miss Andersen dismissed the company, Elizabeth went over to Ben's table and waited while he made some notes in the script. In spite of considerable childishness in his offstage life, Ben was an excellent and thorough assistant to Joe McGill. He looked up at Elizabeth and smiled, a smile that was amazingly gentle and somehow mature for his boyish face.

"Happy, Liz?"

She flung out her arms. "Ecstatic."

"It's an ill wind," Ben said.

"Yes. Bless Dottie."

"Dottie's not going to love you for this."

"Dottie doesn't love me anyhow."

Ben rubbed a long, rather bony finger against his nose. "The Elizabeth-Dorothy mutual hate society, huh?"

"Oh, I haven't anything against Dottie," Elizabeth said magnanimously. "She just doesn't interest me."

"Does she interest Kurt?" Ben started sharpening his pencils with a pocket knife and cast a rather wicked glance at Elizabeth from the corner of his eye.

"Dottie interests most men, I guess." Elizabeth tried to sound casual. "Huntley isn't going to let her interest anybody too much."

"You put great faith in Huntley," Ben said, then added, "Oh, to hell with Dottie anyhow. Liz, I'm glad you got this break. You deserve it if anyone ever did."

"Oh, Ben—" Elizabeth let her breath out in an ardent sigh. "It would be impossible for anybody *not* to act with Miss Andersen directing. Now I really see—I mean, it's not that she shows you how, it's just that she makes you know how. She makes you aware every second with every particle of you, so that you're working much more—more productively, than you ever could by yourself."

Ben stood up. "Think she's better than Kurt?" he asked.

"I don't think you ought to make comparisons. Kurt's lots younger and he works differently. But I don't think you ought to say one way is better than another."

"Oh, Liz," Ben said with a deep sigh, flinging his arm about Elizabeth's shoulders, "life can be such hell."

"What's the matter, Ben?" she asked gently.

"Liz, sometimes you're an awful dope," he said.

"I know, but why in particular?"

"Forget it." Ben started arranging his pencils in a neat row beside the script. His face suddenly had an ageless, simian look of tragedy. "Let's get back to *Macbeth*. We're going to have some good performances next week. And yours is going to be one of them."

Elizabeth sat down on the dusty canvas that covered the floor of the stage and breathed deeply the familiar beloved odor of paint, glue, old coffee, greasepaint, and dust. Beneath her the sea breathed quietly. "I feel kind of guilty about it—"

Ben sat heavily on his three-legged stool. "You and your guilt complexes. What now?"

"Well—Miss Andersen came in when I was doing Jane's scene. If Jane had been doing it, she'd probably be in *Macbeth* instead of me."

"Don't worry about Jane," Ben said. "Jane's okay. She won't hold it against you."

"I know that. It's just that she can't help—well, she can't help feeling badly about it."

"Okay, so she feels badly about it," Ben said. "It's her own fault, isn't it? She and John Peter didn't need to stay swooning on the beach with their recorders when they were supposed to be working."

"Jane has ever so much more experience than I have," Elizabeth said.

"All the more reason for you to get some experience then. You'll learn a lot next week."

"It'll be marvelous," Elizabeth said. "It'll be the most marvelous experience in the world." She lay down on the floor, resting her head on her arm to protect it from the dusty grey canvas, and looked up into the flies. Light came filtering down from a shuttered window above the grid, and long motes of dust twined with the ropes that held up the curtain. "Maybe one reason I feel kind of guilty about Jane is that I'm so happy. If you're too happy about anything, fate usually gives you a good sock in the jaw and knocks you down. Oh, Ben, everything's worked out so marvelously, Soapie having paid room and board for next week and now *Macbeth* and everything. Even if I have to go back to Jordan I can bear it, but now I can't help believing that something will happen so that I won't have to go back."

Ben knelt down beside her. "Liz," he said softly, "you're beautiful, did you know?"

"Don't be silly. I'll do. I can pass for beautiful on the stage with good makeup and lighting, but I'm certainly not beautiful myself."

"That's what you think," Ben said. "It's time to go over to the Cottage for dinner."

He reached down a hand to help her off the floor and they walked back to the Cottage in silence, lost in their own thoughts.

The apprentices were all waiting for Elizabeth and crowded around her, full of excited congratulations, only turning away when the Prices entered, escorting Sarah Courtmont into the dining room for dinner. The actress sat at the Prices' small round table in a corner away from the company and apprentice tables.

Ditta sat next to Elizabeth. "I think it's wonderful, your being in *Macbeth*," she said. "Anything I can do to help you out in any way? I'm afraid I'm not up to box office, but I could do some typing or set tables for you if that would be any good."

"Thanks a million, Ditta. Being in the dress rehearsal tomorrow will make things tight, but I can manage. I don't have to do the box office tomorrow, and as long as Price doesn't give me anything extra, I don't think I'll have any trouble. You're a darling to offer."

"Well, just let me know if you think of anything," Ditta said.

"I will. Good grief, I've got to get upstairs and get dressed for ushering. Some of the flashlights weren't working last night and I have to check them, and if there's time, I want to look over my lines. You can have my dessert."

Ditta laughed. "Thanks. I'll save it for Ben. I've got enough flesh on my bones already."

John Peter brushed by Elizabeth, whispering, "Watch out for Ben. He's going to throw something at the divine Sarah yet."

Elizabeth sighed. "That I would hate to miss, but I have to go change."

She hurried upstairs and got dressed for ushering. She looked quickly at the pictures on her bureau. You'd be glad about *Macbeth*, Father, she thought. I'm sure you would. Then she looked at her mother. I wonder what you'd think? Would you be glad, too? She had seen her mother only once to re-member, and that was after her death. She sat down on the creaking bed and pulled on her sandals.

After the last performance of the drawing room comedy in which Sarah Courtmont starred, supported by Kurt Canitz, Elizabeth ran over to the Cottage to change quickly out of her dress and into blue jeans, sweater, and sneakers, then rushed back to the theatre to meet Kurt.

"A walk on the beach, eh, Liebchen?" he suggested.

"That would be wonderful."

They started down the boardwalk, then jumped onto the sand. Jane and John Peter were already down on the beach, sit-ting on the sand playing their recorders. The music floated on the wind to Elizabeth and Kurt.

Kurt pulled himself onto one of the old barnacled piles,

held out a hand to Elizabeth, and helped her onto the one next to his. He moved beautifully; his actions seemed to pour from his body as smoothly as honey. Elizabeth was agile and strong, but she still moved with the long-legged jerkiness of a very young animal.

"Kurt . . ." she said softly.

"Yes, Liebchen?"

"Do you like it?"

"Like what?"

"*Plaisir d'Amour*. What Jane and John Peter are playing."

"Yes, I like it very much. Why?" Kurt's tone was filled with the gravity an adult uses in talking to a sweet and intelligent child.

"Oh, no reason particularly . . . It makes me think of the sound of the buoys, the way they sound from the ferry at night."

Kurt began to sing along with the recorders, his voice warm in the cool night air:

> *"Plaisir d'amour ne dure qu'un moment,*
> *Chagrin d'amour dure toute la vie."*

"The joys of love," Elizabeth translated softly for herself, "last only a moment. The sorrows of love last all the life long. Do you believe that, Kurt?"

"Sure," Kurt said.

"Don't you think the pleasure lasts too?"

Kurt shrugged. "Why?"

"I don't see why you can't remember the good things as well as the bad."

"Most people have more bad things than good to remember." Kurt's voice was suddenly bitter.

"You sound as though you'd been awfully hurt, Kurt," Elizabeth said tentatively.

"Everybody gets hurt at least once," Kurt said. "I don't get hurt often and I think I will not get hurt again. This is a very dull conversation, Liebchen. Let us talk about something else."

Elizabeth stared out over the ocean. "I should like to sit here sometime at high tide in a storm," she said, "with the water wild all around me."

"You're a funny kid, Liz." Kurt looked at her rather curiously.

"Am I?"

"You're going to get hurt yourself, and badly, if you take everything so hard."

"Am I?" she asked again.

"The tide's coming in."

They lapsed into silence. Then Kurt said, "Dottie's rather upset about losing her part."

"I'm sorry about Dottie, but she asked for it."

"Are you being fair? Don't you think it was— —well, shall we just call it a trifle high-handed—to toss Dottie out like that? But I'm more than happy that you're getting the chance, dearheart, and I don't see why Dottie's making such a fuss." Kurt made his voice annoyingly reasonable. "You should not be so scornful of Dottie, Liebchen. You could learn a great deal from her. She has beauty and assurance. She's an asset to any stage."

"Wouldn't it help if she could act?" Elizabeth asked dryly.

"You don't think she can?"

"No."

"Why not?"

Elizabeth looked out across the water for a moment. Then she thought, Well, he asked me, so I might just as well say what I think. "Most of the time she just poses and postures—like Courtmont, only Courtmont has the—the spark—and Dottie's just an empty imitation. And she hams so, Kurt. Such mugging and—and tearing a passion to tatters."

"Okay, what's your idea of good acting, then?" Kurt asked.

In the dark Elizabeth grinned rather sheepishly. "My favorite second-rate actor's definition."

"Whose?"

"Shakespeare's. When Hamlet coaches the players."

"Say it."

"Oh, you know it, Kurt. You know it better than I do."

"I like to hear you quote. You're such an erudite little thing, Liz. All that college education when you should already have been working in the theatre."

"I know that," Elizabeth said. "Now I just have to work harder. Anyhow, thank goodness I never was an ingenue."

"Back to Shakespeare," Kurt said. "How do you happen to know that particular bit by heart? Now don't tell me you played Hamlet in college."

"Don't be silly, Kurt. Mr. Eakins, one of the professors in the Theatre Workshop, had all his students learn it."

"Go on, then. Let me see if you remember."

Hurrying over the words because she was embarrassed, Elizabeth said, " 'Speak the speech, I pray you, as I pronounced it to you, trippingly on the tongue; but if you mouth it as many of your players do, I had as lief the town-crier spoke my lines. Nor do not saw the air too much with your hand, thus' "—she kept her right hand very still because it was covered by Kurt's, and it seemed that an electric current was flowing between them, passing from hand to hand—" 'but use all gently; for in the very torrent, tempest, and, as I may say, whirlwind of your passion, you must acquire and beget a temperance that may give it smoothness. O, it offends me to the soul to hear a ro-bustious periwig-pated fellow tear a passion to tatters, to very rags . . . Be not too tame neither, but let your own discretion be your tutor—' " She broke off suddenly.

"Go on," Kurt said softly. "I like to hear you. You're hurry-ing so that your voice is all tumbled, like little waves. Con-tinue, heart's dearest."

Elizabeth continued, trying to hurry and yet not give the appearance of rushing. " 'Suit the action to the word, the word to the action, with this special observance, that you o'erstep not the modesty of nature. For anything so o'erdone is from the purpose of playing, whose end, both at the first and now, was and is to hold as 'twere the mirror up to nature; to show virtue her feature, scorn her own image, and the very age and body of the time his form and pressure.' " Again she stopped.

"Well, go on," Kurt said. "Finish."

" 'Now this overdone,' " Elizabeth said softly, very con-scious of Kurt's fingers stroking her own, " 'or come tardy off, though it makes the unskilful laugh, cannot but make the judi-cious grieve—' That's enough, Kurt. Please."

"Why does it embarrass you?" Kurt asked.

"I don't know. It seems sort of pompous, somehow, and—oh, I don't know—my quoting Shakespeare to you."

"You strange, sweet child," Kurt said, and then, changing the subject abruptly, "What do you think of Jane and John Peter?"

"I like them tremendously. And I think they're both awfully talented."

"Do they sleep together?"

Sitting on the barnacled pile in the darkness, Elizabeth blushed. "I don't know. It—it never occurred to me."

Mariella Hedeman paused on the boardwalk and called out good night.

"Good night, Miss Hedeman," Elizabeth and Kurt called back, their voices pulled and torn by the wind like wisps of fog.

"I never realized before Miss Hedeman got after me that I didn't breathe from the diaphragm naturally," Elizabeth said. "Jane does. But I have to make the most awful effort." She held one hand over her diaphragm to see that it was moving properly and let forth with one of Miss Hedeman's voice exercises. Her voice did not lack for power and Kurt put his hands over his ears.

"Hung-ay-oh-ooo-aaaaaaaaaawwwww!" Elizabeth howled.

John Peter called from down the beach. "Shut up! You're interrupting our concert."

Elizabeth shouted back, "You have no musical appreciation. I'm improving. Play *Plaisir* again, will you please?"

"Okay," John Peter called, and in a moment the haunting melody was blown along the sand again to them. "It's funny how that song gets me," Elizabeth said. "It means so many things to me. Particularly . . ."

"Particularly what?"

"Nothing."

"You're a funny kid, Liz."

"You've said that before."

"You're so much more of a child than you seem to be at first."

"I don't mean to be."

"You're really an awful baby."

"And people as tall as I am shouldn't be babies."

"You're much too sensitive about your height."

"I know it."

"You're no giant. How tall are you?"

"Five foot nine and three quarters."

"That's five foot ten."

"Five-nine and three quarters."

"Little fool," Kurt said. He leaned across the pile and kissed her. Elizabeth clung to him and he kissed her again.

When Dottie, strolling down the boardwalk with Huntley Haskell, saw them, she stopped. "My, you two make a pretty picture," she said.

Kurt laughed and grinned up at Dottie. Elizabeth stared miserably out over the ocean, shame and fury battling for uppermost in her mind.

"Good performance tonight, Dottie," Kurt said.

"Thanks. Know your lines, Liz?"

There was immense sarcasm in Dottie's voice, and Elizabeth answered, "Yes," shortly, not looking up. Dottie laughed.

"Too bad about you, Dottie," Kurt said. "I must say I think Andersen shouldn't keep people hanging around the theatre all day and then be surprised if they're not there when she calls a scene. However, if it had to happen, I'm glad our little Liz will have a chance."

Dottie laughed again, a metallic laugh with nothing warm or pleasant about it. "For heaven's sake, don't be sorry for me, Kurt. I wouldn't mind a week off. But I'm not sure I shall have one."

"Oh?" Kurt asked. "What gives?"

"Oh, we'll see, my pet, we'll see."

Huntley spoke for the first time. "Dottie likes to be sphinx-like. Courtmont's throwing a party at Irving's before she leaves tonight, Canitz old boy. Coming, aren't you?"

"Hadn't decided yet."

Dottie's tone was softer. "Oh, do come, Kurt. It won't be any fun without you."

"Want to come, Liz?" Kurt asked.

"Thanks," Elizabeth said, "but I'm not included in the company."

"Oh, you can come if you want to, kiddo." Dottie was the great movie star, graciously condescending. "Bibi and a couple other apprentices are there already."

"I think I'll stay here. Thank you." Elizabeth looked down at the sand holding the old piles steady.

"Okay." Dottie sounded relieved. "Be a good girl and go to bed early."

Kurt leaned close to Elizabeth and whispered, "You don't

mind if I go, Liebchen? I'd rather stay with you, but it would be rude to Courtmont."

"Of course," Elizabeth said. "Have fun."

Dottie took Kurt and Huntley each by the arm and they strolled off down the boardwalk. Elizabeth sat very still on the barnacled pile, listening to the plaintive music of the recorders. After a while she called out in an unsteady voice, "Play something else!"

"You just asked us to play that," John Peter shouted.

"I know, but play something else. Play something silly."

John Peter and Jane obligingly started on a gay Elizabethan madrigal. Elizabeth tried to sing along with them. "In these delightful pleasant groves . . ." But her voice wavered and she put her head down on her knees. In her mind's ear she kept hearing Kurt's happy, unembarrassed laugh when Dottie and Huntley discovered them kissing. I should have laughed, too, she thought. I should have been able to. But I couldn't. It was too important. How could Kurt laugh like that if it were important to him?

And then she consoled herself: But of course he had to laugh. *Especially* if it was important.

The music came thin and delicate as a spider's web from the recorders. As Elizabeth sat there she remembered a conversation she had had with her Aunt Harriet shortly after her father's death.

Elizabeth had been sitting in a corner of the cluttered attic in Jordan pretending with half her mind to be Jo in *Little Women* in order to stop weeping over a packet of her father's letters she had taken up with her to read, when Aunt Harriet called her downstairs. Elizabeth blew her nose and went down the dark attic steps and into the small upstairs sitting room where Aunt Harriet was at her desk working on accounts.

"Elizabeth," Aunt Harriet had said, tapping her pen lightly on the desk and not looking up from her account book.

"Yes, Aunt Harriet?"

"It has come to my attention that most young girls are given a certain amount of pocket money. Therefore in return for your household chores I have decided to give you fifteen cents a week."

"Thank you."

Now Aunt Harriet looked up with the sharp, discompassionate glance of a hawk. "What's the matter?"

"Nothing."

"Crying about your father?" Neither the voice nor the face was unkind; they simply expressed no emotion whatsoever; they were as drained of any feeling as a stream of water in the drought season.

"I'm not crying."

"You are. Well, sit down, sit down. Don't stand there looking all arms and legs."

Elizabeth collapsed into a chair, glaring down at the floor, pressing her lips together in order to hide their trembling.

"That's right," Aunt Harriet had said. "I'm glad to see you making an effort at control. My parents raised me, and then died when your father was a boy, so I did my best to raise him to believe that a display of feelings is weak and unworthy. And

I have been appalled at the lack of emotional discipline your father permitted in you." She looked over Elizabeth's head, at a dark and lurid moonlit seascape that was hanging a fraction crooked on the wall. "Straighten that picture behind you, Elizabeth, if you please."

Elizabeth obeyed.

"That's better. I can't imagine how it got awry. I've forbidden you to roughhouse in here."

"I haven't, Aunt Harriet. I never come in here at all unless you send for me."

"Sit down again, please, Elizabeth. I want you to listen to me carefully. I want you to remember that I expect complete self-control from you at all times. In my house I will tolerate no scenes."

"I have no intention of making scenes," Elizabeth had answered with gangly, thirteen-year-old dignity.

Aunt Harriet ignored her, continuing to speak in the level, expressionless voice that Elizabeth found so disconcerting. "As I said, I have always thought your father was wrong in permitting you to display your emotions in the way that he did. I know you are at what I believe is called the 'difficult age,' but your total lack of control seems to me appalling and thoroughly unnecessary."

"I think I have a certain amount of control," Elizabeth said.

"Elizabeth, will you please have the courtesy not to interrupt me? Remember that what I am saying is for your own good." Everything Aunt Harriet said was always for Elizabeth's good. "And I speak from bitter experience. You think I am unfeeling. But please remember that your father was my brother and that I loved him as much as you did, and more, because I am a great deal older than you are and know more of suffering than you, child, could ever imagine, and because I brought your father up and he was as much my son as my brother."

"He was *my* father," Elizabeth said.

"Please be quiet and listen to me. You must not be hurt because I cannot give you the demonstrations of affection to which you were accustomed from your father."

Since her father had been extremely reserved, and only instinct had told Elizabeth how much he loved her, this took her rather aback; but she held her tongue.

"You can rest assured," Aunt Harriet continued, "that I will behave toward you as I would my own child. And you, on your part, must learn to control your emotions. I do not, for instance, care to be kissed."

"I don't want to kiss you," Elizabeth said, wishing she could get back up to the attic. She stood up.

But Aunt Harriet held up her heavily veined hand. "Just a moment, please, Elizabeth."

Elizabeth's long legs capsized under her again in unwilling obedience.

"You must not wear your heart so on your sleeve," Aunt Harriet said, and for a moment the mask left her face and a look of pain came into her eyes. "I think you are old enough now to learn that people do not like to be loved too much. It embarrasses them. It makes them feel smothered. They feel drenched, drowned. Do you understand me?"

"No," Elizabeth said.

"I suppose it is your heritage, but if you do not wish to be unhappy you must learn to combat it. It is far easier to give love than it is to receive it, and you are always spilling your affections about as though people considered it a privilege to pick them up. Let me assure you that they do not. People are much too preoccupied with their own emotions to welcome being burdened with anyone else's. Love is a very demanding thing, Elizabeth, and you will find that people do not care to have too great demands made of them. Your father—"

"Please leave my father out of it," Elizabeth had cried, not caring if she was rude, not caring if she was displaying lack of emotional discipline.

Even through her hurt she had wondered what experience had made Aunt Harriet feel that she had to talk to her grief-stricken niece in that manner.

Now, sitting in forlorn solitude on her pile, Elizabeth took off her glasses misted by the ocean spray and peered out at the horizon. She felt that there was more than a grain of truth in her aunt's harsh words. It was not good to wear your heart on your sleeve where the Dotties of the world could see it and mock, and Kurt might feel overwhelmed by it.

Ben's voice from up the boardwalk broke into her thoughts. "Liz—Elizabeth!"

She raised her head with relief. "Huloo, Ben!"

Ben came toward her, singing, "Did you ever hear tell of sweet Betsy from Pike? All alone, my dove?"

"Mm-hm."

Ben jumped down off the boardwalk and scrambled up onto the pile Kurt had vacated. "This thing's warm." He wagged an accusing finger at Elizabeth. " 'Who's been sitting in my chair?' asked the papa bear."

"Kurt," she said shortly.

"Where's Kurt gone?"

"To the party at Irving's."

Ben listened for a moment to Jane and John Peter's recorders and said, "How ghoulish," before calling to them, "Play something sad."

"Liz just asked for something silly."

"I want something sad and I'm older than Liz. Play the one about the sailor boys and the girls."

"What?" John Peter called.

"*Les Filles de Saint-Malo*," Elizabeth called back.

"That's what I said, isn't it?" Ben shouted.

Again Jane and John Peter changed their tune. Ben said in very bad French, "*Les filles de Saint-Malo ont les yeux couleur de l'eau* . . . We were able to take down the props for Courtmont's play and put up everything for *Macbeth*. How's that for speedy? Thank goodness Price is too cheap to have elaborate sets. Hey, what's the matter?"

"Nothing."

"Now, don't try to fool Uncle Ben. Kurt upset you?"

"No, heavens, Ben, don't be nuts. I'm violently happy!"

"Hurrah!" Ben said. He leaned over and put his hand on her knee. "Did you want to go to Irving's?"

"No."

"Seen Price yet about using Soapie's room and board for next week?"

"Not yet. Being in *Macbeth* ought to clinch it, though."

"I wouldn't count your chickens before they hatch."

"All right. I won't. But why?"

"I just don't trust Price to do the right thing."

"Okay, Ben. You probably know best."

"I'm glad to see somebody put that hellion in her place. I like Dottie the way I like a cockroach in my bathtub. Listen, Liz, can't anything be done with that aunt of yours?"

"You know she doesn't approve of the theatre," Elizabeth said gloomily.

"Neither does my father. He wants me to be a broker, like he is. He hated it every time I got an acting job when I was a kid. Especially if it meant going on tour with Mother and being gone for months."

"You can hardly blame him for that," Elizabeth said. "It must have been awfully lonely for him. Anyhow, he doesn't *really* make a fuss, Ben, and your mother really wants you to be an actor."

"Mother's a dream," Ben said. "Well, I promised Dad I'd stay out of the theatre for four years and go to college. A hell of a lot of good it's done me. A B.A. degree and everybody on Broadway's forgotten I ever existed. I wouldn't have this lousy assistant stage-managing glorified apprentice job otherwise. It's a pity we didn't go to college together, Liz. We'd have had a lot of fun . . . Hey, Liz, isn't that Price coming along the board-walk?"

It was. Ben poked her in the ribs and Elizabeth called out to him, "Oh, Mr. Price . . ." She jumped down from her pile and stood with her hands on the edge of the boardwalk, looking up at him.

"Yes, Liz, what is it? I'm in a hurry."

"Mr. Price—" she hesitated, then plunged. "I didn't want to bother you before the show was over tonight, but Sophie wanted me to tell you that since she'd paid her room and board through next week and wasn't going to be here she wanted me to have it—if—if that was all right."

J. P. Price had not yet recovered from a disagreeable scene with Dottie and his face didn't soften. "I'm afraid that's a little irregular."

"Please, Mr. Price. You know this summer's terribly important to me, and I've been so happy here. Even a week longer makes a lot of difference. It's—it's not that I want to leave, you know."

"You shouldn't have come if you couldn't stay the whole season. You're depriving someone else of a scholarship and I shall have to find someone to replace you in your work."

"But I didn't know I couldn't stay! I didn't have any idea I couldn't until this morning. My aunt promised me I could. But she doesn't approve of the theatre. Not this theatre—*the* theatre—and—"

Mr. Price relented. "Okay, Liz. We'll let it go this time since Sophie had paid ahead."

"Oh, thank you, Mr. Price! Good night."

"Good night."

"Going to the party at Irving's?" Ben asked.

"That's right," Mr. Price said. "You kids had better go to

bed. There'll probably be a lot of work for you tomorrow."

"All right, we will," Elizabeth said. She climbed back onto her pile next to Ben as Mr. Price strode off.

"There's one man who's in the theatre to make money and nothing else," Ben said. "My God, what a fuss for an extra twenty bucks. I should think he'd realize you're valuable to him. He always makes more money when you're in the box office than anyone else."

"You're cracked."

"People see you and they buy ten tickets instead of two."

In the darkness Elizabeth grinned, touched by Ben's dogged loyalty. "My charm may be fatal but I'm afraid you overestimate it. Look, what train is Courtmont going to take? I didn't know trains ran here in the middle of the night."

"Train, my foot," Ben said. "She's going to drive that emerald green convertible of hers. I think I'll go get a hamburger somewhere. Hungry?"

"Yes. Ravenous."

"Come along with me. I'll treat you."

"You don't need to. A beautiful fat gentleman gave me a dollar tip this evening. That's more than I usually make in a whole week of tips. I'm filthy with money. I'll treat you."

"We'll go dutch," Ben said.

"Listen, after all the hamburgers you've given me you've got to let me treat you this once. For auld lang syne and all that. Now don't be difficult and argue with me, Ben."

"Okay," Ben said. "My mother told me always to give in gracefully."

They climbed down from their piles and wandered along the beach. The stars were thick and low above them; the canopy of sky seemed to be sagging with the weight of the heat.

"Tide's coming in," Ben said, slapping at a mosquito.

They passed John Peter and Jane, who had stopped playing their recorders. John Peter was lying sprawled on the sand, his head on Jane's lap. Jane bent over him, tracing his features with a delicate finger.

"Leaving?" John Peter asked, reaching up a lazy hand to Jane's fair hair.

"Going to get a hamburger. Want to come?"

"Nope. We're too comfortable here," Jane said.

"Mind the tide doesn't come in and drown you. Come on, Liz. Here're some steps. Let's go up on the boardwalk. I'm getting sand in my shoes."

They walked along the rough planks of the boardwalk. Soon the houses became smaller and less well cared for, and then began to give way to shops and booths. There was an amusement hall with a penny arcade, and brightly painted turtles for sale; and a jewelry store full of wedding and engagement rings; and a booth with big straw hats and kewpie dolls and costume jewelry; and a rifle range. The lights were bright and garish and Elizabeth forgot Kurt for the moment and remembered that she could stay another week and that she was in *Macbeth*; and she felt supremely happy as she walked along beside Ben. They came to a milk bar that was still open and Ben said, "They make good hamburgers here and I feel like a quadruple-dip milk shake. Okay with you?"

"Fine," Elizabeth said, and followed him in.

Inside the milk bar everything looked very clean and white. There was white tiling on the floor and the walls, and a man with a mop and a bucket was washing the floor at the back. A white counter ran the length of the place, with high white stools in front of it, onto which Elizabeth and Ben climbed. At one end a man in a chef's hat stood over a big grill, and the smell of ice cream and frying onions pervaded the place.

"Want onions with your hamburger?" Ben asked.

Elizabeth loved onions with her hamburger, but there was a remote possibility that Kurt might come back from Irving's and look for her. "Just pickle."

"One with pickle and one with pickle and onions," Ben ordered. "You want a milk shake, Liz?"

"Chocolate with coffee ice cream. One dip."

"Okay," Ben said. "And make mine chocolate with chocolate ice cream. Four dips."

"Four!" the white-uniformed girl behind the counter exclaimed.

"You heard me."

"You'll have to eat it with a fork."

"That's the way I like it."

"Everybody to his own taste, as the old lady said when she kissed the cow." The girl called over to the chef, "Two, one without," then leaned over the counter toward them. "Say, don't you kids work up at the thee-atre?"

"Yeah," Ben said. "Do we show it that bad?"

The girl grinned. "Well, you're not like the run-of-the-mill customers we get. But I recognized the young lady. You're one of the ushers, aren't you?"

"That's right," Elizabeth said.

"My fiancé and I go most every week," the girl told them. "We like it better than the picture show."

"Hurrah for you," Ben cheered. "It's the difference between canned vegetables and fresh vegetables, isn't it?"

"Say, that's good! Did you think that one up?" the girl asked.

"I wish I could claim it, but it isn't very original. Elizabeth here"—he waved a thumb at Elizabeth—"is going to be in the show next week."

"Gee, honest? I'll have to get my fiancé to get tickets, then. We weren't so sure we'd take it in, being it was Shakespeare and everything, but being as I know one of the actresses I just guess we'll have to go."

The chef called, "Two hamburgers coming up," and she went off to get them and make the milk shakes.

"Want me to hear your lines?" Ben asked.

"Oh, Ben, would you?"

"Got your sides?"

Elizabeth reached into one of the back pockets of her blue jeans and pulled out her sides, her speeches with their cues, typed on half-size sheets of typewriter paper between red paper covers, with MACBETH, GENTLEWOMAN on the outside. The penciled "Miss Hatfield" had been crossed out and Joe McGill had written "Miss Jerrold" underneath.

Ben read the cue in a level, rather expressionless voice. He and Elizabeth had both learned, early in the summer when they cued members of the professional company, that it is disconcerting to an actor who is working on lines to have the person who is cuing him try to act. " '. . . she last walked?' "

" 'Since his majesty went into the field,' " Elizabeth said, " 'I have seen her rise from her bed, throw her night-gown upon her, unlock her closet, take forth paper, fold it, write upon't, read it, afterwards seal it, and again return to bed, yet all this while in a most fast sleep.' "

The girl put the hamburgers and milk shakes down on the counter in front of them. "Which one with onions?"

"Me," Ben said.

"That your part you're saying?"

Elizabeth nodded.

"Go on. Let me hear."

Ben gave her the next cue. " ' . . . heard her say?' "

" 'That, sir, which I will not report after her,' " Elizabeth said.

" '. . . meet you should.' "

" 'Neither to you, nor anyone, having no witness to confirm my speech. Lo you, here she comes. This is her very guise and, upon my life, fast asleep. Observe her, stand close.' "

Ben: " '. . . by that light?' "

Elizabeth: " 'Why, it stood by her. She has light by her continually, 'tis her command.' "

The girl made a face. "Say, that doesn't make any sense!"

Elizabeth laughed. "That's because all I have is my sides."

"Beg pardon?"

"My sides. That's just the speeches I have, with the last three words of the speech that comes before mine as my cue."

The girl shook her head. "It's beyond me. I used to think I'd like to go on the stage or be in the movies or something, but I decided to marry my Jimmy and settle down instead. He's a plumber and makes real good money."

"A lot better than most actors do, I can tell you that," Ben said. "Want me to go on cuing you, Liz?"

"Never mind," Elizabeth said. "I know it."

Ben handed her back the sides. "Gee, eleven sides. I never realized the Gentlewoman was such a good part, even hearing it at rehearsals."

"Miss Andersen's wonderful in that scene," Elizabeth said. "Oh, Ben, isn't she just superb? It's so hard not to sound hammy, but she sends cold shivers down your spine."

"From now on," Ben said, "you'll be the one I'll watch in that scene. Want another hamburger?"

"No, thanks. And I'm paying for this, remember?"

"You can pay for my hamburger but you can't pay for my quadruple-dip milk shake. They cost a fortune."

"Was it good?" the girl asked.

"Out of this world. Can we have the check, please? Do we pay you or the cashier?"

"You can pay me."

"Well, take the hamburgers and her milk shake out of her dollar and my milk shake out of my fifty cents."

"Okay. Hamburgers twenty-five and milk shake twenty-five. Here's your quarter, miss. And the quadruple-dip milk shake. Well, we'll call it fifty cents."

"Thanks, and don't forget to come to the show next week."

"I won't. I'm looking forward to it. Night, now."

"Good night."

When they were out on the boardwalk again Ben said, "Let's go on down to Irving's for a few minutes."

"Uh-uh." Elizabeth shook her head with determination. "I want to work on my part."

"Okay," Ben said. "I'll walk you home. Pardon my curiosity, Liz, but is Kurt *with* anybody?"

"Dottie and Huntley."

Ben looked through the darkness at Elizabeth, and said suddenly, "Listen, Liz, this next week don't do anything silly, will you?"

"What do you mean?"

"You know what I mean. No guy's worth being unhappy about."

"Or worth making a fool of yourself for, don't you mean?" Elizabeth asked, walking on again, angry at herself because she always stopped and looked wistfully at the windows with the engagement rings, angry at Ben for suggesting that Kurt would make her unhappy.

They turned away from the boardwalk and walked down the street toward the Cottage. As they passed one of the larger houses they could hear a phonograph playing loudly, one of *Carmen*'s arias. Elizabeth put her hand on Ben's arm. "Let's listen for a minute, Ben."

They stood there on the sidewalk, letting the music and the light from the windows spill over them. Then the door opened and some people came out, laughing, calling good-nights, and Elizabeth and Ben moved on.

"They're almost always playing records there when we go

back to the Cottage at night," Elizabeth said. "Have you noticed?"

"Yes." Ben nodded. "Golly Moses, but I love music. One of the nicest times I can remember was a winter we spent in Chicago—my father was sent out there on business for a year—and I played all the kid parts in the opera. Not singing, just walking on, sometimes in the mob, and sometimes with a couple of lines. That was wonderful fun. They had a darned good company that winter, too. I suppose I was too young to know it, but my mother did. I've loved music ever since then."

"We like so many of the same things, don't we, Ben?" Elizabeth asked.

"With a few marked exceptions."

"What do you mean?"

"Oh, forget it. I like that opera, *Carmen*. That year at the Chicago Opera Company there was a mezzo who sang Carmen like I've never heard it since. Her name was Anna Larsen. I used to be crazy about her. I was six years old and she was my first love. That's one reason I first noticed you. You look kind of like her."

"Yes, Ben," Elizabeth said in a strained, tight voice. "You see, she was my mother."

"Well, that's no small coincidence," Ben said. "And that explains a lot. About Aunt Harriet, I mean."

"Yes. I guess it does." Elizabeth walked slowly up the path to the Cottage and the uncomplicated elation she had felt at hearing the music flowing out to her from the house fled, and instead her heart began to beat rapidly, as though she were afraid. She sat down on the bottom step and her legs were shaking and she put her head down on her knees. "What do you remember about my mother, Ben?"

Ben sat down beside her and put his arm around her. "Liz," he said, and the strange gentleness was in his voice again, the gentleness that made him seem years older than Elizabeth, a member of a sadder and wiser generation, "your mother was a real artist. That's not just my opinion. Anybody who knows anything about singing knows that. My parents still keep up with some of the singers we met at the Chicago Opera Company that season, and whenever they come to our house they talk about Anna Larsen. She—well, let's face it, she did some cockeyed things, and people are always waiting to jump on anything an artist does, but she was a wonderful person. Didn't you ever know her, Liz? Didn't you ever see her at all?"

Elizabeth shook her head and began plucking bits of grass from a clump that grew up through a crack in the walk. "I went to her funeral. That was the only time I ever saw her to remember. I guess one of the cockeyed things she did was, she left Father—and me—when I was six months old. It seems funny, Ben, she was my mother, and I never knew her, and you did, and I have to ask you questions about her."

"I'll tell you everything I remember," Ben said. "Most of it maybe I don't really remember. What happened then and what's been talked about since is all mixed up in my mind. She was crazy about kids. I used to adore her. Well, I told you that. She'd call me into her dressing room and we'd play games. She had a bearskin rug on the floor, and when she was onstage and I wasn't needed she'd let me lie on it and read. And then we'd play all kinds of games with it, going to the north pole and

African explorers and all kinds of things. It got so I spent most of my time in her dressing room, and then her dresser left, so Mother took over as a kind of combination dresser-secretary for her until she could find someone new. That's why we saw so much more of her than any of the other singers. I remember when she died. I came down to breakfast one morning and Mother was sitting with the paper spread out on the kitchen table in front of her and her cup of coffee spilled all over it and weeping her head off."

"Have you—have you got any of her records, Ben?"

"Dozens at home." Ben gave a fierce swat at a mosquito.

"I tried to buy some while I was at college but they were all out of press or whatever it is. Of course Aunt Harriet wouldn't even have a Victrola, she was so afraid I'd get hold of some of Mother's records. She was always terribly angry if she was reminded of Mother in any way—and I guess I was a constant reminder. Tell me more about her, Ben. What was she like as a person?"

Ben, with his arm still protectively around Elizabeth, said, "Well, the thing I remember most, and maybe just because it was the thing Mother talked about most, was the way your mother loved people, and the way she wanted love. She was affectionate to anybody and everybody, kind of like a baby or a kitten. When she'd sung particularly well she'd come offstage and fling her arms around Mother and kiss her. If Father was around she'd kiss him, too. She always had to have someone to love. And she always had to have someone hugging and kissing her. She couldn't seem to believe that anyone could really love *her*. She always thought it was because she was a star, not just because of her herself, and she always had to be reassured. She kept asking Mother, 'You really do like me? You really are my friend?' And I think she was scared I loved her just because she played with me and brought me presents."

Elizabeth said softly, "You say it makes you understand Aunt Harriet better. It makes me understand things better, too." All kinds of little pieces in the puzzling background of her parentage began to fall into place. Now she could imagine with clarity her father as he must have been when he left Aunt Harriet and the house in Jordan and went to live with his bride in the small town where he taught. Probably he was, in manner, something like Aunt Harriet then, reserved, undemonstrative. Elizabeth remembered his saying to her once, speaking the words with difficulty, "My darling, it is very hard for me to show people that I love them. But you know that I love you, don't you? Even though I can't put my arms around you so sweetly and kiss you the way you do me."

So there was Robert Jerrold, probably even less able to show in the little affectionate ways his love for his wife than he was for his daughter, and there was Anna Larsen, young, volatile, filled with dreams of romantic, ideal love, and yet tragically, utterly unsure of her own desirability . . .

"My mother left my father to go to New York with another man," Elizabeth said. "That was all I ever really knew. Father never talked about Mother. I always wanted to ask him about her, but I was afraid I'd hurt him if I did. Aunt Harriet only talked about her once when I first came to live with her. She told me my mother was a wicked woman and she was going to do her best to see that I didn't follow in her footsteps. And once at school, one of the kids showed me a clipping in a magazine about Mother singing in a nightclub in New York. And then I didn't know anything again until she died when I was in college."

"No matter what anybody said, no matter what she did, she was a wonderful person, a mother to be proud of. Don't ever forget that," Ben said fiercely.

"No . . . Ben—this is the second time in my life I've ever been able to talk about my mother to anybody."

"When was the first?"

"Just after she died, when I went to the funeral. The woman who ran the boardinghouse where she died talked to me . . . That was the only other time . . . and then, of course, it was all too much like a bad dream . . . and Mother had been ill the whole time she was there."

"We'll talk about her as much as you like," Ben said.

"After Father died I found a newspaper picture of Mother in with his papers. I have it in a frame on my bureau now. Haven't you ever noticed it, Ben?"

"What a blind fool I am," Ben said. "You and Jane have your bureau so littered with pictures and there's always such a gang in there . . . Let's go look at it now."

"That's a fine idea," Elizabeth said. "If I stay out here in the dark with you, I shall cry."

"Well, why don't you, Liz? Might be a good idea."

Elizabeth shook her head violently and stood up. "No. I don't want to cry."

"I know," Ben said. "It's okay."

"Most of the time it's as though I'd never had a mother at

all." Elizabeth pretended to be very busy slapping a mosquito. "We ought to have some citronella," she said in a quivering voice. "We used to call it Cinderella when I was a kid. Mosquitoes don't usually bother me much, but they're certainly after me tonight. Let's go in, Ben."

Ben followed her into the Cottage, letting the screen door slam behind them. The lights were all on and a group from the company was sitting around one of the long tables in the dining room playing poker. Mariella Hedeman in a lavender velvet gown was sitting regally at the head of the table and dealing.

Marian Hatfield looked up at Elizabeth and Ben and waved at them. "Come play," she called. "This is Miss Hedeman's lucky night. She's cleaning the rest of us out."

"What about Courtmont's party at Irving's?" Ben said.

"We left about an hour ago, but there are still people there."

"Want to play, Liz?" Ben asked.

"No, thanks. I'm no good at cards. You go ahead."

"I don't want to leave you if you're going to be lonely," Ben said in a low voice.

"I want to work on my part, anyhow. You go on and play, Ben. I don't think I could talk any more tonight. It's silly to get so emotional, but I can't seem to help it. But can we talk about her again?"

"Anytime," Ben said. "Now you get some sleep, Liz. You've got a hard day ahead of you tomorrow with dress rehearsal and everything, and you know you need plenty of sleep."

"I'm going to bed in just a few minutes," Elizabeth promised. "Have a good time and win lots."

Elizabeth climbed the two flights of stairs to the third floor. The hall lights were on but all the rooms seemed to be dark; almost everybody went out on Saturday nights. Elizabeth switched on the bedroom light, went over to the bureau, and stared for a long time at her mother. All of a sudden the woman in the newspaper picture seemed to be a real person instead of an unhappy shadow constantly in the background of her life. It couldn't have been easy for you, either, she thought. And I'm glad Ben liked you.

Elizabeth flung herself down on her bed and concentrated on going over her lines. Later she would think about her mother; not now. After she had worked on her sides for a few minutes she undressed, took a shower, and pulled on her pajamas and a flannel bathrobe. She heard the sound of recorders coming up the stairs and John Peter and Jane entered.

"Hi," John Peter said. "Where's Ben?"

"Downstairs playing poker, I think."

"He wasn't just a minute ago."

"He's probably gone to the party at Irving's then. I hope he behaves himself. He's too young to drink too much."

"It's unattractive no matter how you slice it," John Peter said. He sprawled out on Jane's bed and began to play *Plaisir d'Amour*.

"Don't play that again, John Peter, please," Elizabeth said.

"Why not? I thought you were so crazy about it."

"I am. It— I've just heard it enough tonight."

"Listen, Liz," John Peter said, suddenly putting down his recorder. "Why don't you give Ben a break?"

Elizabeth grew rigid. "What do you mean?"

"Are you such a dope you can't see he's in love with you?" John Peter asked.

"I think you're the dope," Elizabeth said. "Of course he isn't in love with me." She added faintly, "Is he, Jane?"

"I wouldn't know."

"Sure," John Peter said, "as though we hadn't been talking about it half the evening. For heaven's sake, Liz, your feelings are your own business, but either give Ben a break or don't keep him hanging around. I don't care what you do to that bastard Canitz, but I don't want to see Ben hurt."

Elizabeth was trembling with rage and with horror. "John Peter Toller—" she started, her voice shaking. Then, "I haven't any words to say to you. What you've said is so—so—"

"I'm sorry," John Peter said, the beakiness of his nose seeming to sharpen as it did when he was being stubborn, "but it's been on my mind and I had to get it out."

"Ben knows how I feel. We're wonderful friends and that's all and that's that." Elizabeth hoped she sounded more convincing to John Peter and to Jane than she did to herself. She was sure Ben knew that she loved Kurt; that was something she couldn't seem to hide from anybody, no matter how much she wanted to.

"Okay," John Peter said. "If Ben really knows how you feel, then it's his own business, I guess." He did not sound happy or convinced.

Jane dropped her hand lightly on Elizabeth's shoulder. "Don't be angry, Liz. I begged John Peter not to say anything.

It's only because we're so fond of you and Ben, both of you—"

"I don't think I'm angry anymore," Elizabeth said. "I'm just appalled."

"Well, forget it, will you? As long as everything's clear with you and Ben, that's all that matters."

"Ben knows about Kurt," Elizabeth said flatly.

"Knows what about Kurt?" John Peter asked.

"About how I feel about him."

"Ben's been in the theatre a long time," John Peter said. "He's known a lot of Kurts."

"What do you mean?"

"Look, I shouldn't have brought it up. Jane was absolutely right. Forgive me and forget it. Please, Liz."

"Okay."

"And, Liz, honey," Jane said. "One other thing."

"What?"

"It was sweet of you this afternoon to say I was a better actress than you are and try to give me the part, but you shouldn't do things like that."

"Why not? You are."

"In the first place, I'm not; and in the second place it was entirely my own fault for staying out on the beach and being late for rehearsal."

"Oh, piffle," Elizabeth said.

John Peter clapped his hand over one of his cheeks and groaned.

"What's the matter?" Jane asked anxiously.

"My tooth," John Peter said gloomily. "It still hurts."

"You'd better go to a dentist on Monday, darling."

"I'll have to if it isn't any better. But I hate to go here to someone I don't know. I'd much rather wait till I get back to New York. I don't know what makes my teeth so lousy. Every six months it's just as though a gremlin got in my mouth with a small but very effective machine gun." He looked up as there was a sharp knock on the door. "Oh, come in, come in, if you fool you must," he said.

Valborg Andersen stepped into the room and all three of them jumped up in confusion. Elizabeth backed up to the bureau to stand in front of the large picture of the actress herself.

"Miss Jerrold," Valborg Andersen said.

"Yes, Miss Andersen?" Elizabeth reached behind her and put the picture down on its face. The actress saw and smiled slightly.

She looked around her. "Four of you in here? Seems like pretty close quarters. I'm sorry to come calling so very late. Miss Jerrold, might I speak to you for a moment?"

"Of course," Elizabeth said, and followed her out into the hall.

Jane and John Peter looked at each other. "What do you suppose she wants?" John Peter asked.

Jane shook her head. "I don't know, but I'm afraid I can guess."

"Dottie?"

"I'd bet my bottom button."

John Peter looked at Elizabeth's picture of Miss Andersen lying flat on the bureau. "Now why on earth did Liz move the picture?"

"Oh, you know, sweet. I can't explain." Jane gesticulated

vaguely. "It looks like asking for something. Oh, drat that Dottie for slitching things up for Liz."

"Maybe it isn't that."

"What else?" Jane asked.

"Why don't you tell Liz?"

"Tell her what?"

"About Miss Andersen."

"Why, John Peter?"

"I don't know. It might make her feel better or something."

Jane shook her head slowly. "I don't know. I don't see why it would. And I said I wasn't going to tell anybody. I think I'd rather not. Not even Liz."

"Okay," John Peter said. "You do however you feel best about it." Then he took advantage of the moment of privacy by kissing Jane. They drew apart as the door opened and Elizabeth came in quietly, crossed to her bed, and picked up the Gentlewoman's sides. Valborg Andersen stood in the doorway.

"I'm extremely sorry, Miss Jerrold. I wouldn't have had this happen for anything."

"Of course. I know," Elizabeth said. "Here are the sides, Miss Andersen."

"Thank you, Miss Jerrold. Good night."

"Good night, Miss Andersen."

"I was afraid of that," Jane said as the door closed behind the actress.

"What did she say?" John Peter demanded.

"Dottie raised a stink with Mr. Price. Threatened to quit."

"Aw, honey," Jane said. "What a shame."

Elizabeth reached up, took off her glasses, blew on them,

and put them on again. "Miss Andersen said she'd make Price use me if I wanted to, but of course I couldn't."

"It was decent of her to come tell you herself," John Peter said.

"Yes, it was. It was wonderful of her. It wasn't necessary at all. But she said she wanted me to hear it from her. That's why she came so late. And she said she wanted to have me sit in on dress rehearsal if I wanted to, but I was afraid Dottie would object to that, too, and make it uncomfortable for everyone, so I won't. But she was wonderful to bother to think of it."

The door burst open, so violently that it banged against the foot of Elizabeth's bed, and Bibi dashed in. "Miss Courtmont's going!" she shouted. "Are you coming down to say goodbye?"

"We are not," John Peter said. "And for heaven's sake, don't bang that door again. It kills my tooth."

"Isn't she just the most glamorous person you've ever seen! I want to look just like that when I'm middle-aged!" Bibi cried with enthusiasm.

"Why don't you tell her, Bibi," John Peter suggested with a grin at Jane and Elizabeth. "I'm sure she'd be touched. I just know Sarah Courtmont would appreciate being called middle-aged."

"Go say goodbye, Bibi," Jane said. "Say goodbye for all of us."

"Aren't you excited about being in *Macbeth* and doing the Gentlewoman, Liz?" Bibi squealed, paying no attention to Jane. "Gosh, you're lucky."

"I'm not doing the Gentlewoman," Elizabeth said.

"Why not? Who is?"

"Marian Hatfield, same as before."

"You mean Dottie's playing Lady Macduff after all?"

"Exactly."

"If you want Courtmont to say goodbye to you, you'd better hurry downstairs." Jane's pleasant voice sounded unusually impatient.

"*Aren't* you coming?" Bibi asked.

"No," Elizabeth said. "We're not. Goodbye."

"Ben's downstairs saying goodbye."

"He can stay there."

"You needn't be so rude, Elizabeth." Bibi's reedy voice was aggrieved.

"Sorry."

Bibi started for the door. "Jack and I are going back to Irving's after Courtmont goes, so I won't be back until late."

Jane looked at her with distaste. "It's late already."

"If you value your life, don't wake us up when you come in," Elizabeth added.

"I'll be quiet if you don't wake me up tomorrow morning," Bibi bargained.

John Peter took Bibi by the shoulders and propelled her out the door. "If you make any noise when you come in, you'll answer to me." He shut the door and brushed his hands off. "There."

"Liz," Jane said.

"Mm-hm?"

"Now that you aren't doing the Gentlewoman—well, look, I know how much you want to be here just to watch Miss

Andersen next week, and if you'd let me I'd love to lend it to you . . ."

Elizabeth looked at her awkwardly. "Jane, bless you, you're an angel, but Soapie's already paid room and board through next week and I managed to argue Price into letting me stay on that."

"Oh, good, that's all right, then," Jane said, equally awkwardly. "Have you told your aunt yet?"

"No, I should have called her tonight, but I'll do it in the morning so she won't expect me on the train."

Just then a voice called, "Everybody decent?" And without waiting for an answer, Huntley Haskell opened the door a crack and pushed his head in.

"Come on in," John Peter said. "Anything we can do for you?"

"Have you seen Dottie?" Huntley's speech was a little slurred, his gait a little unsteady.

"Didn't she go to Irving's with you?" Jane asked.

"I lost track of her," Huntley said. "She hasn't been there in a coupla hours."

"Did you see Kurt?" Elizabeth asked.

"Not there either," Huntley said. "Darn little bastard. Listen, Jerrold, you might've known you couldn't edge Dottie out of the play."

"That wasn't really my idea, Huntley," Elizabeth said.

"Didn't say it was. Just said you ought to have known you couldn't've done it. Dottie doesn't give. She takes."

Huntley stood swaying in the doorway for a moment. Then

he waved at them, a limp, heavy hand. "So long, kids." He wavered out.

"What a fool," John Peter said.

"John Peter, darling, I want some more coffee before I go to bed."

"Come on, then," he said. "It's late. It's almost three. And I want to go to bed. My tooth hurts."

"I can't go to sleep unless I've had coffee. It's getting to be practically a neurosis." Jane sighed. "Want some, Liz?"

"No, thanks. I'm going to sleep."

John Peter put his arm around Jane. "Come on, darling."

Before Elizabeth could get into bed, Ben bounced into the room, his face white with fatigue, but his dark eyes sparkling as usual. "Courtmont's gone. Thank everything. And congratulate me for being a good boy, Liz. I went to Irving's but I had a pineapple malted milk and a maple nut sundae and a banana split."

Elizabeth groaned. "I don't know which is more lethal, that goo or gin."

"Gin was mother's milk to me," Ben elegantly misquoted from *Pygmalion*. "And tomorrow our little Bibi will be down at the station to meet Mr. Mervyn Melrose, heart-throbbing star of cinema and stage. And what a frappy comedy Price has picked for *him*. The gags in it were hoary in Minsky's day."

"Bibi will love him. It's a pity Soapie's gone."

"Oh, Soapie wouldn't like him. He lives with a dame."

"Well!"

"He's married to her, but she's still a dame. Caramel?"

"No, thanks. Ben, we're awful to be so mean to Bibi and

Soapie. We shouldn't have teased Soapie. It's partly our fault she left."

"And good riddance, too," Ben said with finality. "Soapie didn't have looks and she certainly didn't have talent. The sooner she retires from the theatre, the better. And the same goes for Bibi. Only Bibi has looks, if you go for that type, which I don't, and she's a lot surer of herself than Soapie was, so she'll be a lot harder to dislodge."

Elizabeth lay back on the lumpy bed and stared up at the ceiling. "We're so darned sure of ourselves. We simply assume that we're good and then feel we've a perfect right to criticize and condemn other people wholesale. Sooner or later we're going to get a boot in the behind that'll knock us off our high horses—my metaphor's mixed but you know what I mean— and we'll deserve it, after the way we carry on about ourselves."

"You just got a boot on your high horse from Aunt Harriet and you still feel fairly sure of yourself," Ben said.

"Yes. And *Macbeth*. Sure, but that didn't have anything to do with me. Miss Andersen still wanted me, that's what's important. Losing the part was just politics. Kurt was right this afternoon. We just aren't as good as we think we are. Nobody's that good."

Ben laughed, then asked, "What brought that on?"

"Oh, I don't know. Aunt Harriet's always drummed it into me about pride going before a fall—though she's got the same kind of pride most Southerners have—oh, I don't know. I guess knowing I have to go back to Jordan the end of next week. I was so sure of the summer and everything being so wonderful, and now all of a sudden a whole half of the summer's just vanishing into thin air."

Suddenly Ben sat up with a yell. "Hey, listen, what did I hear you say just now?"

"Could you do that good a double take onstage?" Elizabeth asked him.

"Did I hear you say you weren't doing *Macbeth?*" Ben demanded fiercely.

"You did."

"Dottie?"

"Yes."

"That jerk! Sacred cow, Liz, that's nauseating."

Elizabeth watched a fly crawling slowly across the ceiling and pause to investigate a crack that must have appeared to it like a chasm. "I wouldn't care so much except she must have made it awfully unpleasant for Miss Andersen."

"Somebody's going to strangle her someday. You'll see." Ben nodded knowingly.

Elizabeth sat up. "Miss Andersen told me herself, Ben—I mean, about my not playing the Gentlewoman."

"That was decent of her."

"Catch anybody else taking that amount of trouble over an apprentice? If there were only more people like her, the theatre wouldn't be in the mess it's in today." She looked over at Ben and he was sitting, chin in hand, not listening, an unhappy expression on his face; unhappiness was not a common expression to Ben's features, which were usually alive with laughter, and Elizabeth asked gently, "What's the matter, Ben?"

"I was thinking about what you said about how sure we are

of ourselves," he answered, looking not at Elizabeth but down at his feet. "Does it really seem that way? Do we really seem so darned sure? If I seem sure of myself, it's just a bluff. Maybe I take it out on people like Soapie and Bibi just to kid myself I really mean it, to bluff myself as well as everybody else."

"What do you mean?" Elizabeth asked, aghast.

"Oh, sure I'm sure of myself," Ben said, still looking down at the floor. "I'd have to be sure of myself or I wouldn't be here marking time. Maybe it's different for you. You're just out of college. And John Peter and Jane all full of drama school. But I was on the stage pretty steadily until college. I wasn't ever a star or anything, but I had jobs, I worked, I was part of the theatre. And where am I now?"

"Where are you?" Elizabeth asked gently.

"Nowhere. In limbo. I'm too old to do kid parts anymore. My arms and legs are too long, I'm too skinny, God knows I'm not handsome and I know it, too, I can see my face in the mirror when I shave in the morning. Everything about me's too big for myself now. My nose is too big, my hands and feet are too big. So it's nothing but marking time till I grow up to myself. I'm scared stiff to do Kostya for Miss Andersen tomorrow. It's my type of role but I'll look like a fool."

"You're going to be very handsome someday," Elizabeth said, putting her hand on his shoulder, "and you're a good actor right now. Give Miss Andersen some credit."

"Oh, sure," Ben said, "sure. It's just that it's such a hell of a long wait, Liz. You've got to kid yourself into believing you've got an awful lot of faith in yourself."

"I have faith in you, if that helps any," Elizabeth said.

Ben looked up at her quickly. "Liz, if I—if you—" he started, then broke off as John Peter and Jane came in, bearing cartons of coffee. They had picked up Ditta on the way.

"I think Kurt is coming up to see you, Liz," Jane said, looking at John Peter and raising her eyebrows as Elizabeth sat up quickly.

"Oh," she said too casually.

When Kurt came in, his face fell. "Liz—I wondered—oh, you're undressed." Suddenly he seemed like a disappointed little boy. "I wanted to talk to you."

"Well, sit down and talk," Ditta said. "We don't bite."

For a moment Kurt looked annoyed. Then he sat down on one of the beds. "It's been a long day. I'm tired."

"Why don't you go to bed, then?" Ben asked rudely.

Kurt raised his eyebrows, but answered perfectly amiably. "I thought I'd see how everyone's doing," he said.

"I suppose you know Dottie bitched Liz out of her part," Ben said.

"Yes," Kurt said. "I'm very sorry about that. I wanted to talk to you about it, Liebchen."

"Oh, forget it," Elizabeth said. "If Dottie wanted to raise a fuss, there wasn't anything anybody could do about it."

"Oh?" Ben looked pointedly at Kurt.

But Kurt ignored him and turned to Elizabeth. "Thanks for being such a good sport about it, Liebchen. Mariella Hedeman has a whole gallon of coffee downstairs. Come on down with me and let's have a cup of coffee and we can talk for a few minutes."

Elizabeth hesitated a moment. "I'm in my pajamas."

"Just pull your blue jeans over them then. It won't take you a second."

Elizabeth hesitated again, then gave a small sigh and said, "Okay, Kurt."

But when they got downstairs Kurt stopped in the hall. "Liebchen, I don't want to go in with that mob again, but I couldn't say that in front of your friends, so I used it as an excuse to get you away. Come along to my dressing room for a few minutes so we can really talk."

"All right. But just for a few minutes, Kurt. I'm awfully tired."

"So am I," Kurt said. "That's why I wanted to get away somewhere with you and just talk for a little while. You're wonderfully restful, Elizabeth."

They walked over to the theatre and Kurt pulled out his key and let them in. His dressing room doubled as an office. It was a small room with a desk in it, a filing cabinet, a straight chair, and a studio couch. Sometimes after a particularly late rehearsal (or one of the more rowdy of the professional company's parties) he would spend the night there instead of going up the boardwalk to the Ambassador. Now he said, stretching, "I think I'll stay here tonight instead of going up to the hotel. I'm bone-tired."

Elizabeth laughed a little and said, "Aunt Harriet would certainly think I was a fallen woman, wouldn't she, going into a man's room like this."

Kurt laughed, too, and his laugh was not uncertain like

Elizabeth's. "Your Aunt Harriet doesn't realize that things are different in the theatre. Things that would be all wrong according to the outmoded moral code of wherever it is—"

"Jordan, Virginia."

"—Jordan, Virginia, are all right here and now. Aren't you hot, Liebchen? Don't you want to take off that sweater?"

Elizabeth shook her head. "I'm not hot." Involuntarily she pulled her sweater more closely about her and realized that she was almost shivering. She sat down on the straight chair by the desk while Kurt sprawled across the couch, lighting a cigarette.

"Sweet Elizabeth," he said. "After an evening of Dottie's company—well, I wonder how I can ever be such a fool as to spend five minutes with her when I could be with you. To hell with her Hollywood charms. And, dearheart, I'm terribly sorry about your part in *Macbeth*. I know you must be sick with disappointment."

Elizabeth shook her head. "I am disappointed," she admitted, "but I guess I'm not surprised, and I'm okay about it now. At any rate, I can stay another week on Soapie's room and board and I can see it every night."

"Elizabeth," Kurt said. "I wish I could just go to Price and get him to keep you on a small salary. You're more than worth it. But if I did that, he'd misinterpret my reasons, and this— being director here—is rather a testing ground for me. I bought myself the job, naturally, but if I should wish to return here next summer I must keep on good terms with Price. I didn't do as well as I should have with my two New York plays—of course the scripts were impossible—but I should have done better in any event. Possibly my directing was too European in its approach, and I myself was going through a period of personal chaos, but I should not have allowed it to be reflected in my work. I feel that this summer I am making progress as a director. I was against Andersen coming since she's doing her own directing, but I find I've learned a good bit from watching some of her rehearsals. I am young and now is the time I must leap ahead. I am ambitious, you see, Liebchen. Acting, producing—fine as sidelines. But it is directing that I care about, conducting a play as I might a great orchestra." He looked up at her and blew her a kiss. "Bring me an ashtray, please, Liebchen."

Elizabeth picked up a large glass ashtray from the desk and took it to him. As he reached for it Kurt took her wrist and pulled her down so that she sat beside him on the couch.

"Ah, that's better," he said. "You looked so austere and formidable by the desk, as though we were having a business interview."

Kurt put his arm about her. "Ah, Liz, Liz, you're such a funny creature, so completely different from anybody else I've ever known."

"Am I?"

"I'm maybe five years older than you are," Kurt said, "and yet I'm a million years older. You give me my lost youth and innocence again. I've been old forever, it seems, Elizabeth. I don't think I ever had that quality of innocence that shines out of you like a candle."

Kurt drew her toward him and kissed her then, and she smelled the faint astringent perfume of his aftershave lotion.

Somehow alone with him in his dressing room she found his kisses different from when they were strolling on the boardwalk or sitting on the old piles.

She pulled away. "I ought to go back to the Cottage now, Kurt."

"Why?"

"I just—I'm just terribly tired. So many things have happened today—having Miss Andersen hear me do Nina and give me a part in *Macbeth*—and now not doing it—" And finding out Ben knew Mother, she added to herself.

Kurt ran his fingers over her cheek tenderly. "I'm a selfish brute," he said. "Run along and get your beauty sleep. Did you know your skin is as soft as a baby's? Good night, heart's dearest." He kissed her again, but very gently this time, and she left him.

Act III
SUNDAY

ON SUNDAYS practically no one had breakfast at the Cottage. Elizabeth and Ben sat out in the kitchen with Mrs. Browden, eating chicken livers on toast. John Peter came in while they were eating, and one side of his face was swollen from his toothache. Mrs. Browden clucked over him anxiously.

"I'm full of aspirin," John Peter said, "and it might just as well be bread crumbs for all the help it's given my tooth."

"You better get right off to the dentist, pet lamb," Mrs. Browden told him.

"On Sunday?" John Peter asked gloomily.

"Oh, my soul, so it is. But you just sit down, dear John Peter, and warm your tooth with some coffee, and I'll go call my daughter-in-law. She's got a brother who's a dentist." And she bustled off.

John Peter groaned. "I've got a psychosis about dentists," he said. "I must have been scared by a dentist at an early age."

"That's very possible," Ben said. "I know I was."

John Peter took a sip of hot coffee and groaned again. "This thing's killing me. I suppose I shall *have* to go to Mrs. Browden's daughter-in-law's brother."

"*Le dent de mon oncle est dans le parapluie de ma soeur,*" Ben said.

"What?"

"The tooth of my uncle is in the umbrella of my sister. French. I took it in the fourth grade."

Elizabeth grinned. "Sounds like it."

"All I have to do is go by a sign that says DENTIST and I break into a cold sweat," John Peter said.

"Get him to give you gas," Ben suggested, making himself a sandwich of bread and jelly.

"He'll probably be one of those brutes who won't even use Novocaine. Jane not down yet?"

"No, she said she didn't want any breakfast," Elizabeth told John Peter.

"What's up?"

"Have you forgotten she and Ben are doing their scene from *The Seagull* for Miss Andersen this morning?"

"Oh, Lord," John Peter said. "What with my tooth it flew right out of my head. Poor girl, I know she's frantic."

Mrs. Browden bustled back into the kitchen. "You're to go right over," she told John Peter with enthusiasm.

John Peter groaned. "Thanks, Mrs. Browden. Where does the scene of slaughter take place?"

"You know where Cherry Street is?"

"No."

"Well, you walk down the boardwalk till you get to it. It's just beyond Lukie's. Then you turn on Cherry Street—"

"Which way?" John Peter asked, taking a gingerly sip of coffee.

"The only way there is to turn without your walking into the ocean. Walk down Cherry Street till you come to Oak Street and you'll see a sign saying DENTIST. He's expecting you."

"Please tell Jane I've gone to be slaughtered and wish her good luck on her scene. And good luck to you, Ben. Thanks again, Mrs. Browden."

Mrs. Browden shook her head after him as he left. "Things like toothaches and colds always seem to make actors sicker than anyone else. In all the summers I've been cooking here I never seen one what didn't go to pieces with a splinter in his finger. But they got to be so you have to take them out on a stretcher before you can keep them from going over to that theatre at night."

"The show must go on," Ben intoned.

Elizabeth grinned. "Judging by a couple we've seen, sometimes I wonder why. I'm going to walk over with you so I can beg Mr. Price to use the phone to call Aunt Harriet, and then I'm going swimming. This'll be the first chance I've had to swim all week. Coming upstairs, Ben?"

"Yep. I'd better get Jane."

"Want anything more to eat, my pets?" Mrs. Browden asked.

Ben finished his bread-and-jelly sandwich, stuck a spoon in

the jelly jar, and took a large mouthful. "I think I'll survive. You haven't got a couple of apples we could take in case we get hungry before lunch, have you, Mrs. Browden?"

"Indeed I have," she told them. "Two beauties." She polished them on her apron and gave them to Elizabeth and Ben. "We're having roast beef for dinner and I'll see that you get yours nice and rare the way you like it."

"Angel!" Ben cried. "Come on, Liz. I'm going up to get Jane. I feel as though we were off to be slaughtered ourselves. I'd much rather go have a tooth pulled. Honest."

"Don't be a nut," Elizabeth said sympathetically. "Just don't get excited and overact. You've got to watch out for that."

"Are you going to wait to swim until we are done?" Ben asked hopefully. "Then we can go together."

Elizabeth considered a moment, and said, "Okay. Meet me at the Cottage when you're finished. I want to know right away what Miss Andersen said but I know she'll think you're wonderful."

Upstairs in the bedroom Jane was standing by the window, her fingers clenched till her knuckles showed white, her lips moving swiftly over Nina's words. She had made her bed and dressed herself carefully in a pressed grey cotton dress of rather an old-fashioned cut, and had a fresh grey velvet ribbon holding back her pale hair, and an antique brooch at her neck. Bibi was still asleep, half of her bedclothes tumbled on the floor.

"Where's John Peter?" Jane asked nervously.

"He's gone to the dentist," Elizabeth whispered. "He said to tell you and to wish you luck. Mrs. Browden got her daughter-in-law's brother to take him."

"Oh dear," Jane said unhappily. "Poor John Peter—"

"Come on." Ben's nervousness made him snappy. "Let's go."

"I'm so scared . . ." Jane whispered.

"What *is* this?" Ben asked. "It's not like you to get in a tizz like this, Jane."

Jane looked first at Ben, then at Elizabeth. "Well, I suppose I might as well tell you," she said.

"Tell us what?"

"She's my aunt."

"I beg your pardon," Ben said, "but who did you say was your aunt?"

Jane sat down on the foot of her bed. "Valborg Andersen. She's my Aunt Val. I didn't tell anybody because—well, I didn't want to be known as Valborg Andersen's niece. I wanted to be known as Jane Gardiner. I didn't get this scholarship through her, either. Price doesn't know. But I don't mind if you do. And yesterday—being off down on the beach when I ought to have been rehearsing Nina—I know she was disappointed in me about that, and I care so terribly what she thinks."

"When she sees your Nina it will be all right," Elizabeth said.

"John Peter's tooth hurt and he didn't feel like rehearsing yesterday," Jane said, "but I shouldn't have stayed out on the beach with him. I should have come on in to rehearse anyhow. It was the kind of thing we criticize Bibi for doing."

"Shhh," Elizabeth said.

Jane glanced over at Bibi. "She's sound asleep. Anyhow it's true. If you want to get anything out of being an apprentice at a summer theatre, you can't spend all your time out on the beach."

"Okay, Jane," Ben said, patting her shoulder. "Sure you were wrong yesterday. But it gave Liz a chance to have Andersen see her, and you've got your chance to redeem yourself now. Come along. Let's not be late. That wouldn't help anything. Liz is going to walk over with us so she can call her aunt."

Once they reached the theatre, Ben turned to Elizabeth and said, "Kiss me. It's customary to kiss the condemned before he goes to the executioner."

Elizabeth kissed him on the cheek and then went into Mr. Price's office to use the telephone. Mr. Price was shuffling through some papers at his desk and looked up when Elizabeth hurried in.

"Yes?" he said, and looked back down at his papers.

"Thanks again for letting me have Sophie's room and board. Please, Mr. Price, may I use your telephone to let my aunt know that I'm staying?"

Mr. Price stacked some of the papers together. "If you type these letters up for me when you're done." He got up and handed them to Elizabeth as he left the office.

Elizabeth stared at the phone. Making this call was the last thing she wanted to do. Aunt Harriet would be furious. She took a deep breath, lifted the receiver, and dialed the operator. Acting, she thought. I'll act my way out of this.

When she told her aunt that she would not be returning to Jordan until next Sunday, the world did not end. "I don't approve," Aunt Harriet said, "but at least you won't be there the whole summer."

Elizabeth smiled and opened the door of the office again so she could hear if the others came out. She typed up the letters for Mr. Price, and when she finished she went back to her room in the Cottage to wait.

She pulled out her battered volume of Shakespeare and sat cross-legged on her bed, which she had made before breakfast. Once in a while Bibi grunted or turned in her sleep, but she did not awaken. Elizabeth read until she heard Ben and Jane on the stairs. Then she shut her book and went out into the hall to meet them. "How'd it go?" she asked.

Jane sat down on the top step. "I couldn't have been worse but she was awfully nice about it."

"Jane's an idiot," Ben said. "It may not be the best she's ever done Nina, but it was good and Andersen told her so. I stank."

"You're the idiot," Jane said. "Aunt Val was very impressed with you."

"She certainly tore me apart," Ben said. "I thought she was telling me I'd better give up all idea of ever working in the theatre, and quick."

"Yes, but then when she'd finished she said it was only because you were worth criticizing that way that she'd bothered. And she told you she thought you had great talent and there were very few young people she said that to, and then she said that judging from the little she'd seen she thought we must be a very unusual group of apprentices, and Ben just up and said, 'Oh, we are.' "

"Oh, Ben!" Elizabeth laughed.

"Well, she knew what I meant," Ben said.

"You should have seen him," Jane told Elizabeth. "He was so embarrassed over saying it that he turned almost purple."

"I explained I didn't mean me," Ben said. "I meant Jane and Liz and John Peter and Ditta and all of us."

"Aunt Val's really a wonderful person," Jane said. "She's always been my favorite relative, and at least she didn't seem to want to disown me or tell me to get out of the theatre. Nobody but you two and John Peter knows about her being my aunt, so don't for heaven's sake forget and say anything."

"Of course not."

"Oh, and she spoke especially about you, Liz. Says you have a really unusual quality, that thing that makes people watch you onstage whether you have talent or not, but you have talent, too."

"Did she really?" Elizabeth beamed.

"And she was very nice about my being on the beach yesterday. And I'm glad it happened so she got a chance to see you, Liz, but it won't ever happen again."

"Come on, hurry up," Ben urged. "We can talk more down on the beach. I'm dying to get in the ocean and cool off. I'm in a lather. Get into your bathing suits, quick. I'll meet you on the beach."

Ben trotted downstairs and Elizabeth and Jane went into the bedroom where Bibi was now lying on her back and gently snoring.

Jane took off her dress and hung it up. "I really ought to wait for John Peter," she said, wrinkling her brow anxiously.

"Poor darling, I was afraid his tooth wasn't going to get any better. I just hate to think of his being hurt."

"He'll probably be ages," Elizabeth said, "and I'm sure he'll look for you on the beach first. Come along."

"Okay. I guess I'll go down, then. But poor John Peter, it does seem a shame, and on a Sunday, too." Jane slipped into a two-piece bathing suit, black, brief, and very becoming to her even though her shoulders were burned. Elizabeth's suit was an old green woolen one and had been darned in two or three places where moths had dined on it, but Jane looked at her admiringly.

"That color's beautiful with your tan and your hair. Kurt seen you in it?"

"Yes." Elizabeth blushed.

There was the sound of someone walking heavily down the hall and Ditta thudded in. "Hey, anybody going swimming?" she asked loudly.

Elizabeth and Jane both shushed her and Bibi groaned and turned over. "Oh, sorry," Ditta whispered. "I just came to see if anybody was going swimming." She wore a badly draped flowered bathing suit and had taken her glasses off so that her eyes looked weak and red, something that Elizabeth was grateful that hers, nearsighted though they were, never did.

"We're both going swimming, and Ben's going to meet us on the beach. Come along," Elizabeth told her.

Ditta's whisper was almost as loud as her speaking voice. "How's John Peter's tooth?"

"Do be *quiet*, can't you? Have you no consideration?" Bibi

moaned, and pulled the covers over her head so that her feet stuck out at the bottom. Elizabeth, Jane, and Ditta retreated into the hall.

"How's John Peter's tooth?" Ditta repeated.

"He had to go to the dentist, poor lamb." As she reported on John Peter, Jane looked in pain herself. "Come on. Let's get down on the beach."

At this hour on a Sunday morning the section of beach in front of the theatre was still deserted. Most of the company took full advantage of the fact that dress rehearsal did not begin till three in the afternoon to sleep. Many of the apprentices took advantage of no classes to do the same thing.

Ben was already there and greeted them, calling, "The water's icy! Come on in!" He jumped up and down in the shallow waves, his arms hugged tight around his chest, and shivered.

Jane pulled a scarlet cap out of the pocket of her beach robe and started tucking her hair up under it. Ditta carefully spread a multicolored towel out on the sand, sat down on it, and proceeded to cover herself methodically with suntan oil. "Now tell me exactly what Miss Andersen said to you and Ben," she demanded of Jane as Elizabeth ran across the sand and joined Ben in the water.

"Good heavens, it *is* cold!" Elizabeth cried as she splashed in.

"I never should have come in so soon after breakfast," Ben said. "Those chicken livers Mrs. Browden gave us are having a frightful argument with *my* liver. I've always wondered what it must be like to be liverish. Now I know."

Elizabeth splashed on by him. "I took lifesaving at college. I'll save you."

Ben walked slowly through the water toward her and suddenly disappeared most frighteningly from view under a small wave. This falling down an imaginary hole was one of his favorite tricks, but it never failed to startle Elizabeth. After a moment he came up. "Let's sing underwater," he said, "and see if we can guess what we're singing."

"Okay," Elizabeth agreed, and they submerged.

Ben, holding his nose, sang loudly, large bubbles rising to the surface above him, until he had to come up for air. "What was I singing?" he asked.

Elizabeth laughed and shook her head. "What was it?"

"I'll give you a hint. It might remind you of you. Now see if you can guess."

"Oh, good heavens, 'Sweet Betsy from Pike.' "

"Right the first time. Now you sing."

They submerged again. When they came up, Ben said, "It certainly didn't sound like anything but it was probably that awful song about gopher guts. Am I right?"

"Couldn't be righter."

Ben shivered. "This ocean's too cold for me. Let's go sit in the sun and get warm for a little while."

"You go on in," Elizabeth said. "I'll be along in a few minutes."

The ocean was very calm, the waves scarcely more than ripples. Elizabeth lay on her back and floated, letting herself rest on the deep and gentle breathing of the sea. She thought, Perhaps this is the last chance I'll have to be in the ocean this summer. A small sudden wave washed over her face and she sat up spitting the saltwater out of her mouth.

She shook the water out of her hair, then splashed through the shallows toward the sand. Ditta and Ben were walking up the beach looking for shells. Jane sat on her yellow beach robe, her red-capped head down on her knees. Elizabeth stood by her and hopped, first on one foot, then on the other, to get the water out of her ears. "Aren't you going in the water?" she asked.

"In a minute. Liz, it's awful to love anybody so much."

Elizabeth sat down on the beach beside her, and the soft white sand turned dark wherever she dripped water onto it.

"What's the matter?"

"I had a cousin who knew somebody who *died* because of a tooth," Jane said tragically.

"Oh, Jane!" Elizabeth laughed helplessly.

"I know it's awful," Jane said, "but I love him, so I just can't seem to help worrying about him. I don't think I could bear it if anything happened to him."

Elizabeth let the sand sift through her wet toes and stick to them. "Don't go around asking for trouble, though."

"I know. I'm a nut," Jane said. "But when you love anyone the way I love John Peter, when you're so happy, you can't help being afraid fate is just waiting to give you a slap. Maybe that's my puritan ancestry or something. But—don't you feel that way about Kurt?"

Elizabeth thought for a moment. "I guess I would if I ever really got to know him the way you know John Peter. But it's different with Kurt and me. I—I just come when he calls me.

It's—I can't explain, but we're not *equal* the way you and John Peter are. I think of Kurt when I wake up and when I go to sleep and whenever I'm not with him. But I don't think he thinks of me like that. Yet."

"It was different with John Peter and me," Jane said. "We both knew from the very first minute we met each other. It was at an audition last winter at drama school. John Peter's turn came after mine and I stayed to listen to him just out of curiosity because I thought he looked interesting and then we left the theatre together. And then we went to the Automat for lunch and just stayed there and talked for hours and hours and it seemed as if we couldn't ever stop talking. And looking at each other and smiling. And then we went to a French movie and then we went to an Italian restaurant in the Village for spaghetti and just went on talking and talking. And we just knew. There wasn't ever any question for either of us."

"It—it must be wonderful when it happens that way. But I don't think it does with most people." Elizabeth looked out over the horizon and a sudden feeling of sadness crept over her.

"When John Peter goes out of a room," Jane said, "it's as though he takes part of me with him. I'm not complete unless we're together. I'm talking to you, now, and the sun's warm and I feel it, and I like you more than any of our friends, but part of me just isn't here. John Peter has it. I—I don't know what part of me it is—I can't explain it—but it's just as impor- tant as a leg or an arm. And I keep waiting for John Peter to bring it back. Behind everything I say or do I'm waiting for him."

Elizabeth said slowly, "I don't think it's good to get quite as dependent on anyone as that."

Jane didn't get angry, but she said, "Liz, I don't think you're in love with Kurt."

"Because I don't feel about Kurt the same way you do about John Peter? There are lots of different ways of loving a person and I don't think one is any better than another. Besides, I *do* feel about Kurt that way; that's one of the things that worries me. Wherever I am I'm always aware of him, I'm always looking for him, hoping that he'll come. And whenever he does, my insides feel like an elevator suddenly dropping."

Jane laughed. "Yes. That's the way it is. Only *my* insides feel like an elevator rising. I wonder if it'll always be like that, even after we've been married years and years. I don't think it'll ever change, because it just goes on getting bigger and bigger every day, loving him—and I always used to pride myself on being such an independent person! Have you ever been in love before, Liz?"

Elizabeth shook her head. "Not really. I used to pride myself on being an independent person, too. And from what I knew of love I thought it was something to be avoided except on the stage. Oh, I had kind of a crush on the boy who took the lead in the senior play when I was a freshman at college, but it was just kid stuff. And I dated some at college—they were guys who came over from other colleges to be the men in the Dramatic Association plays. Anyhow, I was always so busy at college I didn't have time to fall in love. All the interesting professors were already married, and I didn't go to many of the dances because I couldn't afford evening dresses and junk and the few I went to I was taller than most of the men I danced with and I hated that."

"You're taller than Kurt," Jane reminded her. "Ben's the only one around here who really towers over you."

"I'm not taller than Kurt," Elizabeth said quickly. "Not when I wear flat heels."

But Jane's face had an expectant, rather rigid look and Elizabeth knew that she was no longer listening. "Here comes John Peter!" she cried, and got up and ran tearing across the sand.

Elizabeth, munching Mrs. Browden's apple, left the beach shortly before the others. Her hair felt sticky from the salt water and she wanted to take a shower and get cleaned up before lunch. She was in the shower and her hair was full of soapsuds when she heard Ben's voice calling up the stairs, "Hey, Liz! You up there?"

"I'm in the shower," she shouted above the sound of water.

Then she heard Ben run thudding up the stairs, three steps at a time.

"You sound like an elephant," she called out to him.

Ben leaned against the bathroom door with such vigor that the whole doorframe shook. "I worked with elephants once. Maybe that's why."

"*You* did, Ben? When?"

"I was in a show about Cleopatra where four live elephants came on the stage at once and I rode on the head of the leader. My mother almost had heart failure every night and twice on matinee days during that run. It flopped in New York, but we toured the darned thing all over the United States *and* Canada. Sixteen weeks in Chicago."

"Ouch, darn it!"

"What's the matter?"

"Soap in my eyes. Tell me more about the elephants."

Ben let out one of his wild shouts of laughter, so that again the doorframe shook. "One place we played they had to bring the elephants in through the basement and then they were supposed to take the elephants up to stage level in a big freight elevator. Well, the elephants hadn't ever been in an elevator before and they were scared to go in it. Ever tried to force an elephant to do anything it didn't want to do?"

"Nope. Never have." With her eyes closed and her face streaming with soapy water Elizabeth started to rinse her hair.

"Elephants don't like to be forced," Ben said. "They started to get mad and the guy who took care of them knew he'd have to think of something else if those elephants were going to get onstage that night. So he sent for me because the lead elephant was fond of me. You know how animals sometimes get about kids. They'll take all kinds of things from a kid they'd ruin an adult for. So this guy told me just to work on the lead elephant, to see if I could get her to go in the elevator with me. You can imagine how important I felt, Liz, their having to send for the kid of the company to cope with the elephants."

Shaking water out of her ears, Elizabeth laughed. "I certainly can. What did you do?"

"I talked to that elephant, and sang to her, and had her

watch me ride up and down in the elevator until she decided it was okay to get on with me. And I might as well admit to you, Liz, I was scared. And I think the others were, too. I know my mother was dying a thousand deaths. This was a nice elephant, and gentle, but if she'd taken it into her head to get panicky she could have crushed me against one of the walls and that would have been the end of little Ben."

"Oh, Ben," Elizabeth gasped as she turned off the hot water and an icy deluge fell over her. "What happened?"

"She was sweet as a lamb," Ben said, "and we just rode up and down and up and down and the other three elephants stood and stared at us and kind of waved their trunks like trees in the wind, and next thing you know I had all four of them upstairs, and the next week the man who managed the elephants gave me a gold fountain pen with my name on it."

"The one you still use?"

"Yep. Why I haven't lost it I'll never know. I certainly lose everything else. And I have lost it at least a dozen times but it always turns up."

Elizabeth pushed against the door. "Hey, move," she called. "I'm ready to come out."

Ben stepped aside and Elizabeth, in her flannel bathrobe, her head turbaned in a towel, emerged.

"Matter of fact," Ben said, "I've come across a lot of actresses who were a lot harder to handle than those elephants. You've got some more freckles, Liz."

Elizabeth sighed. "Yes, I know. It's from being out on the beach this morning."

"Listen," Ben said, "I want to look at that picture of your mother. Okay?"

"Okay," Elizabeth said, and went down the hall to the room. "Come on."

Bibi had left, though her bed was still unmade and she had clothes strewn all over her chair and Sophie's bed.

Elizabeth went over to her bureau, picked up her glasses which she had left there when she went to wash her hair, put them on, took down the double frame picture, and handed it to Ben.

"Here it is," she said. "I don't know when it was taken."

Ben studied it gravely. "Yes. That's Anna Larsen all right. And you certainly look like her, Liz."

"Was Mother hard to handle, Ben?" Elizabeth asked.

"She had a reputation that way," Ben said, "but I know Mother never had any trouble with her. And she certainly never spoke a cross or impatient word to me. And I've never been able to forget her."

"You said you never forget anybody."

"I don't. But I remember your mother more like yesterday than a lot of people right here in the company this summer. Did you ever think about singing, Liz?"

"No." Elizabeth rubbed her head violently with the towel. "I love music, but not that way—just to listen to, not to do. I guess it's a good thing. If I sang it would be even worse for Aunt Harriet than acting, though I don't think she thinks there's much difference between the two."

"Want me to scram while you get dressed?" Ben asked.

"I guess you'd better. It's almost time for lunch."

"I'll wait for you downstairs," Ben said.

After lunch Elizabeth helped Jane clear the tables. Then she went out onto the porch, where most of the company was sitting. Jane joined John Peter and they started off down the walk, Jane hovering solicitously over John Peter, who had had his tooth pulled and was looking very pale and dramatic. Ben and Ditta were sitting on the steps going over a scene from *Oedipus*.

"Anybody want to rehearse *Seagull* this afternoon?" Elizabeth asked.

"John Peter says he doesn't feel well enough," Ditta said. "He and Jane are going down to sit on the beach. But we could work on something else. How about *Twelfth Night*? You said you wanted to try Viola and I'd love to butcher Olivia."

"What about me?" Ben asked. "I don't see myself as Orsino."

"Feste, of course," Elizabeth told him. "You'd make a wonderful Elizabethan clown. If Kurt's around maybe he'll read Orsino for us. Shall we go in and start?"

Ben flung up his arms. "Such energy! Let's relax for a few minutes."

"Anyhow, we wouldn't have any privacy till the professional company goes over to the theatre for dress rehearsal at three," Ditta said.

"Don't you have to be there, Ben?" Elizabeth asked.

"No, Joe doesn't want me until five."

"Hey, listen," Ditta said. "I have an idea. Why don't we rehearse on the beach?"

Elizabeth shook her head. "We tried that before, remember, and didn't get anything done."

Ditta stood up, shut her book, and stretched. "I think I'll go down to the beach till three, then. Coming?"

"I got too much sun this morning," Ben said. "I think I'll take a nap. You can wake me at three, Liz. Throw some pebbles up."

"Okay, and if you don't wake I'll start throwing rocks," Elizabeth warned.

"You coming, Liz?" Ditta asked hopefully.

Ben climbed down from the stone railing. "You oughtn't go back on the beach today, Liz. Your nose is bright red from this morning."

Elizabeth felt her nose. "Yes, I guess it is. I don't get out often enough and my nose peels all over again every week. Poor thing, I'd better stay inside and put some of Jane's sunburn stuff on it."

Ditta stretched again. "In that case, I think I'll follow Ben's example and take a nap, too. That shindig at Irving's last night was too much for an old schoolmarm like me. You can wake me, too, Liz."

Elizabeth laughed. "Okay. You're making me feel sleepy, too."

"Going up to take a nap?" Ben asked her.

She shook her head. "No. I don't like to sleep in the afternoon. I can't wake up the rest of the day."

"Oh, well, I won't sleep either then," Ben said. "Come on

over to the theatre. It's nice and cool over there and we can play some records."

"Good." Elizabeth followed him off the porch. The sun beat down on their heads as they walked through the hot streets to the theatre. The back of Ben's shirt was stained with perspiration.

They bumped into Joe McGill sitting on the rickety back steps that led to the back stage. He was smoking an evil-smelling cigar and mopping his brow with a damp handkerchief. "Hi, kids," he greeted them.

"Hi, Joe. Mind if we go backstage and play a few records before dress rehearsal starts? It's cooler there than anywhere else."

"Go ahead. Listen, Ben, I don't really need you today after all, see. There isn't anything I can't handle myself, and you've been working like a dog all summer so if you want time off, I figure it's coming to you, see. But it's up to you."

"Thanks an awful lot, Joe," Ben said. "But I really enjoy watching Andersen in action, so I'll be there at five."

"That's fine, then," Joe said.

Ben and Elizabeth climbed the wooden steps and went into the narrow corridor backstage that led to the dressing rooms.

Elizabeth put her arm lightly about Ben's shoulders. "He's a nice guy, isn't he?"

Ben nodded. "Best stage manager I've ever met."

It had always struck Elizabeth as interesting the way the different members of the company kept their dressing rooms. All the doors were locked during the day when the dressing rooms were not in use, but each one had a neat typewritten card bearing the name of the occupant. Dottie and Marian Hatfield shared a dressing room, and below the card someone had drawn a crude star in lipstick. Dottie's side of the dressing room always looked as though a hurricane had hit it. Opened lipsticks and tubes of greasepaint and lining sticks lay in disorder on the table with broken eyebrow pencils, false eyelashes, a soiled powder puff and a jar of cold cream discolored by greasepaint. Everything was covered with a heavy film of dark powder. Marian's half of the dressing room was always immaculate, her makeup neatly arranged on a tray covered by a yellow linen towel. Her can of Albolene was covered and a bottle of witch hazel stood in line beside it. Her telegrams were stuck neatly with Scotch tape on the wall around her mirror, and her costumes, instead of being thrown on the hangers any old which way, were neatly hung up and covered with a dust sheet.

Ben went out onstage and snapped on the work light, a naked bulb with a wire cage around it that hung down from the grid. The curtain was raised and row after row of chairs stretched out into the dusty reaches of the auditorium. Elizabeth went to the big box where Joe kept the records that were played during intermission or occasionally during a performance and began looking through the albums while Ben switched on the turntable that was attached to the loudspeaker in the auditorium. Elizabeth handed him the *Rosenkavalier* waltzes.

"Your mother used to sing Octavian in *Der Rosenkavalier*," Ben said.

Elizabeth nodded. "Yes. I thought she probably would have."

Ben put the record on and the music filled the theatre. He turned the volume down. "Liz—"

"What, Ben?"

"You say you went to your mother's funeral. Where was she when she died?"

"A boardinghouse in Georgia."

"What was the matter with her?"

"Her heart. She went south to get away from a northern winter. I don't know just what it was—her heart gave out or something. She was there about six months before she died."

"Well, how did you happen to go to the funeral, your Aunt Harriet feeling the way she does?" Ben was fiddling with the controls on the loudspeaker, but his face was very still and listening, the dark peaked brows drawn together in an intent frown.

"I told Aunt Harriet I was going, and she let me. She gave me my train fare. Maybe she approved of Mother's going south to die. Sort of an indirect compliment because of Father's being a Southerner. Or maybe she just approved of Mother's dying." Elizabeth's voice was light, but she found she could not look at Ben as she talked. She had to concentrate her gaze on the grey canvas floor covering. If she was going to share something as personal as seeing her mother, looking into Ben's intent eyes would bring too much emotion out into the open and above all she did not want Ben to see her cry.

When Elizabeth had announced to her Aunt Harriet that she was going to her mother's funeral if she had to hitchhike, she was extremely surprised at her aunt's lack of resistance.

But dying was the most considerate thing Anna Larsen had ever done as far as Harriet Jerrold was concerned. And since Anna had had the added courtesy to die during Elizabeth's spring vacation from college, Aunt Harriet gave Elizabeth both the permission and the funds to attend her mother's funeral.

Elizabeth remembered with strange clarity the afternoon the telegram came. Even though spring was late that year and there was still snow on the ground, she was sitting out on the porch wrapped in her winter coat and reading a book she was due to give a report on when she returned to college. Inside the house the telephone began to ring. For a moment the shrill insistence of the bell did not pierce Elizabeth's concentration, and when she went into the house to answer it Aunt Harriet was there before her, and handed the receiver to her.

"It's for you, Elizabeth," she said. "It's a telegram."

The telephone table was in a hallway beside one of the registers and Elizabeth remembered standing over the grill and feeling the hot air blow up her legs. "Yes, this is Elizabeth Jerrold," she said.

"I have a telegram for you," the operator said in a voice that was impersonal but that nevertheless prepared Elizabeth for bad news. "Your mother died this morning . . . The funeral will be Thursday . . ." It was signed Ilsa Woolf and gave the address.

Elizabeth had not known that her mother was ill, nor that she was in Georgia. Somehow she had never imagined that her mother would die. A living Anna was much more potent a ghost in Elizabeth's life than a dead one. Elizabeth stood holding the telephone in her cold fingers, shivering inside her heavy winter coat, while the hot air from the register was like an icy blast on her legs. She knew she should say something, but she couldn't imagine what.

Then the operator asked, "Would you like the telegram mailed to you, miss?"

"Yes. Please." Automatically Elizabeth replaced the receiver. Then she said to her aunt, "Mother is dead."

For a long moment Aunt Harriet did not reply. Then, to Elizabeth's intense surprise, she started to cry, turned away, and went up the stairs.

Elizabeth had ridden south in the day coach. All through Virginia and North Carolina, the rain dashed itself against the dirty windows of the train. Night fell and the windows showed only the distorted reflections of the passengers, and Elizabeth sat stiff in her seat, too frightened at the ordeal ahead of her to be able to relax or try to sleep. She sat staring out the window, still shocked into a state of complete numbness, saying over and over to herself in rhythm with the wheels, I am going to see my mother . . . I am going to see my mother . . .

She had grown up with the knowledge that she was never going to see her mother, and now to see her mother even this way, dead, was a shock so great that it seemed to split her life in two.

In Georgia it was also raining, a steady monotonous downpour. She stood on the narrow station platform and looked about her at the rusty cracked branches of the station palms, the dripping masses of Spanish moss on the oaks, an orange peel in the gutter, stained damp newspapers flapping in the wind. Mrs. Woolf, the owner of the boardinghouse, had sent a man to meet her. He greeted her kindly, and drove her through the oak-lined streets of the town until they came to a large, shabby, white-pillared house on a river.

"Mrs. Woolf's expecting you," he said as he took her bag into the hall. "She's in the drawing room."

He led her into a large, dark room with long French windows leading out onto a terrace. A woman with tawny hair streaked with grey was seated at a square Victorian piano playing Bach.

"The young lady's here, Mrs. Woolf," the man said, and the woman rose from the piano and came toward Elizabeth, hand outstretched in greeting. Her grip was firm and cool and somehow comforting to Elizabeth, who was beginning to shiver with nervous fatigue.

"Your hand is like ice, child; you must be exhausted." Mrs. Woolf's voice was deep, rather dark in quality, but clear-cut and clean. "Would you like to go up to your room?"

"I would in a minute." Elizabeth put her hand on a small chest of drawers and braced herself wearily. "But, please, could I ask you some questions first?"

"Of course. Come in and sit down." Mrs. Woolf seated herself back on the piano bench. Elizabeth sat uncomfortably on a straight chair and looked around at the room. It was ugly, filled with massive Victorian furniture. There were, however, no knicknacks around, no scatter rugs or tables, no potted plants or shelves of curios or vases or figurines, none of the horrible little things that were usually in such rooms.

"Your mother is at the undertaker's," Mrs. Woolf said. "Reuben will drive you over whenever you're ready to go. Would you like me to go with you?"

"Oh—please—don't bother—" Elizabeth said quickly. "But please—I didn't even know she was ill. Was it something sudden?"

Mrs. Woolf had very light, very clear blue eyes, and they seemed to Elizabeth to be piercing her like two arrows and pinning her against the wall. "Her heart was bad. She was here for about six months and was ill most of that time."

"Oh," Elizabeth said. "Thank you." She sat in her chair silently for a moment while Mrs. Woolf continued to stare at her.

"Do you smoke?" Mrs. Woolf finally asked.

"No. I don't. Thank you."

The older woman reached in the pocket of her blue tweed jacket and pulled out cigarettes and matches. She put a cigarette in her mouth, struck a match, and lit the cigarette, bending down to the match with a gesture at the same time impatient and extremely careful. She shook out the match, then reached with the fingers of her left hand to the top of the piano where a pair of silver candlesticks stood, ran her fingers over one's heavy base, then over the dark mahogany of the piano. A flicker of annoyance crossed her face. She reached toward the other candlestick, and again ran her fingers over silver, over polished wood. Then she stood up and walked rather angrily to a table and ran her fingers searchingly across its surface until they touched a silver ashtray. She dropped her match in it, took it back to the piano, and banged it down next to one of the candles. "I wish people would learn not to move my things from their places," she said.

It was only then that Elizabeth realized Mrs. Woolf was blind.

"You didn't know your mother very well, did you?" Mrs. Woolf asked.

"I didn't know her at all."

"I wondered about that," Mrs. Woolf said. "But she talked about you a great deal. She wanted me to tell you that it had been hard for her to leave you, terribly hard, and that losing you was the one great regret of her life, and that she loved you more than anyone in the world, even though she was never able to let you know this."

"Thank you," Elizabeth said. She wanted to cry, but instead she asked, "Could you tell me anything else about her?"

Mrs. Woolf leaned back against the piano so that her elbows made two light discords as she put her weight on them. "I really knew very little about her as far as facts went. She so obviously didn't want anyone to question her, and I have been so hounded all my life by prying busybodies that I felt that the least I could do was to refrain from bothering her with any kind of curiosity." She paused for a moment, then said, "Your mother and I got on very well. You understand perhaps the way one can simply *know* someone without knowing anything in the way of past history. And she never pitied me because of my blindness. Your mother treated me like a human being and she—well, we were friends. I was able to give her a small amount of help and comfort. She was the kind of person who needs terribly to be loved and I found it very easy to love her. I shall miss her a great deal . . . I thought perhaps you might like to know that she was loved here and cared for, that she wasn't completely alone."

"Thank you," Elizabeth said. "But was there anybody else—I mean anyone from—from before?"

Mrs. Woolf shook her head. "No, but I think it was of her own choosing. At first she received letters, but she never answered them and gradually they stopped coming."

"Was she alone when she died?"

"I was with her."

Elizabeth stood up. "I think I would like to—to see her now, please."

Mrs. Woolf walked across the room with complete assurance, only occasionally guiding herself with a featherlight touch on a table or chair back. She pulled on a faded petit point pull, and somewhere far off in the house Elizabeth could hear the faint ringing of a bell.

Mrs. Woolf did not ask again if Elizabeth wanted her company but went out to the car with her and got in beside her.

Outside the undertaker's there was a magnolia tree in full bloom. Many of the delicate white petals had fallen to the ground and lay there, bruised and browning. Mrs. Woolf said in a low voice, "I'll have to take your arm now, please, Miss Jerrold," and Elizabeth guided her into the undertaker's establishment; it was a strange feeling, because even in being led Mrs. Woolf moved with authority, and Elizabeth, numbed and bewildered, felt that she was the one being guided.

"Your mother left full instructions for the funeral," Mrs. Woolf said.

"Thank you. I—if there's anything I ought to do, please let me know."

The face of the woman in the coffin was much younger than Elizabeth had expected. She had never been able to imagine in her mind's eye what her mother might look like. Always in her daydreams, in spite of the newspaper picture, the face was amorphous, and somehow she had anticipated someone much older and with more obvious signs of a turbulent career, someone who bore the markings of what, to Jordan, Virginia, was a wicked and glamorous life. But the face in the coffin was small and pale and childish, and the straight fair hair was soft as a baby's. The few lines Anna Larsen bore touched the soft skin gently; only the closed eyelids, bruised like the fallen magnolia petals, bore witness to her illness. Elizabeth stood looking down at her for a long time. Then she went back to Mrs. Woolf.

She remembered Mrs. Woolf taking her in to dinner that night and introducing her in a low quiet voice to the boarders. "Miss Myra Turbcull—Mr. and Mrs. Joshua Tisbury—" Elizabeth murmured how-do-you-dos and stared down at her plate, acutely overaware of the curious and pitying glances of the boarders. Mrs. Woolf said grace in a clear, businesslike manner, and then a maid served the dinner. In front of Mrs. Woolf, however, she put a plate that had been prepared in the kitchen, the food arranged systematically, the meat already cut up in small pieces; and Elizabeth thought with a kind of horror of how Mrs. Woolf must reach out into darkness, into the illimitable void, for every bite she took. But only a strange, sure grace as her steady fingers reached for her water tumbler or broke off a piece of biscuit marked her eating as being in any way different from that of a sighted person.

After dinner Elizabeth said good night to Mrs. Woolf and went to her room. She had seen her mother and now she would never see her again.

Ben was looking soberly at Elizabeth. Suddenly he put his arms around her in a rough, comforting gesture. "Oh, my God, Liz, what a ghastly nightmare for you to have gone through. But that Mrs. Woolf sounds like a fine person."

Elizabeth nodded. "She was. I don't know what I would have done without her—or if she'd been different, the way I'd imagine someone who'd keep a boardinghouse would be. It was such a terribly strange thing, Ben, going down there and seeing Mother that way. There was a quality of—of insanity about it. But Mrs. Woolf let me alone when I ought to be alone and talked to me when I needed someone to talk to me. She made a terrific impression on me, maybe because I met her when I first saw Mother and it was a time that stands out in my life like—well, I don't know exactly like what, Ben, but it was completely unlike anything else and I remember it so clearly that sometimes it frightens me.

"I mean, the theatre, this summer, this is all different, but it's *part* of everything, and that, somehow, was *outside* of everything. Do you know what I mean? And Mrs. Woolf was the last person who'd been close to Mother and the first person I'd ever been able to talk to about Mother—the only other person besides you, Ben. And then, I'd always felt that, because of Mother, I was different, not like other people who had proper mothers, even though I always got on well enough with people. And Mrs. Woolf was different, too. I was different because of Mother and she was different because she was blind. And she'd taken her blindness and made it become something outside of her; she was much bigger than it was, if you know what I mean."

"Yes, I know," Ben said.

"It wasn't that it didn't matter to her, because of course it must have mattered horribly, but she never let it become more important than she was. Aunt Harriet has a friend in Jordan who's blind, and whenever we go to call on her all she ever talks about is how much she's missing and how lucky everybody else is to be able to see, and she never lets you forget it for a minute.

"But with Mrs. Woolf it wasn't like that. Aunt Harriet's friend just dotes on being led around, but Mrs. Woolf got annoyed whenever she had to give in to her blindness in any way, and she didn't give in to it. And somehow she gave me courage—or at any rate she made me value courage a lot more—and I felt stupid for worrying about being different because I didn't have the same kind of mother other people had . . . And she was good to Mother. That was terribly important. They used to talk a lot together and she said that on the days when Mother felt well, Mother used to read aloud to her, mostly plays, Shakespeare and Ibsen, and Chekhov's short stories, and Balzac. She was never well enough to sing, though.

Mrs. Woolf used to play piano for her a good bit, too. She said Mother's favorite was Chopin's *Revolutionary* Étude.

"Oh, Ben," Elizabeth said, "it was so—so sad—to think of Mother dying there all alone and away from everything and everybody she knew and loved. And I was thankful she had someone with her who could understand her and help her a little."

Elizabeth shook her head. "The whole experience was unreal, and—and sort of like a nightmare—but it made me believe in Mother for the first time. I finally felt that I'd been born; that I'd actually had a mother, just like anybody else."

The waltz from *Der Rosenkavalier* had long since played through and the needle was scratching round and round in the final groove. Ben put the playing arm back on its rest and turned the machine off. "Your mother didn't leave you anything?"

"No. I found out later that Mother hadn't paid Mrs. Woolf anything for several weeks before she died, and Mrs. Woolf paid for the funeral. I think Mother lived longer than she had expected to when she went south."

"Your mother must have made a good bit of money, one way or another," Ben said, "but she never knew how to hang on to it. She was always giving presents, and trying to make herself beautiful, so people would love her. Mother said she always needed someone to take care of her. She wasn't strong the way you are, Liz."

"Me!" Elizabeth exclaimed. "But I'm not strong, Ben!"

"Sure you are," Ben said, "even if you don't know it. Probably *because* you don't know it. Tell me some more about this Woolf dame. How did she come to be running a boarding-house anyhow?"

"I asked her that," Elizabeth said, "and she gave a funny kind of laugh and said there wasn't much else an impoverished Southern woman who was blind into the bargain could do."

"She really did make a big impression on you, didn't she?"

Elizabeth nodded. "She was really a wonderful person, Ben. And so good to me. And what I admired most was that in spite of being blind she was so much stronger and—and bigger—than anyone else around her." As she talked Elizabeth remembered the start of surprise with which she had realized that Mrs. Woolf's seemingly unconscious carelessness, the dash, the bravado, was the result of discipline, patience, and courage. From her room Elizabeth had seen Mrs. Woolf walk by the river, watched her fall headlong over an uncovered root and pick herself up unshaken, and continue. After that it had been impossible, somehow, for Elizabeth to turn back to the room, fling herself down on the bed, and weep for lost Anna Larsen. She could love her mother now, because at last Anna was real to her; but she knew that if she wept, the tears would be not for Anna but for Elizabeth herself.

"Ben," Elizabeth said, "thank you."

"What for?" Ben asked.

"For talking to me about Mother. For letting me tell you about it. It's something I've needed to say to someone ever since—ever since it happened."

"Listen," Ben started, and broke off as the screen door to

the stage entrance slammed and someone came hurrying by the dressing rooms and out onto the stage. It was Dottie.

"Thought I might as well be bright and early today," she said. "Anguished Andersen here yet? Oh, hello, Liz. What are you doing hanging around?"

Ben scowled furiously. "She's not hanging around. She's here talking to me. At my invitation."

"I was just going," Elizabeth said hastily.

"Me, too," Ben said.

They walked to the stage door where Joe was still sitting on the steps.

"Say, Ben, since you want to watch Andersen, you might as well stick around now and see the whole dress rehearsal," he said. "You can hold the book for me."

"Okay, Joe. Sure." He turned to Elizabeth. "Listen, honey, don't rehearse too much this afternoon. It's hot as Tophet. Don't wear yourself out." He walked down the path with her. "And tell the others I'm sorry to miss our practice."

"I suppose Miss Andersen's rehearsal will go on till all hours of the morning?" Elizabeth asked.

"Yeah, like as not. It'll be interesting, though. Wish you could watch. You'd learn a lot. That—" he caught himself. "I can't say what I think of Dottie in front of you."

"Oh, Ben," Elizabeth said, "I wish I didn't have to go back to Jordan after this week. I'm going to miss you terribly."

Walking back to the Cottage through the sun-stifled streets, Elizabeth passed various members of the company on their way to the theatre, and when she got to the Cottage she found Kurt stretched out on his back on the stone rail of the porch, smoking lazily and blowing smoke rings into the hot still air above him, his dark hair moist with perspiration, his pale green eyes half closed.

"I came over here looking for you, Liebchen," he said. "What are you doing this afternoon?"

"Well, we thought we'd rehearse *Twelfth Night*. I want to try Viola. And I thought maybe you'd be an angel and read Orsino for me."

Kurt groaned. "Oh, dearheart, not on Sunday and in this heat!"

"You'd make such a beautiful Duke," Elizabeth said. "I imagine Orsino just like you, with beautiful black hair and stone green eyes and long secret black lashes and—"

"Go on," Kurt said. "Don't stop. This is the kind of talk I like to hear. Don't forget my strong yet passionate mouth and my virile body."

Elizabeth sat down on the old wicker swing and began to rock gently, looking over at Kurt so elegantly stretched out. "Don't tease. I mean it seriously. You *would* be a beautiful Duke and you could wear the costumes. So few men ever look anything but silly in Shakespearean costumes."

"Were you planning to use costumes this afternoon?"

"Don't be a nut." Elizabeth gave the swing an extra hard push.

Kurt threw his cigarette into a barberry bush, then rolled over, leaned on one elbow, and looked down through the heavy shadows of the porch at Elizabeth on the swing. "What've you been doing since lunch?" he asked.

"I was over at the theatre talking to Ben."

"Are you in love with Ben?"

His voice was casual but Elizabeth stopped swinging, put her feet on the cement floor, and said in a startled voice, "No!"

"You see an awful lot of him."

"I see an awful lot of Jane and John Peter and Ditta and—and *you*, too." Her voice held a trace of anger. She had managed to put John Peter's words about Ben out of her mind and she did not want Kurt, of all people, bringing the subject up.

"Yes. But usually in a bunch. You're always going off with Ben alone."

In spite of her anger Elizabeth felt a kind of wondering gratification at the thought that Kurt might actually be jealous of the moments she spent with Ben. If Kurt could be jealous, then he really must care. "Ben doesn't find it easy to talk to most people."

"Ben!" Kurt exclaimed. "He never shuts his mouth."

"Yes, but it's all gags. I mean serious talk. We just get along. He's been in the theatre since he was a kid and I love to hear him talk about it. He's told me lots of funny things that have happened, like once when he was about five he was touring with an old-time actor in a melodrama and in one scene at the climax of the play the actor had to come running across a moat with hounds baying behind him and then he had to jump off the moat and land on a mattress and stick his head in a bucket of water so that when he came up it looked as if he was swimming. And Ben said that one night the stagehand who was responsible forgot to put the bucket and the mattress out and when the actor got ready to jump he looked over the moat and saw no stagehand, no mattress, no bucket; but the hounds kept getting nearer and nearer and finally he just had to jump. Well, he landed like a ton of bricks, chinned himself up over the edge of the moat, looked out over the audience, and said, 'By golly, the moat's frozen over.' "

Kurt did not laugh. Instead he said, "If you aren't serious about Ben, I wouldn't see so much of him if I were you."

"Why not?" Now Elizabeth's anger flared.

"People are beginning to talk."

"Who's people?"

"Dottie, for one."

"If you want to take seriously anything Dottie says about me—"

"Calm down, Liebchen. It isn't that important. I don't take it seriously, but other people might."

"I doubt if anybody's that stupid." But she kept remembering Jane and John Peter and their kindly if blundering warning.

"I wouldn't be so sure if I were you, dearheart."

"Don't call me 'dearheart' when you can say things like that!"

Kurt got down from the stone porch rail and came over to Elizabeth on the swing. "Elizabeth, my darling, please do not get angry with me. I shouldn't have told you this thing, but I thought perhaps you ought to know."

"What has Dottie been saying?"

"Nothing of any importance."

"Kurt, please tell me. If she's been saying anything at all about me, it's important."

Kurt shrugged. "It's simply because she was furious with you because of the *Macbeth* business. And she's all the more furious with you because it was her fault, not yours."

"But what has she been saying?"

"Let's just forget it, Liebchen."

"No. Please, Kurt."

"Only that she didn't think you yourself were serious about Ben and she didn't think it was fair of you to lead him on if you weren't."

John Peter's words. Elizabeth went pale with anger. Her rage at Dottie and John Peter and Kurt and Ben and herself was so enormous that no words would come out.

"Elizabeth, you foolish child, it really doesn't matter; it isn't an issue of world-shattering importance."

"It *does* matter! Everything's been so wonderful with Ben and me. I've had such fun with him and we've had such good times together. It's been kind of as though he were my brother. And now it's all spoiled. I'll feel uncomfortable with him. The wonderful thing about Ben and me is that we were always so relaxed together. And now we won't be able to be. At least *I* won't."

"That's foolish, Elizabeth."

"It may be foolish but it's true. I hope you told Dottie I *wasn't* leading Ben on."

"Certainly."

"Has she talked about it to anyone else?"

"I don't know. I doubt it."

"Oh, damn!" Elizabeth cried. She jumped up and walked

the length of the porch and back. "I wish I didn't have inhibitions about swearing. I'd like to really let loose."

"Go ahead."

"I can't."

"Listen, Elizabeth, just forget the whole business, will you? Just forget I ever brought it up." Kurt put his hand on her shoulder in a worried manner.

"Why *did* you bring it up?"

"I never should have. I wish I hadn't. I didn't have any idea you'd take it so hard."

"I'm—I'm terribly fond of Ben," Elizabeth said. "As a friend he's—he's important to me. I can't bear to think of Dottie saying things like that."

"Oh well, nobody pays any attention to Dottie."

But what about John Peter and Jane? Elizabeth thought.

Kurt gave her a little shake. "Come along, Liebchen, forget it. Let's go for a swim."

Elizabeth shook her head. "I was down on the beach this morning. Anyhow, I promised Ditta I'd work with her."

Kurt ran his fingers affectionately over the back of her neck. "You don't mind if I go down to the beach and forget Shakespeare for this afternoon, do you? I'm much too hot to concentrate."

"No, of course not, Kurt. Go ahead. You're wonderful to work with us at all. We really appreciate it terribly. Honestly."

"Now, none of that. But, Elizabeth, forget what I said. I'm extremely sorry I mentioned it, so please just imagine the whole thing unsaid."

"I'll try."

"Except one thing, dearheart."

"What?"

"Are you sure Ben doesn't want more than you can give him?"

Elizabeth answered too quickly. "Of course I'm sure."

"Well, that's splendid, then."

But it wasn't splendid.

She went into the Cottage and walked slowly up the stairs. Maybe Aunt Harriet's right, she thought. Maybe the theatre isn't any place for a reasonable human being after all. It keeps your emotions in such a constant state of upheaval. It's really terribly wearing. I wonder if I could stand it, one emotional upset after the other just going on and on for the rest of my life. It must have been that way with Mother. And I'm afraid Mother wasn't a very reasonable human being.

She climbed up to the third floor and peered into her room. No one was there. She went down the hall to Ditta's room and opened the door gently. Ditta, lying sprawled across her bed, did not move. Her mouth was open and her face had drooped into tired lines. Dark circles made the skin beneath her eyes look bruised; and a copy of *The Complete Works of Shakespeare* had fallen out of her fingers and lay on the floor.

I really oughtn't wake her, Elizabeth thought. She looks so tired. Elizabeth tiptoed out of the room and shut the door gently behind her.

Elizabeth decided to go for a walk, and when she reached the garage she heard someone shout her name and, looking up, saw Jane leaning out of one of the windows.

"Liz," she called, "you aren't going to rehearse, are you? It's much too hot."

Elizabeth shook her head. "Can't find anybody to rehearse with. Ben's over at the theatre and Ditta's sound asleep."

"Let's go for a walk on the boardwalk or something, then," Jane said. "John Peter didn't sleep much last night and he wants to take a nap."

In the Cottage a window screen was flung violently open and Lulu Price stuck her head out. "Will you please be quiet!" she bellowed. "People are trying to sleep. You apprentices are certainly more trouble than you're worth."

"Oh—sorry," Elizabeth murmured sheepishly. She cupped her hands to her mouth and whispered up to Jane, "Come on down."

Jane nodded and joined Elizabeth on the gravel in front of the garage.

"I bet Lulu Price is trying to sleep off a hangover," Jane said. "I hear she got stewed last night at Irving's. That dame is certainly revolting when she's drunk."

"Most people are."

"Yeah, you're right."

As they reached the boardwalk they met Mariella Hedeman going toward the theatre.

"Hi, Miss Hedeman," Jane called. "Thought you were at dress rehearsal?"

"Hello, Jane, Elizabeth," the old actress said. "I am at rehearsal, but Miss Andersen said she wouldn't need me for an hour, so I thought it was worth going down the boardwalk for a glass of ginger ale and a breath of air. My makeup isn't much this week and it's stifling in that theatre with all the lights on."

"I expect the lighting's pretty complicated, isn't it?" Jane asked.

"Yes, but it's going to be very effective. It's been most interesting this week working with Miss Andersen. And she's so courteous to her actors—except, of course, when they misbehave, as Dottie has been doing. So many young people seem to forget that discipline is an extremely important part of the art of acting. I hope you two will remember it."

"We'll try, Miss Hedeman," Elizabeth promised.

"Yes, Elizabeth. I think you and Jane will. I'm sorry you didn't get your opportunity to be in *Macbeth* this week. You'd have been arresting as the Gentlewoman, and Marian would have made a lovely Lady Macduff. However, it seems that such things are out of our hands." She looked at the watch which she wore on an old-fashioned watch chain and had tucked into her belt. "I must go and get into my costume. It's as heavy as a bearskin and just about as comfortable on a day like this."

Jane turned to Elizabeth as Miss Hedeman went off to the theatre. "I guess a bare skin would be better than a bearskin at that."

Elizabeth groaned. "Oh, Jane, that would have been pretty feeble, even for Ben."

Jane pulled out a small, delicate handkerchief and wiped her forehead. "It's the best I'm capable of on a day like this."

"I bet Miss Hedeman must have been beautiful as a young girl," Elizabeth said.

Jane put her handkerchief away. "She's still a pretty grand-looking old dame—if only she'd leave the underwear ribbons and dried flowers out of her hair. Hey, something's going on out there. Let's go see what it is."

Strains of music came from one of the piers jutting out into the ocean, and Jane and Elizabeth stepped from the splintery boards of the boardwalk onto the older and even more rotting planks of the pier. A motley group of people were sitting on folding chairs listening to a Sunday afternoon concert. On a small raised platform a large woman in a violently flowered chiffon dress was singing one of Violetta's arias from *La Traviata*.

"Oh, no, Jane," Elizabeth protested. "I love *Traviata*. She ought to be strangled."

"If you ask me, she already has been," Jane whispered.

Elizabeth tugged at Jane's arm. "Come on. Let's go. I can't stand it."

"Have you no appreciation of *art?*" Jane demanded, but she turned away and they left the pier and started walking down the boardwalk again.

As they passed the milk bar Elizabeth said, "That girl—you know, the one Ben and I told you about—is going to think we gypped her if she makes her boyfriend take her to *Macbeth* next week and they find I'm not in it after all."

"Yes, there you'll be, in your usual place, asking if you can sew them to a sheet."

Elizabeth felt Jane's forehead. "Aren't you feeling well, Jane? Your jokes are getting progressively older and feebler."

"I must be hungry," Jane said. "Want a milk shake?"

"Uh-uh. I'm much too hot to eat."

"That isn't eating. It's drinking."

"I'm too hot to drink, then."

"You could explain to the girl you aren't going to be in the show next week."

"I don't want to explain it to her. It'll be good for her to see it anyhow, and it'll be the best show of the summer so they ought to go."

"Well, come in with me anyhow," Jane begged. "I was so upset over Aunt Val and John Peter's tooth I couldn't eat any lunch. Or breakfast."

Elizabeth sighed heavily. "Okay, but if it's hot in there, for heaven's sake, hurry."

It was hot in the milk bar, even hotter than out on the boardwalk. A different girl was working and Jane ordered a hamburger to go.

"It's almost suppertime and Mrs. Browden's feelings will be hurt if you don't eat," Elizabeth warned.

"Oh, she'll just think I'm still worried about John Peter. I'm having this so I can eat it on the way. Let's get back to the Cottage. Maybe it'll be cooler and maybe John Peter will be awake."

As they neared the Cottage they met Ben coming from the theatre. "Hi," he greeted them. "Help me carry sandwiches and coffee over to the theatre."

Elizabeth looked at Ben unhappily because she could not help remembering Kurt's words.

"Andersen said they could work some and then break for supper at the Cottage, but no one wants to take makeup off.

Mrs. Browden will be so disappointed about her roast beef. Rehearsal's going pretty smoothly in spite of the lighting. I think we'll finish well before midnight."

"It'll be the first time this summer," Elizabeth said.

"Listen, Ben," Jane said suddenly, "what we talked about this morning. I'll do it."

"Swell," Ben said. "That's wonderful, Jane."

"What's that?" Elizabeth asked.

"None of your business," Ben said. "Just something between Jane and me."

"I wouldn't let John Peter know if you're having secrets," Elizabeth warned.

Mrs. Browden had packed two baskets full of sandwiches and had filled two large thermos bottles with coffee. Ben took the bottles and Jane and Elizabeth the sandwich baskets.

"It's going to storm tonight," Ben said. "This heat can't last."

"How's the company holding up?" Elizabeth asked.

"Pretty wilted. That's another reason Andersen wants to get through rehearsal. She said she'd rather have them still alive tomorrow night. Thanks for the help, kids. Can you hang around a minute? Thank God I don't have a costume, so I can eat outside."

"I've got to go back and wash my hair before dinner," Jane said. "Got any shampoo I can borrow, Liz?"

"Sorry, I used mine all up this morning."

"Oh, well, I'll use John Peter's shaving soap. It works pretty well."

"You going to stay, Liz?" Ben asked hopefully.

"Yes, I'll stay."

She sat down on the steps and waited until Ben came back out of the theatre, a cup of coffee and a sandwich in his hands. "How'd *Twelfth Night* go?" he asked.

Elizabeth looked down at her feet in her worn white sneakers. "We didn't do it. Everybody thought it was too hot."

"What have you been doing?"

She shifted her gaze to a clump of Queen Anne's lace growing up between the steps. "Oh, nothing much. Jane and I went for a walk on the boardwalk."

She knew she was not hiding from Ben the strain that Jane's and John Peter's and now Kurt's words had set up in her, and she was not surprised when he asked, "What's the matter, Liz?"

She reached between the steps and picked a piece of Queen Anne's lace. "Oh, nothing. I'm just hot. This is pretty, isn't it, Ben? Some people call it cow parsley, and I suppose it's silly of me but that makes it seem not nearly so lovely as when you call it Queen Anne's lace."

"Yes, but what's the matter?" Ben asked again. "Are you mad at me?"

"Of course not. Why would I be mad at you?"

"I don't know. I thought maybe I'd done something or said something you didn't like."

"No, Ben. Of course not."

"What is it, then? You're not acting like yourself. Maybe you're not mad at me, but you're acting as though something's wrong."

Elizabeth held her breath, then let it out in a kind of gasp. "Ben, have I been leading you on?"

"What?"

"Have I been leading you on?"

Ben reached for her face and turned it so that he could look into her eyes. She met his gaze and stared up at him unhappily.

"Listen, Liz, what are you talking about?" he asked. When she did not answer he said, "Somebody's said something to you."

She nodded, looking up at the long lanky legs above her on the wooden steps.

"Who?"

"Oh, Ben, it doesn't matter."

"It does matter. It matters like hell."

"No. As long as you don't think I've—I've been leading you on, it's all right."

"Was it Dottie?"

Elizabeth shook her head. "It wasn't Dottie who told me."

"You mean Dottie said something and somebody told you?"

"Yes."

Ben stood up, towering above her on the steps. "This time she's gone too far. This time I'm going in and shaking her until the teeth rattle in that beautiful vicious head of hers."

Elizabeth stood, too, and caught at his hand. "No, Ben, please, please, *please* don't!"

"When I'm mad I have to do something about it."

"But it wasn't only Dottie. Jane and John Peter said something, too, only it didn't upset me so much until I heard about Dottie."

"I'll teach John Peter to mind his own business. How I behave and how you behave is our own affair, nobody else's. That's the hell about the theatre, everybody prying into everybody else's private lives. I'm not so surprised at John Peter, but I thought Jane had better sense. Wait till I get at her."

"No, please, Ben, please. I never should have said anything about it, only you guessed something was wrong and I couldn't bear to have it there between us."

Ben sat down heavily. "Listen, Liz, if you're going to work in the theatre, you've got to get used to people slitching other people. There's always someone around who'll do that. You've just got to see it for the pack of lies it is and pay no attention to what people say."

"Aunt Harriet always says where there's smoke there's fire."

"Are you going to start paying attention to what Aunt Harriet thinks at this late date?"

Elizabeth looked down at her feet again. "Ben, you don't"—she started, paused in a panic, and then rushed on—"Ben, you don't want more than I can give you, do you?"

For a moment Ben didn't answer. Then he said, "Listen, Liz, I like things just the way they are. Sure I want more, but so what? I don't want it if you can't give it, and I don't want any Dorothy Dawne whispering things to Kurt Canitz and then having Kurt Canitz whispering them to you and then you getting all upset over nothing."

"How did you know it was Kurt who told me?"

"I don't think he's the only one Dottie's talked to about it, but he's the only one who's bastard enough to come to you with it. Sorry if I defame your idol, but you can hardly expect my feelings about him to be particularly cordial. Now listen,

Elizabeth Jerrold, just put it all out of your head. If you're going to stay in the theatre, you've got to get used to things like that and you've got to get used to paying no attention to them."

"Is there always a Dottie?" Elizabeth asked.

"In all my great experience in the theatre I've never been in a company where there wasn't." Ben finished his sandwich, carefully folded the waxed paper, and put it in his empty coffee cup. "They don't always look alike. In one show it'll be the character man, in another the star, in another the juvenile, in another somebody's wife or girlfriend. Everything's intensified in the theatre. All my life—and I'm a year older than you are and don't you forget it—I've noticed that people who work in the theatre can be much bigger louses than other people; and also they can be much more wonderful. They can live with beauty and integrity and I'm sorry if those are fancy words but they're the only ones that'll do, and they can live like swine. And you've got to learn to walk through a pigpen and not get dirty."

For a long moment Elizabeth didn't say anything. Then, as she was about to speak, a voice from inside the theatre called, "Hey, Ben, Joe wants you," and he stood up.

"See you tonight if we break early enough," he said.

After dinner Kurt telephoned from his hotel over to the Cottage for Elizabeth.

"Come on down to Irving's with me this evening, Liebchen."

"I can't afford it, Kurt."

"This isn't dutch," he told her, his voice far away as though he were not talking directly into the phone. "I'm asking you to go out with me."

She shook her head as though he could see her motion of negation. "I don't think I'd better, Kurt."

"Elizabeth, are you still angry with me for what I told you Dottie said about you and Ben?"

"I don't know."

Now Kurt's voice came clearer, warm and persuasive. "Liebchen, darling, please try to realize I told you only because I love you so and I thought you'd want to know."

"It's all right," Elizabeth said. "I guess you were right to tell me."

"Maybe I wouldn't have told you if you'd been going to stay the rest of the summer, but you've only got one more week, so it will be simple enough just to ease off Ben."

"I won't have to," Elizabeth said. "I told him about it."

"You told Ben!"

"Yes."

"Darling, you're out of your mind."

Elizabeth shook her head stubbornly at the phone. "No. Ibsen says honesty is the only basis for any kind of a relationship between two people, and I like Ben too much not to be honest with him. It's all right, Kurt. Please. Let's just forget about it."

It's a funny thing, she thought. Recently I've been almost fighting with Kurt about so many things and I don't know why.

"That's fine," Kurt said. "I'm all for forgetting it. So come along and let's go on down to Irving's. Come on. To show me you aren't angry."

"All right," Elizabeth said, and felt deep chagrin because she wasn't as happy and excited at the prospect as she ought to be. "I'll have to change."

"Hurry, then, because I'll be right over for you," Kurt said.

She dressed carefully in a red cotton skirt and white blouse, brushed her hair, and put on fresh lipstick. Then she changed out of her sneakers and put on a pair of thonged sandals that Jane had bought and couldn't wear.

"You look lovely, Liebchen," Kurt told her when he arrived.

As they started down the steps of the Cottage they met Marian Hatfield. "Hi, Liz," she said. "I'm glad I bumped into you. I've got a couple of hours before Miss Andersen needs me again and I came over to get a book. Haven't you got Bradley's *Shakespearean Tragedy?*"

"Yes. It's upstairs."

"May I borrow it? I thought I'd like to look up *Macbeth.*"

"Sure. It's in the bottom drawer of my bureau at the tidy end of the room."

"Thanks." Marian started in, then turned back with a grin. "I bet you wish I'd fall down the stairs and break a leg."

Elizabeth laughed. "No. I wish no pox upon you, as Ben would say. I wouldn't want to get the Gentlewoman that way. But I don't think I'd feel much pain if Dottie came down with acute laryngitis."

Marian laughed and went on into the Cottage.

Walking down the boardwalk with Kurt was very different from walking with Ben. With Ben she felt completely relaxed, and as carefree as a child. With Kurt she walked much more carefully, trying not to stride, and feeling very much a woman.

"God, it's hot," Kurt said.

"Ben says it's going to storm tonight."

"Just for fun," Kurt suggested, "let's not talk about Ben tonight. He's caused enough trouble between us already."

Elizabeth looked at him in surprise. "Okay."

"Let's have this evening be just you and me. I'm going to miss you after next week."

"I'm going to miss you, too, Kurt."

Kurt put his hand up to his sleek dark head and smoothed his hair down in a characteristic gesture. "I've never met anybody like you before in my life, Elizabeth."

"Neither have I. Met anybody like you, I mean."

Kurt took her hand and tucked it under his arm. "You'd never met anybody like most of the people around here, had you, dearheart? It must seem rather strange after nothing but college and that town—what is it?—Jordan, Virginia. But I've rubbed shoulders with people all over Europe and America and you're still an enigma to me."

"An enigma? Why, Kurt?"

"I can't figure you out."

"I don't think there's much to figure out," Elizabeth said. "I'm pretty simple, really."

"That's what you think," Kurt said with an odd inflection from his lips.

"But I am. I never keep anything hidden inside me. Sometimes I wish I could, but I never can. I can't ever hide my feelings. People always know whether I'm angry or upset. It's awful!"

"That's not all of you by any manner of means." Kurt reached up and gave her fingers a little squeeze. "You know, Liebchen, sometimes you're just like a pussycat, all cuddly and affectionate, and other times you're like a clam, all shut up in a hard little impenetrable shell. Which is you? Which is the real Elizabeth?"

"Both, I expect," Elizabeth said, rather shortly because she remembered Ben saying that her mother had been like a kitten.

Kurt raised his eyebrows mock-tragically. "Now what have I said?"

Elizabeth laughed in apology. "Nothing. I don't mean to be snappy."

"A kitten and a clam and a snapping turtle. Quite a small zoo, aren't you, my little one? What animal do I remind you of?"

Elizabeth pondered for a while as they walked. The air was heavy and lifeless. "I don't think you really remind me of any animal particularly, Kurt. Perhaps a black panther more than anything else."

He gave a small pleased laugh. "As long as you don't say a snake in the grass or a wolf." He laughed again, and they turned off the boardwalk to go into Irving's. Irving's was the first nightclub to which Elizabeth had ever been; it was a low white building with a striped awning, a uniformed doorman, and potted trees on either side of the door. The neon sign flashed on and off, blinding the night, and a gush of stale cold air blew out at them.

"One reason I wanted to come to Irving's tonight is that it's air-conditioned," Kurt said, holding Elizabeth firmly by one elbow and guiding her in.

The ceiling of Irving's was covered with blue mirrors, and the people moving on the crowded dance floor were reflected in a strange, inverted pattern. The dim blue light turned their tans to an unhealthy pallor; most of the faces, relaxed in the abandonment of dancing, looked cadaverous, or bloated, like drowned creatures floating through blue water. The headwaiter led Kurt and Elizabeth to a small table against the wall. He pulled it out and Elizabeth slipped in, sitting on the blue leather couch. Kurt sat beside her.

"What'll it be?" he asked her.

"Coke, I guess."

"Oh, come now. Why not a drink?"

She shook her head, smiling, but firm. "Nope. Thanks. I had a drink at the Tavern once to celebrate a play at college and it gave me a horrible headache and made me act silly. Anyhow I'm under twenty-one."

"Oh," Kurt said, disappointed. "And I was counting on your getting just a tiny bit tight tonight."

"I can get drunk without drinking," Elizabeth said. "Ben says I'm a dipsomaniac about excitement."

"I thought we weren't going to talk about Ben. Just Elizabeth and Kurt. Yes?"

"Yes, Kurt." She was pleased and touched, and she felt that Kurt was making an effort to be sweet and gentle to make up for what he had said that afternoon. She thought of explaining to him that Ben was the one person to whom she could talk about her mother, but decided against it.

"Want anything to eat?" Kurt asked her. "Salad? Club sandwich?"

"Not yet, thanks. Supper isn't halfway down me yet."

"Later, maybe?"

"Maybe."

Kurt gave the order. "One Coca-Cola and one scotch and soda."

Elizabeth looked around at the people, thinking that perhaps she might see Bibi or one of the other apprentices, but there were no familiar faces. The small orchestra, composed of excruciatingly suntanned men with white teeth that flashed like neon lights, blared out a samba. It was so loud that it almost completely washed out all conversation, though occasionally a voice could be heard bellowing above it.

"Want to dance?" Kurt asked her.

Elizabeth hesitated. "Oh, Kurt—I'm not a very good dancer. I've never had much practice."

"Well, let us practice a bit now, then."

"The floor's terribly crowded—and I'll step all over your feet and dirty your beautiful clean white shoes."

"I'll risk it. And you should not act unsure of yourself, Elizabeth." Kurt stood up, and she had to rise, too. He guided her out onto the dance floor. "Now just relax, Liebchen, and you'll be all right."

In Jane's sandals she was just about the same height as Kurt. He held her tightly, and she could feel his body very close to hers. His legs pressed against her legs and guided her; it was impossible not to follow him.

"You're the most beautiful dancer, Kurt—" she told him breathlessly.

"I like to dance," he said, leading her skillfully through the intricate steps. "It's an art most American men sadly neglect. This bobbing around you see all about you certainly cannot be called dancing. You're doing very well, dearheart. Just try not to be so stiff. I feel as though I were holding a ramrod. Relax!"

"I'm trying to relax," Elizabeth gasped.

"Don't try so hard, then; that's part of your trouble. Just try to forget that you're dancing."

"Then I'll step on your feet."

"No you won't. I'll see to that. Try closing your eyes."

She closed her eyes and immediately became doubly conscious of Kurt's supple body pressed against hers and guiding it. She opened her eyes quickly and looked at the blue faces swirling about her. "Do I look as blue as everybody else?"

"I expect so. Do I?"

"On you it looks good, as Ben would say. Oops, sorry."

In spite of the air-conditioning the dancing made Elizabeth warm. She still did not feel comfortable dancing with Kurt, and she was glad when the music stopped and they went back to the table where their drinks were waiting. If she had been dancing with Ben, she wouldn't have been embarrassed, she thought. She would have apologized if she'd stepped on his feet but it wouldn't have been a matter of grave importance; whereas she writhed at the thought of Kurt having found her clumsy.

"I was terrible. I'm sorry," she said.

"You weren't terrible at all. And one very good thing was something you *didn't* do."

"What was that?"

"You didn't try to lead me. You let me lead you." He raised his glass. "Here's to you, my dear."

She lifted her Coca-Cola and touched her glass to his. "And to you."

"It's nice here, just the two of us, isn't it?"

"Yes, Kurt."

"Nobody from the company, none of the apprentices, no theatre, just Kurt and Elizabeth . . ."

The orchestra was leaving, and in a moment the dim lights were lowered even further and a pair of duo pianists was announced. Two white pianos on a platform were rolled out onto the dance floor and lighted with a green spot which contrasted strangely with the blue mirrors. The pianists, two young men, came out, bowed quietly, and started to play. They plunged into a malaguena and their fingers flew over the keyboards in perfect coordination; it seemed incredible that the music coming in such complete harmony of purpose from the pianos was being made by two separate entities.

"Those boys can play," Kurt said. He beckoned to the waiter and ordered another drink for himself and another Coca-Cola for Elizabeth.

"That's what real ensemble playing on the stage should be," Elizabeth said. "That's the way you have to do Chekhov."

"Elizabeth and Chekhov." Kurt smiled affectionately. "No. Too many implications for me. Your *Seagull*. What does it mean? Symbols within symbols—"

Elizabeth shook her head. "You're trying to make it too complicated, Kurt."

"Am I?"

"Sure. I don't think he's trying to be highly symbolical and I don't think the play's any more symbolical than . . . *Hamlet*, or . . . or *Winnie-the-Pooh*."

Kurt laughed.

"But I mean it," Elizabeth protested. "Chekhov's people are complete four-dimensional people and should be taken as such. They aren't Maeterlinck symbols. As for the seagull itself, it seems to me it stands only for beauty carelessly destroyed. It means more to Nina *personally*, in her grief, than it did to Chekhov or needs to mean to the audience."

Kurt shook his head. "Elizabeth, are you sure you know what you are talking about?"

The pianists were replaced by a young woman in a scanty tangerine gown who swooned over the microphone and sang in a nasal, whining voice. Elizabeth listened to her for a moment with distaste, then turned back to Kurt and said, "It seems to me that one of the reasons that Chekhov's plays confuse the audience is that they—the people in the audience, I mean—are used either to the typical comedy or problem play where they find nothing but types, or the Shavian sort of play where each character stands for one aspect of the author's argument. Chekhov simply wrote about people, and his characters are consistent with the terrible inconsistency of people. Sometimes the ones who go around saying how clear everything is are the most confused. Or they laugh when they're sad or cry when they're happy. If you live with a Chekhov play, if you really work with it, if you look at it simply, like a child, you'll find that there is nothing confusing in the play—it's as simple as life—but, on the other hand, that's the most confusing thing in the world . . . If Chekhov's plays must be cataloged, 'prophetic' is certainly a better word than symbolic."

Kurt laughed again. "Oh, Elizabeth, Elizabeth, anybody would know your father was an English teacher."

After a moment Elizabeth laughed, too. "Sorry. I didn't mean to lecture."

"But I enjoyed it!" Kurt told her. "You get so intense and furious. Have a sandwich now? Hungry yet?"

"I could eat."

"Good. How about a club sandwich?"

"That's too much for me, Kurt. Lettuce and tomato'd be fine."

"Okay. I guess I'll have liverwurst on rye. And they have wonderful dill pickles here. You're looking very lovely tonight, Liebchen. And your hair is beautiful. You ought to wear skirts more often. You look attractive in those jeans of yours but you begin to fulfill your beauty in skirts."

"I only have three dressy summer outfits that are fit to wear. And I have to be careful of them."

"What did you wear at college?"

"I accumulated an adequate number of skirts and sweaters. And we wore jeans a lot, too. If ever I make a lot of money, I'll probably go hog-wild buying dresses and hats and things."

"Don't you ever use nail polish?"

"Nope."

"Why not?"

"Oh, just one of my prejudices."

"What do you mean?"

"Well, if you already have pretty hands it detracts from them; and if you have ugly hands it draws attention to them."

Kurt laughed. He always laughed a good deal, but this evening his laugh seemed to rise out of him like a hidden spring, clear and full of friendliness. "You're an awful little puritan in some ways. But you have very pretty hands. Very strong hands, Liz. I can't imagine your doing anything with them badly. And yet they're not a bit masculine."

The wailing singer gave several deep curtseys and departed, and the two pianists returned to the floor. Elizabeth heaved a sigh of relief. The waiter brought fresh drinks and Kurt ordered their sandwiches.

"What shall we talk about now?" he asked, and smiled at her.

"Let's just listen to the music."

The pianists played for about fifteen minutes. Then their platform was rolled off the dance floor and the dim blue lights came back up. The orchestra returned to its place and dancers began to straggle out onto the floor. The noise of the orchestra and the noise of the patrons once more rolled over the nightclub like a huge wave.

"Would you like to dance again?" Kurt asked.

"I'd rather just sit if you don't mind. Do the pianists play again?"

"They come on again about one-thirty or two. They're new this week."

"They're wonderful."

"Having a good time?"

"Yes, Kurt. Thank you."

"Not angry with me anymore?"

"Of course not. Don't be silly."

"We'll have to see a lot of each other when you come to New York. If I direct a play, I will certainly try to find something in it for you. Will you write me the rest of the summer, so that we can keep in touch?"

"Of course. If you want me to."

"Sure you don't want to dance?" he said to Elizabeth. "That's a good rhumba they're playing."

"No, Kurt. Really. I'm not good at rhumbas and sambas and things. I'm okay with something easy like a fox-trot, but the only thing I've ever *really* had fun with is waltzing. One of the professors at college who used to act a lot for us was Viennese, and sometimes he'd bring a stack of waltzes to the theatre and after we'd finished rehearsal we'd put them on the Victrola and waltz and waltz until when we stopped we just fell down on the stage and everything whirled around for about five minutes."

"Were you in love with him?" Kurt asked.

"Who? Mr. Bergen? He was married."

"Elizabeth, Elizabeth," Kurt said gently. "Everything is so simple with you. 'He was married.' You say that as though that was all there is to it."

Elizabeth looked at him in surprise. Then she said, looking down at the marbleized tabletop, "Oh, I wouldn't put it past me to fall in love with a married man. I'm just that kind of a dope. Only I certainly think it's inadvisable if you can possibly avoid it. After all, there isn't much point to it."

"Why not?"

"Well, it just seems to me it's a little more sensible to fall in love with someone who's—available."

"Some people don't know the meaning of the word 'unavailable,' " Kurt told her. "Sometimes I wonder if there actually is any such word."

Elizabeth picked up her knife and ran the back of it across the table as though she were drawing. "It's just one thing I happen to feel particularly strongly about," she said. "And—well, it's just always seemed to me that the easiest way to decide whether something's right or wrong is to ask yourself whether or not it would hurt somebody else. One of the girls in my house at college tried to get one of the art instructors to fall in love with her. She said she was in love with him and nothing else mattered. But he had a wife who loved him terribly and this girl knew it. That to me was—was really wrong."

"That's all very fine," Kurt said. "I suppose it's just another way of saying the golden rule. Do unto others as you would have them do unto you."

"Well, not quite. I'd like to be done unto, for instance, in ways that Aunt Harriet would loathe. But it's not far off."

"Then if you believe it so strongly, why don't you follow it?"

"I try to," Elizabeth said. "What do you mean?"

"You've as much as said that you're hurting your Aunt Harriet by wanting to work in the theatre."

Elizabeth was silent for a moment. Then, "Yes. You're right, Kurt. I am hurting her. But I can't help it. It—I can't explain—I'd be betraying myself much worse than I'll be hurting Aunt Harriet. I haven't any choice. I *have* to work in the theatre."

"Some people feel the same way when they're in love, even when the person they're in love with is what you call unavailable."

"Maybe you're right," Elizabeth said unhappily. "I don't know . . ."

"And Ben. I may feel about it very differently than Dottie, but I do think you're taking more from him than you're giving."

"I thought we weren't going to talk about Ben tonight."

"Sometimes you can be very intolerant," Kurt said gently. "You can be so sure that you are right."

Elizabeth stared down at her plate, at the crumbs of toast, a shred or two of lettuce, a bit of tomato. "You make me feel— I don't like the way you make me feel, Kurt. I never thought of myself as being a holier-than-thou kind of person, and that's the way you make me feel."

"Liebchen," Kurt said, "don't look like that. I didn't have the intention to start this. You're not holier-than-thou. Come on. Let's have another drink and another dance and then I'll take you back. It's late and you're tired. Another Coke?"

"All right."

She danced again with Kurt and suddenly she felt completely exhausted, mentally and physically. She did not like the picture Kurt had drawn for her of a person bigoted, quick to condemn, yet sure of her own sanctity. Am I really like that? she thought.

"Elizabeth, dear," Kurt said, "all I've done today is upset

you, and that's the last thing I wanted to do. I didn't mean to make you feel badly. I think it's just because I admire you so much as a person that I felt free to say the things I did. You're so sure of yourself—"

"But I'm not!"

"And I'm so terribly unsure."

"*You*, Kurt?"

"Yes, the great Kurt Canitz. I talk as though I were Reinhardt, but I am intelligent enough to know that not everything I want can be bought. If you could know the black moods of horrible uncertainty I go through, you'd laugh."

"I wouldn't laugh."

"No, I don't think you would, Elizabeth. That's very comforting to me, do you know that?" He touched his fingers lightly to hers. Then he paid the waiter, and they left Irving's and the blue light and the chill stale air and went out onto the boardwalk. The night outside was still stifling and heavy with heat and humidity.

"It's like trying to breathe potato soup," Elizabeth said, looking up at the sky where there were no stars visible, only a drooping blanket of foggy clouds. In the distance the thunder rumbled faintly, and out at sea the sky was lit by a feeble sheet of glimmering heat. Then, at the horizon, the sky was silently split by a bifurcated tongue of lightning. Somewhere in the distance a seagull screeched, its voice sharp with the sound of fury and pain.

"I think we will have quite a storm," Kurt said. He put his arm around her waist and they started to walk along the boardwalk.

Elizabeth had seen Kurt walk arm in arm with Dottie; she had seen Dottie walk arm in arm with Huntley, with any other man who happened to be handy; but when she was the one who was walking arm in arm with Kurt, it seemed a very different thing. She felt his back muscles moving under her arm as they walked, and it was an exciting feeling.

The theatre was dark as they neared it, and Kurt said, "Liebchen, all of a sudden I'm terribly depressed. Before I take you back to the Cottage, come and talk to me for a few minutes and cheer me up. We can go into my dressing room."

"Did I depress you, Kurt?"

"No, of course not. It's just me. Do come talk to me. Please, my little darling one."

"I ought to go right back to the Cottage and go to bed. It's terribly late. And I have to get up early to set tables tomorrow."

"Just a few minutes. Come on. Don't disappoint me."

"All right." She was touched and pleased because it seemed so important to Kurt that she come with him, because she was the one he wanted to get him out of his black mood.

She sat on the studio couch and Kurt sat beside her and put his arms around her and kissed her, and suddenly she began to be frightened.

"I thought you wanted to talk," she said, trying to keep her voice light.

"No. Kiss me again, Liebchen. Love me."

She pulled away from him. "I have to go to bed, Kurt. It was a lovely evening and I do thank you for it, but now I'm awfully tired and you're rather drunk. So good night and I'll see you in the morning."

He took her hand and looked down at it. "My sweet puritan."

"I'm not."

"Then why won't you kiss me again?"

"It's too late and I'm too tired and I don't like the smell of somebody else's whiskey."

He leaned over her and spoke gently. "You're old enough to learn a little about life, Elizabeth. How are you going to be able to act if you keep yourself so aloof? I won't frighten you."

She stood up, her heart pounding. "No, Kurt."

"Yes, Elizabeth."

"No," she said again. "I'm going back to the Cottage now."

He moved so that he was between her and the door. "Why are you afraid? I'd never hurt you. You ought to know that."

"I'm not afraid. But please let me go, Kurt."

"You're a coward." His voice was taunting.

All of a sudden her confusion left her and she was angry. She gave him a violent push that took him off guard and she ran by him, out of the dressing room and out of the theatre. As she got out onto the boardwalk the thunder crashed, the heavens opened as the rain came in a great downpour, and a huge cool wave of air washed over her. She walked rapidly, paying no attention to where she was going, her face held up to the rain. Her white blouse was plastered against her flesh, her drenched red skirt blew soppingly about her legs, and her feet sloshed in Jane's sandals, but she kept on walking. If only the rain continued for long enough, perhaps she might feel clean again.

Act IV
MONDAY

ELIZABETH WOKE UP EARLY, as exhausted as though she had not been to bed at all. Around her the house lay sleeping. She rose and dressed quietly, putting on a clean white shirt, her blue jeans and her sneakers, and went downstairs. Her heart lay within her like a weight of misery; her whole body ached with the pain of it.

She left the Cottage and walked slowly toward the ocean. As she neared the theatre she thought suddenly, I must talk to Kurt. It was only because he was drunk, and I handled it so stupidly. I must make everything all right between us again.

She had the key to Mr. Price's office in the pocket of her jeans and she let herself in quietly and walked across the auditorium toward Kurt's dressing room. But he will be asleep, she thought. I can't wake him.

Then she heard the sound of voices from Kurt's dressing room and she pressed back quickly into the shadows. The door opened and Dottie emerged, with Kurt behind her, leaning lazily in the doorway. Dottie blew him a kiss and hurried across the auditorium. Kurt shut the door. Neither of them had seen Elizabeth.

It was as though a needle filled with Novocaine had been plunged into her heart. There was no more pain, only a cold light feeling. She stayed motionless until she was certain that Dottie would have had time to get out of sight. Then she left the theatre and walked briskly back to the Cottage. It was almost time to set the tables.

Ben was not yet down, but Mrs. Browden was in the kitchen and eager to talk. Elizabeth set the tables quickly and gulped down a cup of coffee, but the hot liquid had no warming effect on the coldness within.

"Anything the matter, my pet?" Mrs. Browden asked.

She shook her head.

"Aren't you going to eat any breakfast?"

"I'm not very hungry."

"Then there *is* something wrong," Mrs. Browden declared. "You and that Ben usually eat so it does my heart good."

"I guess I ate something last night that didn't sit too well," Elizabeth said lamely.

"Something I cooked?" Mrs. Browden threw up her hands in horror.

"Heavens, no!" Elizabeth reassured her. "It must have been a frankfurter or something from the boardwalk. You're the most magnificent cook I've ever encountered."

"I could be if I had something to cook with," Mrs. Browden said complacently. "Mr. Price doesn't give me enough money more than to barely manage and I can't get the cuts of meat I'd like and there's *never* anything left over for sauces or desserts. I don't know why I go on doing it summer after summer when I could get a good job in a hotel or restaurant and have plenty of butter and eggs to cook with, except I've got myself kind of fond of theatrical people, crazy though they be. And I'm afraid if I left, Mr. Price would never find anybody else to feed you as good as I do on so little. Elizabeth, my lambie, are you feeling sick? You look pale."

"I've just got a kind of pain in my stomach," Elizabeth said, pressing her hand against her diaphragm. "I think I'll go out for a little walk before time for classes. Tell Ben I've done everything but put on the toast, would you please?"

"A walk would be just the thing, my pet," Mrs. Browden said. "And the air's all clean and cool after the storm last night. My, that was some storm! I hid in my broom closet till it was over. I knew a woman once who was struck by lightning in her own bed, and another who saw a ball of lightning run across the kitchen floor. That is something I hope never to see. To my mind lightning is an invention of the devil and I intend to do all in my power to keep away from it. Now have a good walk, and if you get hungry before lunch, come out to me and I'll make you a roast beef sandwich."

"Thank you, Mrs. Browden," Elizabeth said.

Outdoors the air was cool and light and a breeze blew in from the ocean. The sky was blue and pure and small white clouds scudded across it. Everything in the world around Elizabeth sparkled, and she walked along aware in her mind of the beauty but participating in none of it. She moved with her usual long-legged grace, but it seemed that she herself was totally anesthetized to feeling. Yes, yes, this day is beautiful, she told herself with sternness, but she felt nothing.

She headed almost unconsciously toward the theatre, not toward the theatre of Kurt and of Dottie but the theatre of Joe and Ben, the theatre of the people who worked hardest and received least credit. She did not go near the front, to the auditorium or to Kurt's or Mr. Price's offices, but to the stage door entrance. She climbed the wooden steps and found the stage door unlocked. Joe was sweeping the stage with a battered broom. He looked up when he heard footsteps and smiled when he saw it was Elizabeth.

"Hi, kid," he greeted her, waving the broom.

"Hi, Joe. How'd dress rehearsal go last night?"

"Okay, I guess. We broke a little after midnight, see. Ben looked for you, but Jane and John Peter said they thought you were out with Canitz."

"Yes. We went to Irving's."

"Had your breakfast?" Joe asked her.

"Yes."

"I'm off for a cup of coffee. If you want to stick around to play a record or something, it's okay with me."

"Okay, Joe. I think I will. Thanks."

When Joe had left, she went to the record box and fingered through the records but did not take one out. Then she sat down on the three-legged stool by the stage manager's desk and picked up and put down Joe's flashlight, then looked with exaggerated intentness at his row of pencils and the master copy of the week's script. Usually Elizabeth loved looking at the master; it contained not only the words of the play but the blocked-out movements of the players, the property lists, and the lighting plots as well.

She was sitting there when Ben came hurrying by the dressing rooms and onto the stage. "Liz," he said shortly.

"Hi, Ben."

"What's up?"

"Up? What do you mean? Nothing."

"Mrs. Browden said you didn't eat any breakfast."

"My stomach was kicking up. It's okay now, though."

"Sure?"

"Sure."

"Then come along back with me and have breakfast."

Elizabeth sighed helplessly. "Okay."

"Listen," Ben said, plunking himself down on the floor at her feet. "Dottie kind of cut up at rehearsal last night and I heard Miss Andersen whispering to Miss Hedeman that she wished you were in the show and Dottie was out. And she said she was tremendously impressed with your Nina."

"Nina's always been my part, somehow," Elizabeth said slowly, "even if I'm not right for her. Maybe because she says the things I believe. Remember, Ben, 'For us, whether we write or act, it is not the honor and glory of which I have dreamt that is important, it is the strength to endure' . . . Chekhov says that over and over again."

I know more about Nina now than I did, Elizabeth thought. Then I felt it, but now I know it. Now I know about Nina and Boris Trigorin. I know it's possible to love someone and have it not turn out all right. Somehow in spite of everything, in spite of Mother and Father, in spite of Nina, I thought that if you really loved anybody, somehow it was bound to turn out all right . . .

"Liz," Ben said, "you're upset about something."

She bent over the *Macbeth* script. "I was just thinking about Nina and Trigorin. She thought he loved her and he didn't, and she should have had sense enough to have known all along that he didn't. But I guess people never have sense about things like that till too late . . . It's nice and cool today, isn't it, Ben? Now the *Macbeth* people won't be so hot in their costumes."

Ben stood up. "Come on, Liz. Breakfast."

"Okay," Elizabeth said, and followed him out of the theatre.

As they went up the steps to the Cottage they saw Kurt and Dottie standing together on the porch. Dottie, noticing them, looked significantly at Kurt, but Kurt simply waved and called, "Top o' the morning to you!" in an atrocious Irish accent, and, ignoring Dottie, vaulted over the porch rail onto the grass and hurried off in the direction of the theatre.

Ben and Elizabeth, followed a moment later by Dottie, went in to breakfast. Dottie wore a ruffled red-and-white polka-dotted sunsuit and had her hair pulled up into a psyche knot with matching ribbon. She looked at Elizabeth and said in a voice like caramel, "Poor thing, you look *so* tired. Out late?"

Ben, who had gone into the kitchen, came back out with a plate of scrambled eggs and bacon in time to hear this and plunked it down in front of Dottie. "All you need to complete your outfit, Dottie, is a pair of diapers showing under your drawers. My sister's brat has a sunsuit just like yours. It looks real cute except where she's faded it from wetting her pants." He turned to Elizabeth. "Scrambled eggs and bacon?"

"No, thanks. Just coffee, please."

Bibi sat down at the other end of the table and said, "Good grief, you got home late last night, Liz. What were you doing?"

"Oh, I was out." Elizabeth poured milk into the cup of coffee Ben put in front of her.

"Yes, I know you were out. The point is, where were you? I came in just before it began to storm and you didn't come up to bed till way after it stopped. And this morning I noticed that your red skirt was simply soaking wet. You weren't *out* in the storm, Elizabeth Jerrold, were you?"

"Quite the little detective, aren't we?" Elizabeth was painfully conscious of Dottie's gaze on her. "As it happens, I like storms. I must have witch blood in my veins. Guess it's the influence of *Macbeth*. 'When shall we three meet again? In thunder, lightning, or in rain?' "

Unwittingly Dottie rescued her by turning to Huntley Haskell and saying, "I was certainly surprised by Andersen letting us off when she did last night. I thought she'd probably keep us till daybreak. Be just like her. And the way she picked on me during my scene was laughable, it was so obvious."

Ditta, who had pushed back her chair and was about to leave, asked, "What was obvious?"

"Oh, that she has it in for me. I'm sure I don't know why, except jealousy."

"We're all just dying of jealousy over you, Dottie." Elizabeth finished her coffee and rose. "Ditta, be an angel and hear me do my voice exercises."

She and Ditta went out to the small patch of lawn behind the garage. Elizabeth did her voice exercises, but Ditta was lying on her back on the grass, her knees raised, staring up at the sky.

"Hey, you weren't listening," Elizabeth protested.

"Yes, I was." Ditta sat up hastily. "You were superb. Liz, can we just talk for a few minutes?"

"Okay, what about?" Elizabeth asked.

"Oh—" Ditta paused, then finished rather lamely, "the theatre."

"Well, do you mind if I ask you a question then?" Elizabeth counterattacked.

"You can ask."

"What do you want to get out of the theatre, Ditta?"

A light shone briefly behind Ditta's eyes. "I just love it. I just want to have something, anything, to do with it, even if it's just teaching schoolkids. If I can teach them to love it, too, it'll be worth it."

"I think that's wonderful," Elizabeth said.

Ditta lay back down on the grass again and rolled over onto her stomach. "Oh, no, it isn't. What I really wanted was to be an actress. This is just a substitute because I have enough sense to know I haven't enough talent to be a really good actress, and I couldn't bear to be a second-rate one. Anyhow, I know I'm ugly as a mud fence and I don't improve on the stage the way some people do. Miss Andersen, for instance. She looks just like anybody else offstage, but onstage she's a raving tearing beauty. Onstage I'm still ugly as a mud fence."

"Ditta, you're nuts," Elizabeth said.

"Oh, no, I'm not. I know what I look like. And once or twice I've heard snatches of conversations that weren't meant for my ears. Don't get me wrong, Liz. I'm not sorry for my-self. I'm really very contented with my lot. And nobody can ever take away from you what you've had, and even if I never have anything else—I mean something like that—it was so wonderful it's really enough."

"What was it, Ditta?" Elizabeth asked softly. "Do you mind talking about it?"

"Most of the time I do." Ditta pressed her face into the grass and her voice came out muffled. "But I'd rather like to tell you about it. I was—I was terribly in love once and the amazing thing was he was in love with me. It was rather like beauty and the beast in reverse, and when I was with him I was different—I really *looked* different. He made me feel that beauty was a quality that comes only from the inside, and when I was with him I was beautiful inside so I expect some of it ac-tually was reflected on the outside, too."

"How did you meet him, Ditta?" Elizabeth asked, feeling that she ought not to be looking at Ditta's face partly hidden by the grass, her eyes closed, because as Ditta talked her face changed and mirrored what she was feeling, and it was sud-denly as though the usually well-disciplined face was un-dressed, as though Ditta had taken off her daily covering of control and was inadvertently letting Elizabeth see something intensely private. And at the same time that Elizabeth felt she ought to look away she also knew that she had to watch. She had to watch Ditta not only because instead of seeming plain and drab Ditta was beautiful in the same way that a leaf cov-ered with dew is beautiful, or a hollyhock searching upwards toward the sky, or anything reaching out fully toward life is beautiful; but she had to watch Ditta in the same way that she watched Valborg Andersen on the stage, or Jane working on a part, or studied a spider spinning a web, or read Marlowe's *Edward II*, or listened to Bach on the radio, or felt the way each grain of sand pushed up between her toes on the beach and each wave reached out to touch her body in the ocean. She had to watch Ditta this way because it was the way she learned; this was what taught her to act. One part of her was listening to Ditta and feeling the sharp thrust of Ditta's pain, and another part of her was excited and very aware and trying to store up the inner quality of everything that Ditta was saying and doing.

Once, Mariella Hedeman had asked the apprentices how you could tell an actor from anybody else; satisfied with none of their answers, she told them that it was because an actor had to be more alive than other people. An actor walking down the street and seeing a blind man *was* for the moment that blind man; or seeing the tragedy behind the gaudy trappings of a prostitute, he was that prostitute. And because an actor merged himself into other people's personalities, he was the first to help the blind man across the street, to offer his seat to an old woman on the bus. You could tell an actor because he was a greater participator in life than anyone else. "Nice, though a bit romantic," Ben had whispered to Elizabeth. "Some actors are self-centered stinkers. But maybe she's just talking about *real* actors."

Now Elizabeth was participating in Ditta's pain, but she was also adopting that pain as part of her wardrobe of acting; it was there for her to utilize whenever she needed it. Miss Hedeman had made this seem like an ideal process; Elizabeth always had a guilty sense of thieving, but it was an unavoidable theft.

"It was during the war," Ditta was saying. "I was teaching at a day school then, so I had more time to myself—too much time. There was a big naval air station just on the outskirts of town and he was a friend of a friend of the math teacher's so she looked him up and had him out to tea. That was how I met him. He didn't know anybody else—I guess that's why I saw so much of him at first—and then there wasn't anybody in the world but the two of us. If I'd never believed in heaven before, I would have believed in it then. Right in the middle of this life I've been to heaven, Liz. Not many people have. I'm terribly lucky, really."

"What happened?" Elizabeth asked.

"We were going to be married, but he was waiting for his orders to go overseas and we thought it would be better to wait till he got back. It was toward the very end of the war— we both felt that it mightn't be long, and that it might be over even before he had to leave. But he did leave and his plane crashed over the Pacific the day the war ended. Or was supposed to have ended."

"Oh, Ditta—"

"No, Liz. Don't be sorry for me. It was—something that happened and that neither of us could prevent, but there wasn't any bitterness in it. I can think of him with nothing but love. Even our occasional quarrels were—gay and loving. I have nothing bad to look back on. If anything ever happens to John Peter and Jane—I mean if something should happen to their love—it wouldn't be anything either of them would want to remember. They'd try to shut out their time together. But my memories are like a fire in winter—whenever I'm cold I can warm my hands at them." Without warning, the mask of restraint closed over her face again. "I'm sorry if I sound sentimental."

"You don't!" Elizabeth cried. "Oh, Ditta, you don't!" She wanted to say something to show Ditta that she understood to the depth of her own experience and beyond, but she could only say, "Oh, Ditta," very softly, very helplessly. After a while she said, "Ditta—"

"What?"

"You know all the gabbing we do—talking till three and four in the morning—"

"Yes."

"And we hardly ever talk about the world—and war—and stopping war—We're so terribly selfish—"

"Well," Ditta said, "the war didn't really touch any of you. It wasn't fought here. You weren't bombed, you had enough to eat, you didn't walk through streets full of rubble and dead bodies, you weren't quite old enough to have people you were madly in love with in the war—and even people who were really in it, who went through the worst of it, want to forget it. It's only human nature."

"But, Ditta—when you see the papers—everything's so awful—the people at the heads of countries do such awful things—and we don't do anything about it. We just sit around and eat hot dogs and talk about people and the state of the theatre."

"Is this the first time that's occurred to you?" Ditta asked.

"No. But it just hit me harder than usual. In college we used to be terribly concerned with the world, but here the whole world seems to be the theatre. If there were only something we could do to stop war so things like what happened to you wouldn't happen."

"It's a funny thing," Ditta said. "You know I wouldn't have met him if it hadn't been for the war . . . I wonder if there *is* any way to stop war? People say it's impossible because there have always been wars, but they said radio was impossible, and telephone, and airplanes. They said if God had meant man to fly He would have given us wings. I believe that God likes us to do things for ourselves, to develop our own potentialities. And as for war—all I can do, personally, to try to stop it, is to re-member it, and try to teach my kids at school about it, sort of sandwiched in between lessons in acting. I like teaching, you know, Liz. I've gotten so that it's really a creative thing with me; I feel that it's a creative art just as much as acting or paint-ing or writing music—and it makes me happy that my kids at school like me; and in the summer I have this. I say I come to summer theatres because I think it's the best way I can keep my theatre knowledge fresh and new for my kids, but I don't know who I think I'm fooling. I come simply because I dote on it. I've met more people this summer that I'd like to go on know-ing than I ever have before—you and Ben and Jane and John Peter and Marian Hatfield. You knew Marian was in the play Kurt directed in New York last winter, didn't you?"

"Yes, he told me." The moment Kurt's name was mentioned the warm emotion that Ditta's story had roused in Elizabeth retreated. She felt cold and wary and she looked at Ditta almost with antagonism.

"I didn't know until Marian told me last night. We went out for a hamburger after she was through rehearsal. She's an awfully good actress, I think, and not a bit upstagey. By the way"—Ditta cast a sidelong glance at Elizabeth, then looked down at the grass—"did you know Kurt was once married?"

"No," Elizabeth said after a long pause in which she felt as though Ditta had kicked her violently in the stomach. Though why? Why should Kurt not be married?

"He never told you about it?"

"No."

"Well, maybe it's because he's still upset about it. It busted up pretty unhappily."

Elizabeth wanted to ask Ditta how, and also how she knew about it, but it seemed that she had no voice. She opened her mouth to speak and nothing came out.

Ditta, still looking down at the grass, answered her unasked question. "His wife went off with another man. Marian says she was probably the only woman he's ever really been in love with."

"Oh," Elizabeth whispered.

Ditta continued, "I think maybe that's why Kurt is so unsure of himself."

"Kurt!"

"Yes, Kurt. He seems so self-sufficient on the surface and so important to us. He's the important young Broadway director and we're lowly apprentices. But on the whole we're probably a lot less afraid than he is. I'm not feeling sorry for him, mind you. I think Kurt's quite a bit of a bastard. But I think it's—interesting—to understand why he's a bastard. He got kicked in the teeth by the person he loved, so now he keeps having to be reassured that women can and do love him. You. Dottie. And one night when I went down the boardwalk with him for something to eat he even made a few passes at me."

"Oh," Elizabeth said, thinking with part of her numbed consciousness that this must have been why Ditta had told her own story, because she was planning all along to talk to Elizabeth about Kurt.

Ditta laughed. "When anybody like Kurt makes a pass at me he must be pretty desperate." Then she said, "Listen, Liz, I couldn't sleep last night it was so hot, and I was lying at the foot of my bed looking out the window after the storm was over and I saw you coming back to the Cottage. I knew you'd been out with Kurt and I thought maybe he'd done something to upset you. And I thought maybe it would help you to understand, if you knew—what I've just told you." Elizabeth didn't say anything and Ditta went on. "I certainly don't think it excuses Kurt for the way he sometimes behaves. And in case you want to know how I know about Kurt's wife, Marian told me. The bust-up happened during the show last winter."

"Oh. Well, thanks, Ditta."

"Thank you for not being furious at me. You have a perfect right to be. But, Liz, you're too smart a person to go on being such a fool."

"Hey!" a voice behind them called. "Having secrets? Tell me all about it!" and Ben appeared around the corner of the garage, tried to vault over a barberry bush, missed it, and landed on his nose in the grass. He sat up, rubbing his nose sorrowfully. "Whenever I have delusions of becoming a ballet dancer, something like this always happens. Last night I dreamed I was on the stage of the Met doing absolutely millions of entrechats, far more than Nijinsky ever did, and everybody was applauding me wildly. Miss Hedeman sent me to tell you Joe says we can have the stage for half an hour for our voice lessons. So come on."

Elizabeth and Ditta got up from the grass, Ditta exclaiming, "Horrors, that grass was *wet*. I've got to go up and change. I'll be over in a little while."

"You wet, too, Liz?" Ben asked.

"Not noticeably. Not enough to change for, anyhow."

Ben walked beside her, but he did not link arms with her as he usually did, and Elizabeth could not think of anything to say to him that would not be the wrong thing to say; so they walked to the theatre apart and in silence. Elizabeth thought about Kurt's words about love in Irving's the night before; and she thought about Ditta's words that morning. Now she understood Kurt better; she no longer hated him; and she no longer was in love with him.

But the understanding that had come could in no way take the place of the love. It was powerless to fill the vacuum that the loss of loving Kurt had created. Walking to the theatre with Ben, she felt that she would have to go all her life with a great hole of longing unfilled inside her.

Kurt sought her out before lunch and pulled her off into a corner of the hall. "Liebchen."

"What is it, Kurt?"

"Not mad at me, are you?"

"No."

"What's the matter, then?"

"Nothing."

"Okay, Liz, no more of this. You're acting as though you were ten thousand miles away from me."

"I guess that's the trouble, Kurt."

"What do you mean?"

"I *am* ten thousand miles away from you. More than that, I guess. We just live in different worlds, that's all, and it isn't any use trying to go from one world to another."

"Don't be melodramatic, Elizabeth."

"I didn't know I was. I didn't mean to be."

"Then stop talking this nonsense about different worlds."

"But that's the way it seems to me. We say the same words and they don't mean the same thing." Because even if he knew I knew about Dottie, she thought, he wouldn't understand.

"What kinds of words, Liebchen?" he asked, his voice gentle.

"All kinds of words. The things we're saying now. The things we've said all summer."

Kurt caught her by the wrist. "Didn't you expect me to want—what I wanted of you last night?"

"I don't know. That really doesn't have very much to do with it." Elizabeth tried to pull her wrist away, but, as he did not release her, she let it lie in his hand as heavy and impersonal as a block of wood.

"Then what are you talking about? I don't understand you."

"I told you we didn't speak the same language, Kurt. It—it all just means something different to me than it does to you."

"The theatre isn't college, Elizabeth."

"No. It's not. But I'm still Elizabeth Jerrold, whether I'm in college or the theatre."

"You've had too much Aunt Harriet." He let her hand fall.

"It didn't have anything to do with Aunt Harriet."

"No?"

"No. It just had to do with me."

"Well—" Kurt said, and for the first time as he looked at her white, unhappy face, the assurance left his eyes and a kind of diffidence came into his voice. "I'm sorry we don't see things the same way, Elizabeth."

"I'm sorry we don't, too, Kurt."

"I don't like to think that I've upset you."

"It doesn't matter."

"Then I have upset you?"

"It doesn't matter, Kurt."

"But it does," he persisted. "What can I do to make it all right with you?"

"Nothing. Just leave me alone—please—"

Jane came out into the hall waving the big dinner bell. "Lunch!" she shouted up the stairs above the clanging of the bell. "Hey, time to eat, you two," she called down the hall to Elizabeth and Kurt.

"Please let me go eat," Elizabeth said to Kurt in a shaky voice.

At last he moved aside and let her go into the dining room.

After lunch Elizabeth went upstairs to write Aunt Harriet.

She was sitting cross-legged on her bed when Ben banged on the door, shouting the question, "Are you decent?"

"Yes, come on in," Elizabeth called, and wondered, Will it always be this way now with Ben and me, strained and difficult?

Ben plunked himself down on the bed beside Elizabeth and gave her a resounding kiss on top of her head. "Lie down, I want to talk to you," he said.

Elizabeth gave him a shove and he rolled onto the floor and lay there, legs waving in the air. "Get up, you goon," she told him.

"I can't. You've injured me for life," Ben said, scrambling up onto Jane's bed and falling flat on it. He watched her anxiously for a moment, then asked casually, "What're you writing?"

"A letter to Aunt Harriet. My phone call to her yesterday was brief and my explanation even briefer. I don't want things to be more awkward than they have to be when I see the rest of the summer out in Jordan."

Ben's look was probing, but then he sat up and reached for Jane's hand mirror and began studying himself in it. "You are moving to New York sooner rather than later, right?"

Elizabeth nodded. "But it will probably be much later than I want. I have to have some savings to move. Everybody in Jordan thinks I'm awful to want to work in the theatre when Aunt Harriet's so against it. They think I ought to do what she wants me to do."

"What does she want you to do?" Ben asked, opening his mouth and examining his teeth.

"I don't know. She doesn't think much of marriage."

"She doesn't know much about it, does she?"

"Well, she *was* engaged, but her fiancé died a few weeks before they were to be married."

"I guess she'd be enough to kill anyone off."

"Oh, Ben, she's not that bad. She's like lots of people in Jordan. I've just shown you the worst side of her."

Ben put the mirror back on the bureau and picked up the picture of Anna Larsen. "Thank goodness you're not like old Harriet. If your mother wasn't blond and didn't have straight hair, anyone'd think that picture was of you. Golly, but she was lovely to look at. Listen, what I came up for was to say Huntley doesn't have to be at the theatre till four and he'll rehearse *Mourning Becomes Electra* for an hour if we want to. Joe doesn't want me till dinnertime so I'm free, too."

"Good," Elizabeth said. "The more work I can get in this week the better. Just let me end off this letter."

Ben waited patiently until Elizabeth finished, folded the letter, and put it in an envelope. Then he said, "Huntley told a new story out on the porch after lunch. Want to hear it?"

"Is it dirty?" Elizabeth asked, searching for a stamp, and grateful for Ben's noble efforts at normality.

"No. It's just silly."

"Okay, then. Let's hear it."

"Well, it seems there was this knight in King Arthur's day and he was so small he couldn't ride a horse, so he rode a St. Bernard dog instead. But in spite of his size he was a marvelous knight and went about rescuing fair maidens from dragons and all kinds of things. Well, one day he was out riding on his trusty steed and he met this other knight and they jostled or joisted or whatever it was they did with those long poles, and he threw the other knight into a pond to cool off, and then started home. But he'd ridden a long distance that day, and fighting with the other knight had wasted time—"

" 'I wasted time, and now doth time waste me,' " Elizabeth declaimed.

"Will you kindly not interrupt me with William Shakespeare or anything else," Ben said with dignity. "As I was saying, the knight was tired and daylight had already gone when he came to the forest he had to cross to get to his castle. Anyhow, the knight and his dog were about halfway through the forest when it began to thunder and lightning and rain, and the knight got all wet inside his armor. It had gotten kind of dented in his battle with the other knight and so it was leaking and you can imagine what leaky armor would feel like."

Elizabeth began to giggle, but Ben glared at her. "Wait to laugh till I've finished," he admonished, and continued. "And the knight's trusty St. Bernard was soaking, too, and her fur was all draggled and she was so tired she could barely drag one foot in front of the other. And then, just as the knight thought they could go no farther, they saw a light through the trees and they rode up to it, and the knight, still seated on his trusty steed, leaned forward in his saddle and knocked at the door. An old man in a nightcap, holding a candle, answered it and said gruffly, 'What can I do for you?' And the knight said, 'Oh, sir, as you can see, my trusty steed and I are wet and tired and my castle is on the other side of the forest. Would you give us shelter for the night?' The old man looked at them for a moment; then he said, 'All right. Come on in. I wouldn't turn a knight out on a dog like this.' "

Elizabeth groaned, "Oh, Ben!"

But Ben was rolling on Jane's bed in spasms of laughter and after a moment Elizabeth began to laugh, too. The two of them laughed until they were weak and Elizabeth was reminded of the hysterical, joyful, abandoned laughter of childhood. This was a laughter that was almost as much of a purge as tears.

John Peter shouted up the stairs at them. "Elizabeth! Ben! Huntley's ready for us! Come on down!"

"Oh, Ben, what fools we are." Elizabeth sighed, getting up and wiping her eyes.

"Yes, but don't you think it's funny?" Ben asked.

"I think it's sweet—but it isn't funny ha-ha the way we were acting."

"It's better than your story about the lobsters going to the movies."

"That's a wonderful story!" Elizabeth protested, running a comb through her hair. "Come on, Ben. Race you downstairs."

They ran madly down the stairs, Elizabeth arriving breathlessly a hair's breadth ahead of Ben.

"Where's the fire?" Huntley asked from the living room. "All ready, kids? Where's Bibi?"

"I think she went down to the beach before you said you could work with us," Ditta said.

"Of course it didn't occur to her to ask. Most of you apprentices think you're here for a suntan and nothing else. Okay, we can manage just as well without her. We'll start with the scene Ben and Elizabeth and Sophie are doing."

"Soapie's gone," Ben reminded him.

"Oh, yes, so she has. Jane, read her part, will you? You

might as well take it over. Here's a script. How's the furniture? Arranged all right?"

Ben was tugging at one of the big chairs. He looked at it critically, sat down on it, moved it a few inches, and sat down again. "Okay now."

After they had been working a short time Huntley said, "Elizabeth, remember what I told you last time about moving on that line?"

"Oh, yes, Huntley. I forgot. I'm sorry. May we go back?"

A moment later she missed a cue and Jane prompted her.

When they had run through the scene Huntley said, "Now let's do it again. Liz, it strikes me that your mind is not on your work this afternoon."

"I'm sorry. I'll try to concentrate better."

"See that you do," Huntley said, rather severely. "Maybe you kids get tired of Miss Hedeman's talking about discipline every two minutes, but the old girl's got the right idea just the same. If you want to work in the theatre, you don't let your mind wander during rehearsal. It doesn't matter if you've received a telegram saying your mother's just died or you've discovered your boyfriend is two-timing you or the doctor's just told you that you have six months to live. When you come to rehearsal the only person whose emotions you worry about is the character you're portraying. And see that you don't forget that. I'm not saying this to Liz in particular but to all of you in general. I'm very sorry Bibi and one or two others I can think of aren't here to hear it. Ben, you're much too apt to clown. You've worked in the theatre long enough to know when to cut out the funny business. Ditta, you usually concentrate but you're so darned intellectual about it that half the time you forget that emotions spring from the heart and not from the brain. Jane, you do just the opposite. You need more objectivity. You get the emotions, all right, but you hug them inside you and forget the audience wants to be let in on the secret. Sincerity doesn't hide or excuse lack of technique. Not that your technique's bad for a kid, but most of the time what you need is just a touch of plain old-fashioned ham. Watch Mariella Hedeman closely to see what I mean. John Peter, you're a selfish actor. Remember that you're not the only person onstage. I don't mean that you do it deliberately; you don't upstage people or anything; but you don't give enough to the other actors. And most important of all, kids, you've got to make the audience believe in you. If they don't believe in you as whatever character it is you're playing, you might as well get off the stage, but quick. Okay, let's start the scene again."

Elizabeth had noticed with wonderment that while Huntley was speaking to them his whole face seemed to change. The puffiness seemed to recede, his eyes sprang to life, the bitter lines eased themselves from his mouth. Why, he could be a wonderful person if he only would, she thought.

Then she forgot Huntley. She forgot Elizabeth Jerrold. She was interested only in the scene she was working on and the characters it involved.

"Huntley's got so much sense about some things," John Peter said after Huntley had left for the theatre. "It's a shame he's such an ass about his private life."

"Oh, well, there's no accounting for love," Jane said. "After all, I love you."

"I am not *Dottie Dawne*," John Peter announced.

"I should hope not!" Ben said.

"Do you suppose if I'd made a couple of lousy movies I'd have Dottie's morals and her delusions of grandeur?" Jane asked.

"Dottie this, Dottie that. Let's stop talking about Dottie," Elizabeth said.

Ben got down on the floor and started doing push-ups. "Got to broaden my shoulders," he panted. "I can do fifty push-ups at a time, now." After twenty he collapsed and rolled over onto his back. "Listen, who's doing tables tonight?"

"John Peter and I," Jane said.

"Well, come on, we've got just enough time for a quick swim before supper if Liz and I help you set the tables when we get back. Okay, Liz?"

"Sure."

"I'll help you, too," Ditta said.

As they started toward the stairs Jane said in a low voice to Elizabeth, "You seem kind of muted today, Liz. Anything wrong?"

"Muted? Good heavens, I'm not muted," Elizabeth said, and gave forth with one of Miss Hedeman's exercises in a voice that would have carried to the farthest ranges of the highest peanut gallery and that brought Lulu Price out into the hall, a glass of whiskey in her hand.

"Will you apprentices please be quiet! I'm working on the

books. Was it you who was making that frightful noise, Elizabeth Jerrold? It's a good thing you're leaving next week. I don't
think we could have stood you for an entire summer. Every
year I beg J.P. not to have apprentices and every year he goes
on having them. I'm sure I don't know why."

"I know why," Ben said as she disappeared. "He makes a
nice fat sum of filthy lucre on people like Bibi and Soapie.
Come on, kids, let's get dressed. Race you to the garage, John
Peter."

John Peter shook his head. "Not me you won't. I'm too old
for that sort of stuff now. All my joints protest whenever I
stand up. At least I no longer have a toothache."

"Yeah, I guess old age is creeping up on you," Ben said. "I
hope none of the other oafs are over in the garage. They'll
want to go with us. Meet you on the beach, kids."

The beach was crowded. They stepped over the tanned bodies
of the sunbathers and splashed into the surf. Ditta scooped water in her palms and dashed it into her eyes.

"Ditta, what on earth are you doing?" Ben asked.

"Getting saltwater into my eyes. It's supposed to be good
for them."

"But it stings."

"I have stoic blood," Ditta said, submerging. When she
came up she explained, "If I splash a little in first, then I can go
under and open my eyes."

"Good heavens, is it good for your eyes?" Elizabeth asked.
"That's wonderful. I always open mine and look around when I

go under. I'd adore to go down in a diver's helmet and see what it's really like. Wouldn't Shakespeare have loved to do that, though! 'Full fathom five' is one of my favorite verses in the world. 'Of his bones are coral made. Those are pearls that were his eyes. Nothing of him that doth fade but doth suffer a sea change into something rich and strange . . .' Isn't that shivery beautiful, though! And wouldn't he have had fun down on the bottom of the ocean looking at everything through a diver's helmet?"

"Liz," John Peter said, "you talk about Shakespeare as though he were some friend of your father's who lived down the street from you and whom you liked a lot."

Elizabeth cupped some sand and water into her hand and looked at it. "I feel lots closer to him than that." She let the sand sift through her fingers. " 'To see the world in a grain of sand, and a heaven in a wild flower, hold infinity in the palm of your hand, and eternity in an hour.' That, for your information, my children, is Mr. William Blake."

"Gad." Ben sat down in the shallow water with a splash. "We are poetical today, aren't we?"

Elizabeth grinned. "Sorry. I get attacks of quotitis every once in a while. It's a very rare disease with no cure. It usually attacks older people, and here I am afflicted with it at my tender age."

Ben snorted.

Elizabeth looked up and caught her breath. She had not seen Kurt on the beach as they crossed it to get to the water, but now he walked over the sand to join them, and she felt herself reddening. This is a mess, she thought, if I'm going to blush every time I see Kurt from now on. I've got to control myself. Please let me be able to control myself.

"Hi, kids," Kurt said. "Good rehearsal?"

Elizabeth lay on her back and floated, letting little waves lap over her face as Jane said, "Pretty good. Huntley couldn't work us very long; he had to get over to the theatre."

The breaking of the waves against Elizabeth's body was gentle and compassionate, and she lay there and tried not to mind the fact that she was close to Kurt and nothing inside her reached out to him. Her heart beat rapidly but it was no longer with joyful excitement. She hoped above all else that he would not come nearer to her.

"We've got to get on back if we want to get the tables ready," she heard Jane saying, and Elizabeth stood up, shook the water off like a dog, and ran her fingers through her wet hair.

After dinner Elizabeth hurried into her ushering dress and out of the Cottage. Kurt was on the porch, and called out to her.

"Let's go for a little walk, Liebchen."

"Sorry," she said hurriedly, "I've got to get over to the theatre," and she ran down the steps of the porch. The theatre was still dark when she got there, but she sat on the steps until it was time to go in, watching the people walk by, looking across the boardwalk to the ocean stretching out till it was lost in the sky. As head usher she had to be at the theatre before the others, so she hoped that Kurt would think that her excuse was a legitimate one, that he would not think she was avoiding him. After all, she thought, and tried to keep her thinking dispassionate, it's not his fault if I've been a fool. It's myself I'm angry at for having been such an idiot as to think I meant anything serious to him.

She stood up, gave herself an angry shake, and went into the theatre.

The house was packed for the opening performance of *Macbeth*. J. P. Price had even put extra chairs at the side. Elizabeth stood at the back of the house and suddenly nothing existed for her except *Macbeth*, except the magic that was being created onstage.

"Lordy, Andersen's magnificent," John Peter said at intermission, and Elizabeth was too speechless to do anything but nod. For these few hours she was no longer Elizabeth Jerrold caught up in her own muddled personal problems but a sensitive receiving instrument ready to receive things that were greater than herself or her sorrows, so that even in the midst of a turmoil which might be making her feel passionately unhappy she could also be capable of feeling great joy.

But after the curtain had come down, after Valborg Andersen had taken her last curtain call and the houselights had come up, she lost her mood of exaltation and fell plummeting down into loneliness. Loneliness is a chilling thing, and she shivered in her light dress.

After the audience had left and she had folded the seats to the chairs and stacked her programs and flashlights for the following night, she wandered backstage. Most of the cast had already removed costume and makeup. She caught a glimpse of Jane in Valborg Andersen's dressing room, talking earnestly and seriously to her aunt. Miss Andersen was listening, laughing once in a while, and then the two of them left the theatre. Ditta and Marian were standing at the stage door with Ben, laughing in the companionship of a shared joke; then they called good night to Ben and left. Elizabeth went into the wings and sat on Joe's empty stool, putting her head down on the promptbook on the table. She heard the final slamming of dressing room doors, the clink of keys being hung on the rack, feet hurrying down the steps, good-nights being called out; and she sat there, hidden in her corner, and felt for the first time alien and not part of the life around her.

But this *can't* happen because of Kurt, she told herself in consternation. The way I felt about Kurt doesn't have anything to do with the way I feel about the theatre!

After a while she looked up and saw Ben coming toward her. "Hi, Liz," he said.

"Hi, Ben."

"Liz, I want to talk to you."

She sighed. "Okay. What about?"

"You. And Kurt. And me."

She flung her arms wide in a mock-dramatic gesture. "All is over between Kurt and me, if that's what you mean."

He gave a slightly sardonic grin. "Well, I rather gathered that. Listen, so all day we've been kidding. I've known something was wrong and you've known something was wrong, and every time I thought I was going to get up courage to ask you I'd make another sappy crack instead."

"Well, now you know." She put her head down on the promptbook again.

"I know you and Kurt had a fight or something but I want

to know more than that. You've been acting toward me as though I had leprosy or something and you were being kind to me out of auld lang syne but really you didn't think you ought to get close to me. What does busting up with Kurt have to do with me? It's more than your being unhappy. Sure, I understand you're unhappy and I'm sorry as hell, but if busting up with that bastard means the end of you and me too, then I want to know why."

Now Elizabeth raised her head and looked at him in consternation. "Oh, Ben, I'm so sorry, but—"

"But what?"

"It hasn't anything to do with Kurt, it's—"

"What?"

"Ben, I guess I've been kind of a stinker about you, only I didn't realize it, honestly, and I—well, that's what it is. That's what's between us. What I told you about yesterday."

"Oh, damn Dottie!" Ben shouted furiously. "Damn John Peter and any other interfering busybody who's been shooting off his mouth." Then he calmed down. "Okay, listen to me. I'm so glad whatever happened with you and Kurt happened I could sing. I'm not a bit sorry. Does that make us even?"

Elizabeth smiled rather wanly. "I don't know."

"Okay, then, listen to this. This is a promise. I'm going to ask you to marry me. Not now or in a month. Not for at least six months. I don't want you on the rebound. But it might interest you to know that my intentions are strictly honorable. Might be rather amusing for a change."

"Oh, Ben—"

"Listen, in the theatre everybody goes around arranging

other people's lives. After the first day everybody decided you were for me. Then Kurt comes along and puts a crimp in it. So everybody's mad. Everybody thinks I'm being done dirt. Rot. You were already twined tightly around Kurt's little finger before I tumbled to the fact that you were my girl. Okay, so I could wait. I knew the Kurt thing wouldn't last. I was right. And get this straight. I'm not asking you to accept me now. I wouldn't have you now. But in six months I'm going to court you properly and you might as well know it now. Okay?"

Elizabeth sighed again but she smiled up at Ben. "Okay."

Ben sighed, too, and sat down on the floor beside her. "Now that I've announced my oh-so-honorable intentions, I'm going to be a stinker. About this business with Kurt. I think you ought to get it out of your system and better me than anybody else. You didn't do anything you shouldn't do, did you? Not that it would make any difference to me if you did, but I know it would to you."

"No, Ben. I didn't."

"I shouldn't have asked you that."

"It's all right. I don't blame you for asking." She looked down at her feet in the gold evening sandals on the dusty ground cloth. Underneath them she could hear the soft lapping of waves against the piles holding the theatre up. The work light above her was swinging slightly and the shadows moved about on the walls and the canvas flats, grotesque and menacing.

"No. I should have known you well enough to know I didn't need to ask it," Ben said.

"It's all right. I've made a fool of myself about Kurt in every other way. I wouldn't blame anyone for thinking I might have in that way, too."

Ben didn't say anything. The light above them was still now; its slow swinging had stopped; but the shadows pressed about it so that it made only a faint small pool of solace.

"Ben, I've been making such an idiot of myself all summer. Agonizing so obviously when he went out with Dottie or anyone else. I was—I was *crude*."

"It wasn't as bad as all that," Ben said. He took her glasses, which she was twirling unhappily, out of her tense fingers and laid them down on the table.

"The trouble is," Elizabeth spoke in a muffled voice as though the shadows which were muffling the light were also muffling her, "that I've let it color everything. The way I feel about you, and Jane and John Peter and everything. I guess I've gone to the other extreme. I've begun to look at things as though I were Aunt Harriet."

"What things?" Ben asked gently.

Now Elizabeth looked up and focused her eyes on a sandbag hanging from the flies. "Oh—things like the way you and John Peter are always in our room sitting around. I never thought of it as being anything wrong. I never thought of it as 'men in the room.' It was just the nicest place for all of us to be—out of the way of the professional company and where we could talk and have fun. I never thought of it as anything wrong."

"It wasn't anything wrong," Ben said with finality.

"Aunt Harriet thought it was wrong."

"Nothing went on in that room that couldn't have gone on in the living room, did it?"

Elizabeth gave a half grin. "Lots more goes on down in the living room than ever goes on in our room."

"Well, then?" Ben asked.

"But, Ben——" Now Elizabeth looked away from the sand-bag, but she could not look out into the theatre because the asbestos was down and she and Ben were hemmed into Dunsinane, into the dark, relieved only by the single bulb of the work light in its small wire cage, and it seemed that there was nothing of comfort on which she could rest her eyes.

"What, Liz?" Ben asked.

"I went to Kurt's dressing room. At night, I mean."

"Oh," Ben said.

"And that——that was wrong, wasn't it?"

"I don't know," Ben said. "I feel like I've been in the theatre so long I don't know how people on the outside look at such things. But to my way of thinking, whether or not it was wrong depends on *why* you went to his room."

"I don't know why," Elizabeth told him.

"I mean, what did you expect?"

"I——I expected him to kiss me. But he'd kissed me out on the boardwalk. I didn't think it would be any different in his room than it had been out on the boardwalk. At least I don't think I did. But it was."

"Well," Ben said reasonably, "that's something you have to find out for yourself, isn't it?"

"Is it? That's what I don't know. It seems to me I should

have known. I should have known that talking to you and John Peter up in our room was different than going to Kurt's room."

"Well, now you know," Ben said.

"But I feel so dirty, Ben. I feel ugly and cheap."

"Listen, Liz, I told you you had to learn to walk in the mud and not get your feet dirty if you wanted to work in the theatre."

"But I feel as though I *had* got my feet dirty."

"Maybe your shoes," Ben said, "but not your feet. And you can always change your shoes."

"I shouldn't have bothered you with all this," Elizabeth said. "I should have worked it out for myself."

"You *are* working it out for yourself."

Elizabeth shook her head. "Oh, Ben, I'm not. That makes it all the worse. It seems to me that everybody knows about it. Oh—they don't know I went to Kurt's room or anything, but they know I'm upset about him, that I was a fool about him. I suppose that's just false pride on my part, being bothered because people know. And I'm a fool to let it get me down now—I mean the fact that it was all spoiled, that I don't love him anymore. I don't even hate him. I just feel—drab— about him. Me, I'm such a romantic idiot. I always thought that the first time you fell in love nothing could spoil it, that you treasured it for the rest of your life, the way you keep pretty stones in a box to look at when you're small. But I don't want to treasure this. I don't want ever to have to look at it again. I'm glad I'm not staying after this week. It would be awful just to go on seeing Kurt every day and act as though nothing had happened."

She had not intended to speak in this manner, but once the first few words were out, the rest followed, one stumbling over the other, rushing out like a small waterfall.

"You could do it if you had to," Ben told her rather fiercely.

Elizabeth shook her head from side to side the way an ill person moves his head restlessly against the pillow which gives no comfort no matter how many times it is smoothed and turned to the cool side. "Oh—I guess I could. But it gives me one really good reason to be glad I have to go back to Jordan. And Ben—"

"What, Liz?"

"You see, there's another awful thing: it's made me feel differently about the theatre. Not just Kurt alone but Kurt and—and—and Dottie—and the way the kids drooled over Sarah Courtmont and the way they apple-polish Miss Andersen without really caring or understanding what a great actress she is— oh, you know what I mean. I've always thought about the theatre like a Christmas tree, all shining and bright with beautiful ornaments. But now it seems like a Christmas tree with the tinsel all tarnished and the colored balls all fallen off and broken. That's a corny way of saying it, but you know what I mean."

"Sure, I know what you mean, Liz. And it's both ways. If you can be corny I can be, too. Some of the ornaments fall and break and some stay clear and bright. Some of the tinsel gets tarnished and some stays shining and beautiful like the night before Christmas. Nothing's ever all one way. You know that. It's all mixed up and you've just got to find the part that's right for you. Now isn't my corn as good as your corn?"

"Yes, Ben, I guess it is." Elizabeth stood up and her limbs

were stiff from sitting so long crouched on Joe's three-legged stool. She walked about the stage for a moment, rather aimlessly, then returned to the stool. "Ben, I'm terribly sorry."

"What about?"

"Talking like this. To you, of all people."

"What do you mean, to me of all people? If you can't talk to the man who's going to be your husband someday, who the hell can you talk to? I don't mean to sound sure of myself, but we're too right for each other not to get together eventually. And all this—well, everything is experience, Liz. Anything you feel really deeply will help you as an actress."

Elizabeth said, struggling to hold back her tears, "I'm such a damned fool!"

"Sure you are. And you shouldn't swear."

"You're right. I'll stop. I'm sorry."

Ben reached over and patted her knee with infinite tenderness. "Let's go over to Lukie's and have some ice cream. I'll treat you."

She didn't even argue with him but said, "Okay, Ben. Thanks."

They walked down the boardwalk in silence. When they got to Lukie's, brilliant light came from the windows and pushed away the night. Music from the jukebox, loud voices, the indiscriminate smells of beer and cigarette smoke overpowered the fresh ocean air.

"Let's sit outside," Elizabeth said.

Ben nodded, and they went to one of the empty tables lining the verandah that was crazily added to one side of the rickety building. Lukie's was built crudely over a pier that stuck out from the boardwalk into the water on insecure, barnacled legs, so that, even more than in the theatre, one had the feeling of being at sea. The tables on the verandah were empty after sundown except on the hottest nights, because they were damp and dirty, and spray from the ocean blew over them, and nothing but ice cream and soft drinks could be had there, and those only by self-service. After the storm the night before, the air was windy and chill, and Elizabeth shivered in her light cotton evening dress.

Ben perched on the rickety rail. "What kind of ice cream do you want?"

"Butter pecan. Thanks, Ben."

"That's okay." He jumped down and pushed his way into the crowded building, looked over his shoulder as he disappeared, and said, "By the way, I love you. In case I forgot to mention it before."

Now Elizabeth could not help smiling at him, and then she curled up on the hard bench to wait for him and to try to reconstruct in her mind Valborg Andersen's brilliant performance, to hear again Shakespeare's words become alive and powerful as she had never known they could be.

It was almost half an hour before Ben came back with the ice cream. "Sorry I took so long. Golly, Liz, aren't you frozen?"

Suddenly she shivered. "Yes, I guess I am."

"For heaven's sake, put on my coat."

"Don't you need it?"

"I've got on a sweater." Ben pulled off his coat and held it out for her. "Here."

"Thanks, Ben. It's lovely and warm." Then she said, "Ben, I—I can tell you how I feel about—about everything. I think you're the best friend I've ever had. I—I'd lie down and die for you if you wanted me to."

"Honey," Ben said. "When I get you to lie down for me it won't be to die."

"Don't laugh at me."

"Why not?"

She looked at him somberly for a moment and then she began to laugh. "You're right as usual. Why not?" She smiled across the table at him. "Why not laugh? Why not see what happens in New York?" She took a spoonful of ice cream. "This is good. Lots of nuts. What on earth are you doing with your teeth?"

"Pushing them in. They keep coming out."

"What?"

"They stick out."

"You idiot."

Ben winked at her. "Here comes Bibi the heebie-jeebie."

Bibi came trotting down the boardwalk, peered in the door, caught sight of Elizabeth and Ben sitting outside, and came over to them.

Elizabeth squinched up her eyes, trying to see her. "Ben! I left my glasses in the theatre. We have to go get them!" she exclaimed tragically.

"Calm down," Ben said. "You aren't missing anything. You've seen it all before. We'll stop by on our way back."

Bibi waved at them. "Hi. What are you all doing?"

"Playing Russian Bank," Ben said. "Can't you see the cards? Listen, Bibi, will you answer me something truthfully?"

"Sure."

"Do you want to 'go on the stage'?"

"Of course. What do you think I'm at a summer theatre for?"

"Well, there has been some difference of opinion," Ben said.

"What do you mean?" Bibi asked indignantly.

Elizabeth shook her head at Ben gently, but he winked and ignored her and Elizabeth turned away to face toward the ocean, listening with only half an ear. The stars were soft and blurred, but she knew that since they were at least visible to her they must be sharp and clear against the darkness of the sky. The lights of Lukie's were reflected on the water and moved under the swell; and if she blotted out with her mind the jukebox and the voices from Lukie's, she could hear the waves lapping against the piles of the pier and the muted breathing of the ocean sighing, deeply at rest after last night's storm.

"Wouldn't you like to get married?" Ben asked Bibi.

"Naturally."

"Well, I think you'd better get married, then."

"But marriage doesn't need to interfere with my Career!" Bibi said career with a capital C.

"When did you decide you wanted a Career, tootsie pie?" Ben asked.

"This winter."

Ben thumped his fist down on the rotting boards of the table and demanded, "What decided you?"

"I did Nora in *A Doll's House* at school if it's any of your business," Bibi said.

"And everyone thought you were wonderful and ought to be an actress?"

"Well, I *was* good. And I bought Stanislavsky."

"Did you read him?"

"Well . . . not yet. But I'm going to. It's such a big book. I don't see why you're asking me all these questions all of a sudden. You want to be an actor, don't you?"

"Want some ice cream, Bibi?" Elizabeth asked, taking pity on her.

"No. I'm going inside to see who's there. Kurt said something about meeting him somewhere, but maybe it was Irving's."

"Listen, little one," Ben said, sounding a hundred years old, "you're going to get an awful kick in the pants someday unless you learn that the theatre isn't an arty prep-school production."

"It wasn't prep school, it was college, and anyhow I don't see what it's got to do with you. I don't understand why your crowd is always so mean to me," Bibi complained. "The actors in the professional company are nice to me. Kurt asked me to go on a double date tomorrow night with him and Dottie and Jud Hancock."

"We're not mean to you, sugar," Ben said. "You're just riding for a fall and I'm trying to give you a word of warning."

"Who's Jud Hancock?" Elizabeth asked.

"He came up with Mervyn Melrose for next week's show and he's just darling."

"Well, isn't that too, too ducky," Ben said.

"I'm going inside. I'm certainly not going to stay out here with you two." Bibi turned on her heel, her little nose up in the air, and disappeared into the crowded interior of Lukie's.

"Ben, you were awful," Elizabeth said sternly, turning away from the ocean and looking at the pleasant pink blur that was Ben's face to her without her glasses.

Ben scraped his ice cream dish. "Was I?"

"You know you were."

"Well, if you must know, she made a few nasty cracks about you this evening and I was sore at her. Little slitch. She couldn't wait to get that in about Kurt."

"She's at perfect liberty to go out with whomever she chooses," Elizabeth said rather pompously.

"Maybe she is, but she hasn't any right to make cracks about you."

Elizabeth shrugged. "Oh, well."

Ben put his spoon back in the dish. "I've finished my ice cream. Want some more?"

"No, thanks." Inside Ben's coat Elizabeth shivered as a soft mist of spray wet her cheeks.

"Mind if I do?"

"Of course not."

"I'll try not to be too long. I'll get you some more anyhow and if you don't want it I'll eat it. Warm enough?"

"Mm-hm."

"Olive oil."

"Abyssinia."

He leaned over her and kissed her very gently, then turned and walked away.

She watched him push his way indoors and try to get up to the soda fountain. She could see that it would take him at least as long as it had the last time, if not longer. Now she was tired; she wanted nothing more than to leave Lukie's and go back to the Cottage and to bed, but after all, she thought, this is the least I can do for Ben, to be here when he comes back with his ice cream.

She looked around, forgetting momentarily that she couldn't see; but the stars were still half obscured and she could not tell where the ocean met the sky. The people in Lukie's were blurs of colored dresses and dark suits and light suits, with blobs of pink for faces and hands. She rubbed her eyes and wondered if this would be the last time she would ever be at Lukie's. Oh, God, if only I could go to New York next week, she thought. If only I didn't have to go back to Jordan.

The boardwalk was emptying now. Only occasional couples strolled by, heading for the more crowded spots beyond Lukie's pier. After a while she saw two women walking toward her and turning off on the pier. They stopped at the main entrance, and one of them went in and looked around, then came out and rejoined the other. They started down the boardwalk again, suddenly caught sight of Elizabeth's lonely figure, and came back.

"Liz! Liz! We've been looking all over the place for you!" It was Jane's voice.

Elizabeth looked up and grinned. "Hi, Jane. What's up?" She couldn't see the woman standing in the shadows by Jane well enough to identify her. She thought it might be Marian or Ditta or perhaps even Mariella Hedeman, who was very fond of Jane.

"Liz, it's Aunt Val," Jane said. "Where on earth are your glasses?"

Elizabeth scrambled to her feet. "Oh, I'm sorry, Miss Andersen, I—I couldn't see you in the shadows. I left my glasses in the theatre. Pl-please forgive me," she stammered.

"It's all right, Miss Jerrold. Sit down." Valborg Andersen smiled at the clumsy nearsighted figure in the evening dress and the rough tweed jacket. She herself sat down in Ben's seat while Jane perched on the rail.

"Miss Jerrold, my niece Jane and your friend Ben have been talking to me about you."

"Oh—" Elizabeth said.

"Now I am not interested in having protégées or being deus ex machina, but your readings of Nina and the Gentlewoman have convinced me that you're worth helping and Jane tells me that at this point you need help. Is that so?"

"I—Yes," Elizabeth said.

"I'm afraid I can't do anything for you this summer. Jane tells me that you have to leave next week."

"Yes. I do."

"But if you can manage to get to New York in September, I'll definitely be doing a play. I'm not sure whether or not it will be *Macbeth* and I'm not sure whether or not I'll be able to offer you an actual part. But at any rate, I think I can promise you an understudy, which would earn you not a grand living but enough to scrape by. Would that appeal to you?"

Elizabeth sat down and stood up again. "Oh—yes!" Her voice rose in a childish squeak.

"I'll get your address from Jane and my secretary will be in touch with you. Incidentally, I was talking to Ben backstage this evening and he told me your mother was Anna Larsen. I knew her slightly and thought her immensely talented." She smiled down at Elizabeth's eager face and touched her shoulder briefly. "I think you've got what it takes. I'd like to help you. Good night, my dear."

Elizabeth opened her mouth to speak and closed it again. Her fingers clenched and unclenched helplessly, since no adequate words of thanks were forthcoming and she could not bring herself to speak the inadequate ones. Tears rushed to her eyes.

Valborg Andersen understood. She smiled, pressed Elizabeth's shoulder, and left.

Elizabeth crumpled down on the bench and huge sobs tore out of her. All the tears that had been shut in, not only during the past few weeks, but her whole life since she had realized what she wanted to make of it and the obstacles which stood in the way, were loosed by a happiness that was too overwhelming to bear quietly. Her sobs at first were tight, tense, then they became loose and free like a child's. Jane gave her shoulder an occasional friendly pat, but said nothing.

When Elizabeth looked up, shamefaced, and dried her eyes, she met Jane's affectionate smile; and there was Ben coming out with the ice cream.